TALES OF THE VELVET COMET #1

EROS ASCENDING

MIKE RESNICK

A SIGNET BOOK

NEW AMERICAN LIBRARY

Copyright © 1984 by Mike Resnick

All rights reserved. For information address New American Library.

A hardcover edition was published by Phantasia Press.

SIGNET TRADEMARK REG. U.S. PAT. OFF. AND FOREIGN COUNTRIES
REGISTERED TRADEMARK—MARCA REGISTRADA
HECHO EN CHICAGO, U.S.A.

SIGNET, SIGNET CLASSIC, MENTOR, PLUME, MERIDIAN AND NAL BOOKS
are published by New American Library,
1633 Broadway, New York, New York 10019

First Signet Printing, November, 1984

1 2 3 4 5 6 7 8 9

PRINTED IN THE UNITED STATES OF AMERICA

To Carol, as always,

And to Hank and Martha Beck,
For cherished memories, past and future.

A CHANGE OF IDENTITY . . .

"Activate."

The computer screen flickered to life.

"This is Harry Redwine, Identification Number 00345, code name Fixer. Please scan my card and identify my retina pattern. Once you've ascertained my identity, compare it against my Access Authorization under the code name Fixer."

The computer flashed a completion message a few seconds later.

"Has my skeleton card activated this room's security system?"

The computer gave him a negative response.

"Is this terminal currently being monitored?"

Negative again.

"All right. Institute Priority Code 03G6673H2."

The computer winked in acknowledgment, and the Fixer began to change forever the past and future of the most unique ship in space, the *Velvet Comet*. . . .

SIGNET Science Fiction You'll Enjoy

PROLOGUE

The *Velvet Comet* spun slowly in space, resembling nothing more than a giant barbell. Its metal skin glistened a brilliant silver, and its array of flashing lights could be seen from literally tens of thousands of miles away.

It orbited about the planet Charlemagne, a tepid green-and-blue world that was barely visible beneath a layer of swirling white clouds, but it was owned by the Vainmill Syndicate on the distant world of Deluros VIII. Seventeen different engineering firms had worked on its design, thousands of men and machines had spent literally millions of hours on its construction, and it housed a permanent staff of more than six hundred men and women.

During its brief twelve years of existence it had become a byword for opulence and elegance, a synonym for hedonism and dissipation. Its fame quickly spread throughout the worlds of the Republic, and while its Sybaritic luxuries and even its air of exclusivity were often imitated, they were never equalled.

The *Velvet Comet*, after more than three decades of gestation, had been born in space, and less than a century after its birth it would die in space, mourned by few and forgotten by most. But in the meantime, it did its living with a grace and style that would not be seen again for many millennia.

It was the crown jewel in the Syndicate's Entertainment and Leisure Division, a showplace where the rich and the famous—and occasionally the notorious—gathered to see and be seen, to conspicuously consume, and to revel in pleasures which were designed to satisfy even the most jaded of tastes. For while the *Velvet Comet* housed a compendium of the finest shops and boutiques, of gourmet restaurants and elegant lounges, while it boasted a fabulous casino and a score of other entertainments, it was first and foremost a brothel.

And it was the brothel, and the promises of secret delights that it proffered, that enticed its select clientele out to the *Comet*. They came at first by the dozens, then the hundreds, and eventually from both nearby and distant worlds. Money was no object to these men and women; they came to play, and to relax, and to indulge.

All except one man. His name was Harry Redwine, and he had come to do a job.

1

"Activate."

Whiskey glass in hand, Harry Redwine leaned back in his fur-covered contour chair and watched the holographic screen flicker to life.

"Main memory bank, please."

The screen remained blank. Redwine sipped his drink, stared at it for a moment, then spoke again.

"Financial data bank, please."

There was no reaction, which didn't surprise him.

"This is Harry Redwine, Company Identification Number 00345, code name Fixer. Scan me, check out my retina identification pattern, and bring up the main memory bank, please."

This time there was a reaction, and it *did* surprise him. Six life-sized nude bodies—three male and three female—suddenly appeared in the holographic field and happily began enacting every sexual combination and permutation that had yet been devised.

"Cancel."

The screen went blank, and Redwine poured himself another drink.

"Okay, we'll try again. Activate."

The screen came to life.

"This is Harry Redwine, I.D. 00345, code name Fixer. Please tell me what procedure is required to bring up the financial data bank."

This time a single nude woman popped into existence,

9

lips and legs both slightly parted. She ran her left hand through her long, flowing hair, then down over her breasts and belly, and kept going.

"Cancel," said Redwine.

The woman vanished.

Three more attempts to bring up anything other than erotic images were unsuccessful, and finally he awarded the first round to the machine.

"Intercom."

A young woman's face appeared almost instantly.

"Yes, Mr. Redwine? How may I help you?"

"I have been trying, without much success, to get something besides pornography on the screen for the better part of ten minutes."

"If you will turn to Channel Z, you will find a complete listing of our holographic and video services," she said smoothly.

"Perhaps I expressed myself poorly," replied Redwine. "I don't want your stock quotations or your newspaper or your morning line either."

"Channel Q is an open channel. If you desire any particular stage play, opera, sporting event, or cinema that is not in our current listing, I will be happy to see if we have it in our library and patch it through to you."

Redwine shook his head. "I need to tie in to the ship's main computer."

"I'm afraid that's off-limits to our guests, Mr. Redwine."

"I don't doubt it," said Redwine patiently. "But I'm not a guest."

"I'm sorry, but I find you listed as a guest."

Redwine looked mildly amused. "Come off it. You know who I am, and you know what brought me here."

"I just came on duty five minutes ago, Mr. Redwine," she said with impressive innocence. "However, I'll be happy to look into the situation if you desire."

"Your loyalty is admirable, but misdirected," replied Redwine. "Sooner or later you people are going to have to cooperate with me. In the meantime, I'm drinking valuable liquor and taking up a valuable suite, neither of which bothers me half as much as it ought to bother *you.*"

"I'm so glad you've already found the liquor," she said sweetly. "We always provide a bottle of a fine Deluros blend for our guests."

"Found it?" he repeated sardonically. "I practically fell over it when I opened the door."

"I hope you didn't hurt yourself. As for your other problem, I'll do what I can, Mr. Redwine," said the woman, showing no sign of tension or irritation. "In the meantime, I will append a list of auxiliary entertainments to our standard listing on Channel Z." She broke the connection.

Redwine, who had expected no more initial help than he had thus far received, finished his drink, left the parlor, and walked through the bedroom to the bathroom. He hesitated briefly until the sensor in the low-hanging chandelier registered the heat and motion of his body and illuminated the room, then stepped carefully around the oversized sunken marble tub and stopped in front of the sink. He held his hands under the water tap, muttered "Cold," waited for the water to come rushing out, and rinsed his face off. Then he returned to the parlor, poured himself another drink, and picked up one of the books he had brought with him. He considered going to the bedroom and stretching out on the huge circular bed, but decided that the mirrored ceiling would prove too distracting, so he sat once again on the contour chair and began reading.

He found that he had trouble concentrating, even without being able to see the ceiling. Visions of the holographic display kept racing through his mind: pie charts suddenly resembled breasts, tall columns of numbers seemed strikingly phallic, and he realized after fifteen minutes had passed that he couldn't remember a single thing he had read.

Finally he put the book aside, picked up his computerized room card, and decided to see what it could do besides unlock the door. He placed his thumb on a colored square, and an elegant fireplace, aglow with a roaring though heatless fire, suddenly materialized. He pressed a second square and found his chair tingling pleasantly, then touched a third and set the entire room to rocking gently. He got to his feet and checked out the other squares which, alone or in combination, started water flowing in the whirlpool, activated the sauna, dimmed the lights, filled the suite with a pleasantly musky odor, piped in a strikingly erotic symphony, dilated the door to a closet he had not previously noticed, and slid back a section of the wall to reveal a fully-stocked wet bar.

When he had finally seen all the features that the suite had to offer, he went over the card again, restored the rooms to their original condition, sat down, and tried once more to focus his attention on his book. He was more successful this time, and wasn't even aware that he was no longer alone until he heard the door slide back into the wall.

Startled, he looked up and found himself staring at a striking brunette. Her hair was piled high in the *haute couture* fashion of the day, and she wore a diaphanous purple gown that had never been intended to hide the exquisite body that lay beneath it. Her cheekbones were high, her nose small, her lips full, her pale blue eyes slightly tilted and oddly catlike.

Redwine estimated her age at eighteen or nineteen. He also guessed that she had packed one hell of a lot of living into those years. She looked like the suite: elegant and expensive, and just a bit overwhelming. He suddenly found himself wondering if the two went together.

"I didn't know anyone carried *books* around anymore," she said at last, and he noticed as she approached him that she possessed a supple feline grace that went with her eyes.

"I'm old-fashioned," replied Redwine.

"It's so much easier to read a screen."

"It's easier to read *this* screen, that's for sure," he said ironically. "By the way, I'm Harry Redwine."

"My name is Suma."

"Do you come with the room?"

"Occasionally."

He had the feeling she was laughing at him. "But not today?" he asked.

"I thought you came here to work, Mr. Redwine," said Suma, arching a perfect eyebrow.

"That's what *I* thought too, but I'm having a little difficulty gaining access to the material I need."

"I know."

"*Everybody* knows," said Redwine wryly. "But nobody seems to want to do anything about it."

"You mustn't feel persecuted, Mr. Redwine," said Suma. "I'm here to help."

"Can you patch me in to your financial data bank?"

"I can take you to someone who can."

"Good," he said, walking to a closet. "Open," he commanded. The door dilated and he reached in and withdrew a briefcase.

"I hope you haven't been waiting long," said Suma.

"A couple of hours." He opened the case, quickly checked its contents, and then closed and locked it.

"Is your suite satisfactory?"

"It's a fabulous suite of rooms, but I can't work here."

"But this is one of our finest facilities. It's close to the restaurants and the casino and—"

"I'll be happy to spend my nights here, but there are just too many distractions. I'll need a plain little office with a chair, a computer terminal, and a steady supply of coffee."

"I don't know why you can't do your work here," said Suma. "I find these rooms charming."

"May I suggest that your job specifications are likely to be just a bit different from mine?"

Suma stared at him, and for just an instant her mask of elegant sophistication slipped and Redwine thought he could glimpse a predator lurking beneath. He wondered what she would be like ten or fifteen years up the road, when she had better control of the mask, and decided that the only word for her would be *formidable*. Then the instant passed, and she smiled.

"We'll certainly endeavor to provide you with what you need, Mr. Redwine."

"Thank you."

"That's a very interesting pin you're wearing," she noted. "Does it mean anything?"

Redwine looked down at his jerkin and adjusted the small gold pin. "It means I won't get arrested for impersonating an accountant."

"How very amusing. Shall we go, Mr. Redwine?"

"Lead the way," he replied, following her out into the long corridor that led past some forty doors on the way to the elevator banks. "And call me Harry."

"If you wish, Mr. Redwine."

He smiled and chose to ignore the remark. "You know," he said, changing the subject as they continued walking, "this is the first spaceship I've ever seen that had bas-reliefs on the corridor walls."

"We prefer to think of ourselves as an orbiting resort rather than a spaceship."

"Well, *resort's* as good a name as any," he said with a shrug.

They reached the open area in front of the elevators.

"Nice frescos, too," he said, looking at the ceiling.

"*We* like them."

"Are they all pornographic?"

"They are all *artistic*," she replied.

The elevator arrived, and a smartly-tailored elderly woman got off, nodded pleasantly to them, and began walking down the corridor.

"A customer?" asked Redwine, watching her until she vanished around a corner.

"One of our best," said Suma, entering the elevator. "And we prefer to call them patrons."

"I suppose it's better than Johns and Janes," he remarked, stepping in after her.

The elevator ascended three levels, then let them off in a large, opulent foyer decorated by muted tapestries and furnished with antique chairs and sofas from a period when the French were more concerned with making love than losing wars. A number of people, their clothes running the gamut from expensively casual to expensively formal, sat or stood in small clusters, conversing in low voices about topics ranging from business to politics to the selection of one of the *Comet*'s restaurants. Suma wended her way among them, finally passing through an archway into a truly opulent lounge. There was a long, polished bar made of a wood that Redwine couldn't identify, a number of small marble-topped tables at which people were eagerly consuming everything from dainty pastries to exotic coffees to triple-strength drinks, and stationed in one corner, partially hidden by a fountain, was a quartet of musicians in formal dress.

They went through the lounge, passed a pair of restaurants—one a formal, candle-lit affair featuring crisp linen tablecloths, fine china and silver, and servants dressed in powdered wigs and Revolutionary America costumes, the other a huge silk tent in which the customers sat or reclined on large cushions and ate off a very low table—skirted the casino, and came at last to an ornate door.

"We're here," announced Suma.

"Good," said Redwine. "For a while there I thought we were in training for a marathon."

"That's not the kind of marathon we run here, Mr. Redwine."

She waited for the door to slide open, gestured to him to step through it, then followed him inside as the door closed behind them.

At first Redwine couldn't decide whether he was in an office or just another sumptuous suite. There were two couches facing each other across an angular chrome table, a strikingly original metal lounge chair made of some incredibly reflective substance, a massive wet bar, and a fruitwood secretary. Then he saw a number of small lights flash and realized that the secretary was actually a computer in an elegant cabinet.

The plain, wheat-colored carpet was not as thick as some of the others he had seen, but it looked more expensive, as did the *objets d'art* that were discreetly displayed around the room. An alien musical instrument resembling a harp was in one corner of the room, and a pair of chairs framed an ancient and priceless chess table in another.

Redwine walked over to the chess table and examined the carefully-crafted inlays, the beautiful unity of design, the exquisitely-carved legs.

"What do you think of it?" asked a low voice.

"It's stunning," he replied. Then he suddenly realized that he was not speaking to Suma, and he turned around and found himself facing a tall, auburn-haired woman.

She wore a low-cut jumpsuit made of some iridescent blue-green lizard skin. It fit like a second skin, and the millions of tiny scales dazzlingly reflected the light of the room. Her only other items of apparel were long leather gloves and a pair of calf-high boots that possessed spiked heels. She wore no jewelry except for a pair of delicate wire earrings that sounded like tiny chimes when she moved her head.

She used very little makeup, nor did she require much. Her green eyes appraised him frankly, and finally she extended her hand. He took it, and was surprised by the strength of her grip.

"You're Harry Redwine?" she asked.

"Right. And you are . . . ?"

"You know perfectly well who I am, Mr. Redwine."

"True," he admitted. "But I'm not quite sure what to call you. The only name I could get from our comptroller was the Leather Madonna."

"Well, then you *do* know what to call me after all, don't you?"

Redwine saw a grin of amusement spread across Suma's face, and decided to change the subject. "Where did you find the table?" he asked.

"On a colony world near the Spica system," she replied, absently stroking the polished wood. "I spent seven years looking for something of that quality."

"Where are the pieces?"

"There aren't any."

"A chess table with no pieces?" he said with a smile.

"When I find a set that's worthy of the table, I'll buy it."

"What do you use in the meantime?"

She raised her head and met his gaze. "I don't play chess, Mr. Redwine."

"Strictly a collector, eh?"

"No," she responded. "I just don't play games that I can't win."

"Pity," he said.

"You disapprove?"

"Not at all," said Redwine. "I just liked it better when I thought I was the only one who felt that way."

"Well," she said, turning to him, "I don't imagine you're here to talk about chess tables." She gestured toward a couch. "Won't you sit down?"

He did so, and she walked around the chrome table and seated herself on the opposite couch.

"Can Suma get you a drink before she leaves, Mr. Redwine?"

He turned to Suma. "I'll have a whiskey, no ice, no water."

"And the usual for me," added the Leather Madonna.

Suma quickly poured his drink and then set about mixing some concoction for the Madonna in a long-stemmed crystal glass. As he waited for her to finish, Redwine turned his attention back to the Leather Madonna and tried to estimate her age. It was more difficult than he anticipated, and he finally concluded that she was in her late thirties, give or take a decade.

"Thank you," said the Leather Madonna when Suma finally handed her an iced, bluish drink. "Come back in about two hours."

Suma nodded, gave Redwine his glass, and left the room.

"I don't think we'll have two hours' worth of things to discuss today," offered Redwine.

"I quite agree," she replied. She took a small sip of her drink, and placed the glass down on the tabletop. "I trust everyone has treated you courteously since your arrival?"

"Absolutely," said Redwine, leaning back and extending his arms along the top of the couch. "It's been the most courteous runaround I've ever experienced."

She smiled, unperturbed. "Well, you must admit that your particular needs are not those we're used to serving."

"Lady, I'm just an accountant trying to do my job."

Her green eyes scrutinized him for a long moment. "You're too modest, Mr. Redwine," she said at last. "Somehow I feel you have many other talents."

He shrugged noncommittally. "Well, maybe one or two," he replied, wondering exactly how much she knew about him. "But one of the talents I seem to lack is the ability to gain access to the material I need."

"I thought you might be tired after your trip," explained the Leather Madonna. "Otherwise, I would have had everything ready and waiting for you."

He gave her a look of open disbelief.

"You seem dubious, Mr. Redwine," she noted.

"True. But I'm willing to be shown the error of my ways," he said. "I'll expect complete access to the computer's data banks by tomorrow morning." He paused. "And I'll want a tour of the facilities."

"Somehow I was sure that you would," said the Leather Madonna.

"Look," said Redwine reasonably. "We seem to be getting off on the wrong foot, and there's no reason for it. We both work for the same company, and we both want your operation to make as much money as it can. We have a lot more in common than you might think."

"Mr. Redwine," she said, "I run the finest brothel in the galaxy, and you spend all your time counting other people's money. What could we possibly have in common?" She finished her drink, then shrugged and smiled courteously. "Still, there's no reason why we can't work together in relative harmony. You'll be given access to the material you need tomorrow afternoon."

"What about tomorrow morning?" he persisted.

"I thought you wanted a tour of the ship." She noticed his empty glass. "Can I offer you a refill?"

"Well, as long as I'm not working tonight, why not?" he said amicably.

She pressed a section of the tabletop, and a moment later a tall, bronzed, blond man, heavily muscled and wearing nothing but sandals and a lioncloth, entered the room.

"Mr. Redwine will have another whiskey, without ice or water," said the Leather Madonna.

He nodded and went over to the bar. She turned back to Redwine and was about to say something when the top of the chrome table glowed with a dim phosphorescence and suddenly came to life, displaying the image of a middle-aged man in formal attire.

"Yes?" said the Leather Madonna.

"We have a counter at the blackjack table," said the man.

"Who is it?"

"Esteban Fuentes."

"How many decks are you using?"

"Two."

"All right," said the Leather Madonna. "Use five decks. If he can keep track of *them*, he deserves to win."

The tabletop went blank.

"I thought the casino was out of your bailiwick," remarked Redwine.

The Leather Madonna sighed. "Mr. Redwine, while we keep time aboard the *Velvet Comet* as a matter of convenience for our customers, in point of fact there *isn't* any day or night up here. We're an around-the-clock operation, and even our pit boss has to sleep every now and then. The man working the current shift is new to the job, and still unsure of himself in potentially awkward situations. Now, Mr. Fuentes is a very good customer of *all* our facilities, and one doesn't offend a very good customer when it can be avoided—or do you think we should have forbidden him to gamble until the pit boss wakes up and has breakfast?" She paused. "I realize that the company has its own ideas concerning our chain of command, but we're dealing with people here, not figures in one of your ledgers— and no matter how much money the casino brings in, it's still an adjunct to our main business. And I don't propose to let them offend *my* patrons." She watched him carefully for his reaction.

"I'm not here to tell you what to do or how to do it," said Redwine, noticing that she seemed to relax slightly as the words sunk in. "I'm just here to observe."

"I thought you were here to audit the books."

"And to appraise and evaluate the business," he added.

"And how many brothels have you appraised and evaluated in your long and varied experience?" she asked, arching an eyebrow.

"Not a one," he admitted. "In point of fact, I've never even been in one before today."

"Then please feel free to call on me for any assistance you may require."

"I just may do that," said Redwine, wondering if she had just propositioned him, and deciding to ignore it rather than make a fool of himself in case it had been a totally innocent remark.

The young blond man walked over, handed Redwine his drink, and looked questioningly at the Leather Madonna.

"That will be all," she said.

He inclined his head slightly, then left the room.

"Does he ever speak?" asked Redwine.

"When he has something to say," replied the Leather Madonna with a smile.

"We could use someone with that attitude back at headquarters," he commented dryly.

"How long have you been with the Vainmill Syndicate, Mr. Redwine?"

"More than twenty years, in one branch or another," he replied. "And you?"

"About ten. Have you been to Deluros?"

"I've been stationed there for the past three years," said Redwine, feeling a bit of the tension between them easing away as they moved on to other subjects. "It's a hell of a world. I wouldn't be surprised to see the Republic move its headquarters there one of these days. Earth's a little too far from the center of things."

"I've been there once," she remarked. "That's where they *should* have constructed the *Velvet Comet:* in orbit around Deluros."

"They'd have had to pay off too many politicians."

"Prostitution and gambling are legal in the Deluros system," she pointed out.

"I know," answered Redwine. "But orbital space is at a premium. They must have ten thousand spaceship hangars and customs stations circling the damned planet. It costs a lot of money to put something in orbit there, more than the *Comet* can afford."

"Not more than we could afford if we were *there*," responded the Leather Madonna, and Redwine heard a note of defensiveness creep into her voice.

"Maybe you're right," he said agreeably. "I suppose seven billion bureaucrats must have a lot of excess time and money on their hands."

"Not that we aren't very successful right where we are," she added quickly. "It's just that Deluros is . . . well . . . *Deluros.*"

"The biggest of the big apples," nodded Redwine.

"Exactly. We're the biggest and the best, so we ought to service the biggest and the best."

"You'll get no argument from me," he replied pleasantly. "However, I don't make the decisions. I'm just a two-bit bookkeeper."

"So you keep saying," commented the Leather Madonna. "By the way, what does 'two-bit' mean?"

"It's a holdover, from before we converted to credits."

"And what *was* a two-bit?"

He shrugged. "I haven't the slightest idea. I gather it was pretty trivial."

The tabletop came to life again, this time displaying a young woman's face.

"We've come up with a minor scheduling problem," announced the woman.

"The Gemini Twins again?"

The woman nodded.

"I'll get back to you in a minute," said the Leather Madonna, and the screen went blank. She looked across the table at Redwine. "I don't mean to be rude, but is there anything further we have to discuss that can't wait until tomorrow morning?"

"No," said Redwine, rising to his feet. "I certainly don't want to keep you from your work." He walked to the door, then turned to her just as she was reaching down to activate the screen. "Ah . . . there is *one* thing, I'm afraid."

"Yes?"

"I'm lost."

She smiled, walked to the secretary, uttered the word "Map," and received a piece of paper an instant later. She then crossed the room to where Redwine was standing and showed it to him.

"You're *here*," she said, using a pen she had withdrawn from the secretary and indicating a tiny rectangle on the incredibly complex map. "If you'll follow this line I'm drawing, it will take you to the elevator banks leading to your suite. You do know the number, I trust?"

"Yes," he replied.

"Then that's all there is to it," she concluded, handing the map to him. "If you decide to dine in one of our restaurants instead of using room service, just sign your name to the check; you have an unlimited line of credit, except at the casino and the shops."

"What about an occasional companion for the evening?" he asked.

"As I said, you have an unlimited line of credit."

"Much appreciated," he said. "I'm rather surprised that I don't feel like a kid turned loose in a candy shop. I guess that reaction sets in later."

"I really couldn't say, Mr. Redwine," she replied, as the tabletop came to life again. "And now, if you'll excuse me, I really must get back to work."

"See you tomorrow," said Redwine, walking out of the room and staring at the map.

As he passed one of the restaurants he decided that he could do with a meal after all, and shortly thereafter he was dining on a sumptuous feast of real meat, sautéed in a white wine sauce that he couldn't identify but decided on the spot to order again before he left the ship. Finally, when he had finished his flaming dessert and a superbly-blended after-dinner drink, he withdrew the map from his pocket and found his way back to his suite with less difficulty than he had anticipated.

He checked the tiny device he had attached to the back of the commode, and was not surprised to discover that both his room and its computer terminal were still being monitored. He entered his darkened closet, made a show of getting out a change of clothes, and managed to remove his skeleton card from his briefcase and slip it into the formal jacket that he would shortly don. Then he stepped back into the brightly-lit bedroom, opened his briefcase again, seemed to check its contents, nodded with satisfaction, locked it, and placed it back in the closet.

This done, he shaved, showered, dressed, and left his suite, ostensibly to enjoy a few hours in the casino, where formal wear seemed to be *de rigueur*. He strode down the corridor, entered the elevator, and ascended one level.

When he got out he found himself in a corridor almost identical to the one he had just left, waited until he saw a middle-aged woman and a handsome young man emerge from a suite about eighty feet away, and walked toward their door, pacing himself so that he reached it after they had entered the elevator.

He pulled out his skeleton card, inserted it in the lock, and entered the suite's elegant parlor an instant later. Wasting no time, he walked directly to the computer's holographic screen and held the card up.

"Activate."

The screen flickered to life.

"This is Harry Redwine, Identification Number 00345, code name Fixer. Please scan my card and identify my retina pattern." He waited a moment, then continued. "Once you've ascertained my identity, compare it against my Access Authorization under the code name Fixer. Let me know when you're done."

The computer flashed a completion message a few seconds later.

"Has my skeleton card activated this room's security system?"

The computer gave him a negative response.

"Is this terminal currently being monitored?"

Negative again.

"All right. Institute Priority Code 03G6673H2."

The computer winked in acknowledgement, and Redwine rattled off four more multi-digit codes in order.

"Now, computer, I want you to prevent anyone from

monitoring or interfering with this terminal for the next 300 seconds, and then I want you to wipe all trace of these 300 seconds from your memory banks." Five minutes, he had decided, was about as late as he could be and still claim unfamiliarity of the ship as an excuse.

"Now please bring up your Personnel File on Harry Redwine, Identification Number 00345."

The computer did as it was instructed, and the Fixer set out to discover just how much anyone on the *Velvet Comet* actually knew about him.

2

Redwine was just finishing his breakfast when he looked up and saw the Leather Madonna approaching him.

She was wearing a different jumpsuit, composed of small strips of beige, tan, and dark brown leather in a chevron pattern. Her gauntlets and knee-high boots were both tan, though the boots possessed gold heels that matched her golden belt. Again she wore no jewelry except for a very simple pair of earrings.

"Good morning, Mr. Redwine," she said pleasantly, sitting down opposite him. "Did you enjoy your breakfast?"

"It was delicious."

"And your suite?"

"All the comforts of home," he replied. "Plus a few dozen that home never had."

"I'm told that you didn't avail yourself of the most enjoyable of them."

"It was a long, tiring day. Besides," he added, "I'm not quite sure of the procedure."

"Just use your intercom and tell the person at the other end what you want," she said. "Or, if you prefer, let me know and I can arrange it for you."

"Much obliged," said Redwine. "Shall we get down to business?"

"I was *talking* business," laughed the Leather Madonna.

"*My* business, not yours." He pulled out the map she

had given him the previous day. "Before we start, I've got a couple of questions."

"I'll do my best to answer them."

"When my ship approached the *Velvet Comet*, I noticed that it was shaped kind of like a barbell," said Redwine. "Now, I gather that the section we're in is called the Resort."

"That's right."

"And this long section here"—he pointed to the map—"which looks like the bar of the barbell, is called the Mall."

"Yes. That's where we have all our shops and boutiques."

"Right. But I can't seem to find the other bell on the map."

"It's called the Home," she explained, "and we don't include it on the patrons' maps for the simple reason that it's off limits to them."

"And to me?" he asked.

"Of course not. You have run of the entire *Comet*, Mr. Redwine. In fact, I'll be taking you to the Home during your tour, since you'll want to see our security headquarters. Also, I have an auxiliary office there which you can work in, if it meets with your approval."

"The Home also holds the crew's quarters, I presume?"

"Among other things. It also houses most of our technical equipment, our staff infirmary, our administrative offices, and various lounges and other recreational facilities for off-duty personnel." She paused. "Did you have any other questions?"

"I'll ask them as they come to me," he said, rising to his feet. "Shall we begin?"

They spent the next hour going through most of the restaurants and lounges. The Madonna answered each of his questions pleasantly and thoroughly, and he noticed that the previous day's coolness and undercurrent of tension seemed to have vanished.

Finally, when they had gone through the sixth and

last of the kitchens, the Leather Madonna removed her
ornate belt buckle, turned it over, and touched a certain spot on it. A series of tiny lights blinked in a
repeating pattern, and after staring at it for a moment,
she replaced the buckle on her belt and turned to
Redwine.

"It seems that all of our fantasy rooms are in use for
the next hour or so. I can either show you some empty
suites, which are very similar to your own, or we can
take the slidewalk past some of the shops."

"I suppose if you've seen one million-credit suite
you've seen 'em all," said Redwine with an attempt at
levity that elicited a polite smile. "Let's take a look at
the shops."

She led him out through one of the restaurants and
past the huge reception foyer. They received a number
of stares along the way, but he couldn't decide whether
it was due to the fact that the madam herself was
showing him around the ship, or simply because of the
striking contrast between her own brilliant outfit and
his businessman's gray-on-gray.

Finally they reached the Mall, the two-mile-long store-
lined bar that connected the two bells of the *Comet*.
The domed ceiling was about thirty feet high, and try as
he would, Redwine couldn't spot the source of the
indirect lighting.

The main walkway of the Mall was some eighty feet
wide, with a sixty-foot strip of polished parquet flooring
separating the two slidewalks that ran in front of the
stores. At first Redwine thought the stores weren't doing
much business, but then he realized that the sheer size
of the Mall tended to make it seem far less crowded
than it was. Once he began concentrating on the
shoppers, he was surprised to find that there were well
over two hundred of them within his field of vision,
riding the slidewalks, walking across the parquet floor
from one side to the other, or browsing at various
windows.

The shoppers were grouped in twos and threes, with

one party of eight particularly catching his attention simply by virtue of its size. From this distance he was unable to see the discreet little badges that identified the *Comet*'s personnel, and found to his surprise that he was frequently unable to distinguish client from employee. A few were dressed formally—the women in gowns, the men in the pleated tunic tops and dark pants that had become so popular on Earth and Deluros— but most of them wore stylish leisure clothes, some very exotic, some less so. Here and there he could spot a woman in a particularly revealing dress or costume, but based on his brief observations in the *Comet*'s casino and restaurants he wasn't sure whether they were prostitutes or patrons.

A juggler in mime's makeup suddenly walked out into the center of the floor about a quarter-mile from the Resort and began putting on a truly remarkable display of expertise. He drew a crowd of perhaps twenty people, but most of them, after watching for a moment, applauded politely and went back to the slidewalks to continue their tour of the shops.

"Does he work for you?" asked Redwine.

"The juggler? He's one of the technicians. He just likes to entertain the patrons during his free time."

They stepped onto the slidewalk.

"Fascinating place," he said.

"Didn't you pass through it when you arrived?"

He shook his head. "They put me on some kind of tramway system. I assume it runs beneath the Mall."

"That's right."

"VIP treatment?" he asked.

She laughed. "*Employee* treatment. They knew you worked for the Vainmill Syndicate. We like our VIPs to have a chance to spend their money at the shops."

"Chardon of Belore, The Ice Crystal, DeLong's," he read as they passed a trio of boutiques. "It looks like the lobby of the Royal Hotel back on Deluros."

"You might try thinking of the *Velvet Comet* as an exclusive resort that provides a number of luxuries, including sexual assignations, rather than as simply a brothel," commented the Leather Madonna. "After all, our clientele can certainly purchase any sort of sexual partners they want without going to the trouble of coming out here. We have to offer them a total experience."

"Makes sense," agreed Redwine.

"You wouldn't believe how hard I had to fight the Vainmill Syndicate before *they* saw the sense of it."

"The shops are new, then?" he asked.

"The shops, the quality of the restaurants, the headline entertainers in the nightclub, even some of the fantasy rooms," she answered. "They've all been installed over the past six years, always after initial opposition—and they've all turned a profit." She turned to him suddenly. "I *made* the *Comet* what it is, Mr. Redwine," she said passionately, "and no one is going to take it away from me."

"Nobody's trying to."

"Then why are you here to appraise the operation?" she demanded.

He shrugged. "Who knows? Maybe I can spot a way for you to make a little more money."

Her expression said that she wasn't satisfied with his answer, but she decided to accept it for the moment, and Redwine went back to surveying the stores and shops.

"Sovereign & Crown," he said, gesturing to an office on the far side of the bar. "Isn't that a brokerage house?"

"Yes."

He looked puzzled. "All the suites have computers. Why the hell should a bright outfit like Sovereign's think they could do any business up here?"

Suddenly two men walked out of the office and took the slidewalk back to the reception foyer.

"A bright outfit like Sovereign's thought our clientele would like the human touch of conversing with a live broker," said the Leather Madonna. "Evidently they were right."

Redwine shrugged. "That just goes to show how much an accountant knows," he said self-deprecatingly.

The Leather Madonna turned to face him. "I want to apologize for flaring up at you a minute ago," she said.

"It's already forgotten."

"No," she insisted. "I'm sure coming here wasn't your idea. I was rude and ill-mannered. I promise that it won't happen again."

He smiled. "You're about to embarrass me, which is something even the so-called entertainments I saw on the holoscreen last night couldn't do."

She laughed. "All right, Mr. Redwine. The subject is closed."

"If you really want to make peace," he said, "why not start calling me Harry?"

"Harry it is."

"By the way, your comment about Sovereign's brings up an interesting question," he said, stepping aside to allow a middle-aged man who seemed in a hurry to pass him.

"Yes?"

"I notice that about every sixth or seventh shop has somebody working in it. Isn't that unusual?"

"Certainly—but our patrons can afford it, and they like the personal touch of dealing with people rather than machines. Also, the nature of the stores demands it. Whoever heard of a computer acting as a custom tailor? Usually one employee services half a dozen clustered shops. If you require personal service, simply announce it when you enter and someone will be with you as quickly as possible."

They rode in silence past a pair of lingerie shops, (one expensive and tasteful, one expensive and wildly exotic), a hair styling salon, a very discreet shop that sold very discreet sexual aids, a florist with the too-cute sobriquet of The Blooming Idiot, a dealer in alien art objects, a store that seemed to deal exclusively in fur wraps and feathered boas, and a jeweler of galactic renown.

"I think I've seen enough," remarked Redwine, stepping off the slidewalk and onto the polished parquet floor.

"Is something wrong?" asked the Leather Madonna.

"No," he said. "But I'm supposed to be inspecting the premises, not window-shopping. I don't imagine the ambience changes much in the next mile."

"No, it doesn't," she agreed. "But there's something that I want you to see."

"Oh?" he said, as she took his hand and gently pulled him back onto the slidewalk. "What is it?"

"That would be telling."

"Well, what the hell," he said. "I had planned to do a little shopping anyway."

"I gather you have a little more to spend than you did yesterday," she noted. "Or so the Duke tells me."

"The Duke?"

"Our pit boss. He says that you have a very complicated wagering system."

He chuckled. "*Very* complicated. I watch the roulette table until red comes up five times in a row, and then I bet on black."

"Very *effective*," she replied. "Or at least it was last night."

"That's because I know enough to quit when I'm ahead." He flashed her a grin. "The soul of an accountant."

"What made you become an accountant?" she asked as they barely avoided colliding with an elderly woman who was emerging from a jewelry shop.

"It took less work than being a lawyer."

"That hardly sounds like a man who is passionately dedicated to his work," said the Madonna.

"I'm passionately dedicated to paying my bills. Accounting is the best way I know how."

"Is there much challenge to it?"

"Some," he replied. "Not much." He paused. "I trust you're noticing the tact with which I have avoided asking you the very same questions."

"It must be quite a strain."

"It is," he confessed.

She laughed. "Some evening we'll sit down with a couple of drinks and I'll tell you all about it."

"I'm sure it'll make better listening than the story of *my* career."

"We'll see," she promised. Then she looked ahead of her. "Ah! We're almost there."

They stepped off a moment later, and she led him to an elegant little antique shop that displayed an ancient spinet in its window.

"Another chess table?" he asked, following her inside.

"No. There's only one of those."

"Then what?"

"Come along," she said. "You'll see."

They went to the back of the shop, and suddenly Redwine found himself confronting a huge bookcase, filled from top to bottom with leather-bound volumes from Earth itself.

He stepped forward and reached out gingerly. "May I?" he asked.

The Leather Madonna nodded. "Of course. They're what I brought you here to see."

He pulled out a copy of Shakespeare's *Sonnets* and began turning the pages very carefully.

"I got the impression from Suma that she'd never seen a book aboard the *Comet*," he remarked.

"Suma has probably never made it past the dress shops," said the Madonna. "But when she mentioned to me that you had brought some books along with you, I knew that I had to take you here."

"Do you collect books too?" he asked her, replacing the volume and withdrawing another.

"Let's say that I *prefer* them."

"I'm not quite sure of the difference," said Redwine.

"I like the *feel* of a book in my hands," explained the Madonna. "However, since books are very expensive and I can call up anything I need from the computer's library, I don't actually own very many. But I come here and borrow them quite frequently."

"I'm surprised the owner allows them out of his sight," said Redwine.

"The owner only gets up here once every two or three weeks."

"You know what I mean."

"He's a very nice man," she said. "I arrange for him to use our facilities on occasion, and he lets me borrow books and keeps an eye out for certain antiques that I want. It's one of the perks that go with the job. With *both* our jobs, for that matter."

"Sounds like an equitable arrangement," remarked Redwine. "Who's your favorite author?"

"Tanblixt."

"I've never heard of him. Or is it a her?"

"I doubt that even Tanblixt knows," she said, amused.

"An *alien*?"

She nodded. "The poet laureate of Canphor VI."

"What does he/she/it write?"

"The most passionate and lyrical poetry I've ever read."

"Sexless love poems?" he said dubiously.

"Your provincialism is showing, Harry," she said. "Perhaps I'll loan you a copy."

"I'd appreciate it. I don't suppose they have any here?" he said, indicating the rows of books.

She shook her head. "These are all human authors."

He went back to examining the books, finally withdrew a copy of Dante's *Inferno* that contained replications of the Gustave Doré engravings, took it up to the front of the store, and had the computer withdraw the purchase price from his home account. He then laid it very gently on a wrapping machine, waited a few seconds for the mechanism to encase it in colorful plastic and affix a satin bow at one corner, and then joined the Leather Madonna, who was waiting at the door for him.

"Pleased with your purchase?" she asked him.

"Very. I've been after a copy for maybe six or seven years."

"How many books do you have, Harry?"

"Oh, maybe five hundred," he said. "But fine volumes in fine bindings? Very few. That store's a treasure chest."

"I guess I know where you're going to be spending your spare time," said the Madonna.

"Only as a browser. I think one of these every couple of weeks is about all my budget can stand."

"I find it odd that an accountant should be so interested in the classics."

"I find it equally odd that a madam should be so interested in love poems."

"There's a lot of difference between sex and love."

"I suppose there is at that," he conceded.

She began walking across the parquet floor toward the return slidewalk, skirting two men and three women who were standing and talking midway between the slidewalks, and he fell into step behind her, studying the curve of her hips and the firmness of her buttocks and concluding that she probably still had what it took to entice a customer if the need arose.

"That large structure down toward the other end of the Mall—toward the Home," he said, pointing. "Is that where the most of the ships dock?"

She nodded. "That's the main airlock."

"They really *do* have to exercise sales resistance on the way to the Resort, don't they?"

"And on their way back out," she added.

"And what's on the other side of the airlock?"

"Storage rooms, food freezers, laundry facilities, a small hospital, things of that nature."

"A hospital?" he repeated, surprised. "Just how many sick people *are* there around here?"

"Very few. But given the nature of our clientele, if they *should* become ill they require the finest medical care available until they can be moved."

"By the way," he said, as the Leather Madonna nodded a friendly greeting to a nearby couple, "I thought I saw a shuttlecraft leaving the *Comet* as I was approaching yesterday. I assume you use it to transport patrons from Charlemagne?"

"That's right—though Charlemagne provides us with no more than fifteen percent of our business these days. If we could install some form of FTL motive power in the *Comet*, so that we weren't stuck in orbit around Charlemagne, I think we could encourage a real bidding war for our services." She watched him out of the corner of her eye for a reaction. "Deluros to the contrary, most Republic worlds would pay through the nose if we'd agree to take up orbit around them."

"It's a thought," he said noncommittally.

"If the Syndicate would spring loose the money to take us away from Charlemagne, it would be *more* than a thought," she persisted. "It would be a very profitable reality."

He smiled. "I don't know how much clout you think I've got, but I have a feeling you're overestimating it."

"I guess so," she said. "Anyway, it *would* work," she concluded stubbornly.

"Probably." He stepped off the slidewalk.

"What's the matter?" she asked, following him.

"I just want to stop here for a minute," he said, entering a surprisingly crowded tobacco shop. "I'm running short of cigars."

He made his purchase while she remained outside, then rejoined her.

"I may go broke before the tour is over," he remarked, transferring the cigar box to the same hand that was holding the book.

"It's a nasty habit anyway," she commented as they once again got on the slidewalk.

"It's nasty habits that keep most people in business."

"Then how fortunate it is for me that there are so many people like you," she said with a smile.

He laughed, and they fell to discussing books again

until he saw an elderly couple going into a furrier that specialized in the skins of alien animals.

"Which one of *them* is the prostitute?" he asked, genuinely puzzled.

"Neither," answered the Madonna. "They're a married couple from one of the Capellan colonies. I think they made their money in mining. Anyway, they come here once every three months, shop their way up to the reception foyer, part company for a week, and then shop their way back to their ship." She looked fondly at them through the display window, and smiled when the man waved to her. "I think they're adorable."

"Unusual, anyway," said Redwine.

They rode the short distance to the ornate reception foyer, which was relatively uncrowded. Two men and five women, none of them employees, sat in large, comfortable leather chairs, reading the latest stock quotations from the main Republic markets on a number of small computer screens, and a handful of other patrons and prostitutes sat in pairs, conversing quietly.

"How do you spot gate-crashers when this place is packed?" asked Redwine.

"They never get this far," replied the Leather Madonna. "Except for the casino, all the financial arrangements are taken care of before our patrons arrive. Once the payment has been transferred to our account, each patron is given a code number, and he can't get through the airlock until our security crew clears him."

"Seems like a waste of manpower," commented Redwine. "Couldn't a computer check them out just as easily?"

"Yes—but a computer couldn't stop them from entering without sealing off the entrance and causing serious inconvenience to any legitimate patrons who happen to be in the airlock at the same time. Why chance offending a good customer by forcing him to remain there against his will until the problem is solved?"

"Yeah, I can see where that might ruffle a few over-anxious feathers."

"Anyway, after a patron has been identified and approved, he or she comes to the reception area and is given a suite, just as you were, and if any arrangements were made in advance, a preselected companion is waiting in the bedroom."

"Is that standard—reserving a companion before arriving?"

She shrugged. "It varies. Some of our more popular employees, such as Suma and the Gemini Twins and a few others, are frequently booked four and five months in advance."

"The Gemini Twins?" he repeated. "I heard you refer to them yesterday. I keep picturing a pair of gorgeous young blondes decked out in very revealing togas."

The Leather Madonna laughed. "The Gemini Twins are a pair of young men who have been surgically altered to appear identical. They work only as a team."

"Are there many requests for multiple companions?"

"Quite a few. Our customers are very sophisticated people with very sophisticated tastes, and by and large they're here for a unique experience—which we do our best to provide."

"I assume you charge proportionately more for extra bodies."

"Extra *companions*, Harry," she corrected him with obviously mock severity. "Yes, we do."

"Do you get many requests for full-scale orgies?"

"Of course. In fact, we have a specialty group that we call the Demolition Team."

He laughed. "That's a hell of a name for them."

"They received it from the Governor of Belore's granddaughter—and I might add that she coined it with a *great* deal of respect."

"I don't doubt it," replied Redwine, amused. He paused to light a cigar. "Demolition Team, Gemini Twins, Duke, Madonna. Does anyone around here ever use their real name?"

"Very rarely. Our customers seem to prefer it. It

lends a certain air of mystery, a little touch of the exotic."

"And of course not knowing names makes it a lot harder for a patron to try to form a permanent relationship," added Redwine.

"Harry, I think you're a secret romantic," said the Leather Madonna. "People don't come to a brothel to form permanent relationships."

"Nobody's ever tried to get one of your prostitutes to run off with him?" he persisted.

"I take it that you haven't read our employment contract?"

"I'll bet it's a beauty."

"The best."

"Getting back to your customers—"

"*Patrons*," she corrected him.

"Excuse me: patrons. What if they *haven't* made a prior arrangement?"

"Then they go to their suites, and at such time as they feel like selecting a companion they instruct the computer to produce holographic displays of all of our available employees as well as a list of their interests."

"You mean their specialties?" he asked.

She shook her head. "You're still thinking of this as some kind of planetbound meat shop, Harry. People come up here to unwind and relax, and sooner or later—usually sooner—they will want a personable partner as well as a passionate one. All of our employees are sexual professionals; the holographs inform our patrons of their *other* qualities."

"What happens when you get someone who finds pain stimulating?"

"*Everyone* has unique needs," responded the Leather Madonna, "whether it's a salt-free diet or regular medication or an interest in the more exotic sexual disciplines. We ask our customers to inform us of them when they make their reservations, so that we can be prepared for them."

"Ever get a sexual request you couldn't fulfill?" he asked, curious.

"Infrequently."

"Such as?"

"You really wouldn't want to know, Harry."

"No," he admitted after a few seconds' reflection. "I suppose I wouldn't."

She paused for a moment, then checked her belt buckle again, and announced that two of the fantasy rooms were now available for his inspection.

"Up or down?" he asked, trying to remember the details of the map as he followed her to an elevator bank at the far end of the foyer.

"The fantasy rooms and athletic facilities are on the upper decks, above the public rooms, and the suites are below them."

The elevator doors opened, and they quickly ascended to the Resort's highest level. They stepped out into a narrow, brightly lit corridor, and Redwine stepped aside hastily to avoid a huge, muscular young man and a petite blonde woman who were hurrying to catch the elevator.

"Wasn't that Gamble DeWitt?" asked Redwine as the doors slid shut.

"Yes. Do you know him?"

He shook his head. "I saw him fight once, on Spica VI, before he beat Nkimo for the title. It must have been, oh, seven or eight years ago. I think he retired about half a year back."

"Eight months," said the Madonna.

"Does he come here often?"

"He works here."

"Under a pseudonym?"

She smiled. "That would be rather silly in his case, wouldn't it?"

"True enough," agreed Redwine. "I would imagine they're lined up halfway to Deluros for *his* services."

"Not really," said the Leather Madoona dryly. "There's

a vast difference between blood sports and bedroom sports."

"Then there's hope for me yet," he grinned.

They walked down the corridor, turned to their right, and finally came to a halt before an oversized door.

"Open," commanded the Madonna. The door slid back into a wall and they stepped into the room.

Redwine found himself on a flat outcropping of rock that overlooked a tropical lagoon. Opposite him was a small waterfall, and to his left was a glade of fruit-bearing trees. A number of brightly plumaged birds flew overhead, and off in the distance he could see what appeared to be a small, dormant volcano, its peak hidden behind a layer of mist. A pleasant breeze carried the scents of jasmine and honeysuckle.

It was cooler and less humid than he would have anticipated from such a setting, and somehow he knew that the water would always be a perfect 68 degrees Fahrenheit. He turned to his right and saw a small thatched hut some fifty feet away. Next to it was a pair of coconut trees with a hammock strung up between them, and behind it a path climbed up a small hill to a lush tropical forest.

"What do you think of it?" asked the Leather Madonna.

He looked around for another moment before answering.

"I'd like to retire to a place like this someday," he said at last.

"There *are* no places like this," she replied gently. "A real tropical island is hot and muggy, and has about ten thousand hungry insects per cubic yard. Jasmine doesn't grow in that kind of climate, and the place is likely to smell of rotting fruit. That's why we call this a fantasy room."

"I take it that you're not much of a romantic," he remarked wryly.

"Only when I'm paid to be."

"I thought you were strictly an administrator," said

Redwine. "Do you still get out into the field, so to speak?"

"I was being facetious, Harry."

"I wasn't."

She shrugged. "I still service an occasional special customer. Why?"

"Just curious. Do you enjoy it?"

She smiled. "I'll answer that when you can prove to me that it's essential to your work."

"Touché!"

"Would you like to see the other room now?"

"In a minute," he said, walking to the edge of the outcropping and looking down into the lagoon. "How big is this room, anyway?"

"I think the actual dimensions are something like ninety feet by two hundred."

"That small?"

She nodded. "Most of what you see are holographic projections."

"What's real?"

"The rock structure, part of the lagoon, some of the grass—though of course it's artificial, the hut and hammock, a few trees. The rest is illusion."

"It's one hell of an illusion, let me tell you." He looked down into the lagoon, then over to the glade of fruit trees. "There's *got* to be a setting like this somewhere in the universe," he said wistfully.

"There is," replied the Leather Madonna. "You're standing in it."

He turned to her with a sardonic grin on his face. "*I* may be a romantic who spends his life dealing with columns of numbers, but *you're* a professional paramour with the soul of an accountant."

"Maybe that's why we're getting along so well," she laughed.

"Maybe," he agreed. He took one last lingering look, then turned and stepped back from the edge of the rock. "All right. I'm ready for the next illusion."

"The next one isn't an illusion," she said, walking

toward what appeared to be a tree and murmuring "Open." The door slid back and they stepped out into the hall.

"It's just next door," she told him, walking about one hundred feet down the corridor and ordering the next door to open.

Redwine followed her into a much smaller room, perhaps forty feet deep, thirty feet wide and twenty feet high. The walls were heavily padded, and there were no props or holographic displays of any kind.

"I've heard of this one," he said, looking up toward the padded ceiling. "It's the free-fall room, isn't it?"

"That's right. I suppose it's the most famous fantasy room we have. Sooner or later everyone wants to try it out." She paused. "I wish I'd never gotten the bright idea of installing it."

"Why not?"

She looked at him. "Have you ever fucked in free-fall, Harry?"

"No. I never have."

"Well, don't. You can sprain everything you've got."

"I'll take it under advisement," he replied. "Where are the controls?"

"There aren't any," she answered. "Oh, we could put a panel over here by the door—or anywhere else for that matter—but it's pretty unlikely that our patrons would be anywhere near it when they decided to turn it off."

"So how does it work?"

"By voice command."

"Maybe you'd better spell out the command words so I don't inadvertently say them and go floating off," he suggested.

She laughed. "Don't worry. The room is deactivated until it's scheduled for use, to avoid just such a possibility."

He looked around. "No music, no light show, no nothing?"

"We had them originally, but it's hard enough to

concentrate on what you're doing in free-fall without added distractions."

"If you say so."

"You look unconvinced. Someday you'll have to try it and see for yourself."

"Is that an invitation?" he asked her.

"A prophecy," she replied. "And Harry?"

"Yes?"

"When you do try it, make sure you do it on an empty stomach."

"My friend the romantic," he muttered.

"My friend the hard-headed businessman," she shot back.

Redwine took a last brief look around the room, then turned to her. "Well, what's next on the agenda?"

"I suppose we'll end the tour with our Security section, unless you've an undying urge to see the hydroponics garden."

"Not really."

"Just as well. We've turned part of it into a picnic area, and it tends to be a little crowded this time of day. Anyway," she added, "after we're through with Security, I'll turn my auxiliary office over to you."

"What about the casino?"

"I thought you saw that last night," she replied, and he detected a note of tension creeping into her voice.

"True enough," he replied quickly, following her out into the corridor. "Security it is, then."

They walked to a different elevator bank and rode down to the public room level, emerging just outside a restaurant that was decorated to resemble a sanitized and opulent version of one of the notorious drug dens of Altair III. The waiters looked like blackhearted villains, and a sultry, olive-skinned girl, an unlit analog of a hashish cigarette dangling from her lips, was doing a slow, sensual dance to the music of a single flutist. Redwine noted, however—as he had earlier in the day— that the food was as well-prepared and carefully-served as in the other restaurants.

Suddenly the Leather Madonna's belt buckle beeped twice, and she turned to him. "Wait here just a moment, won't you?" she said, walking over to a small visual intercom on a nearby wall. She returned a minute later.

"I'm afraid a little problem has come up," she said apologetically.

"Nothing serious, I hope?"

"It won't be if I attend to it quickly. We have a very assertive lady who has decided to extend her stay, and a very demanding gentleman who has booked her suite and insists that no other rooms are acceptable."

"Can't your computer come up with a solution?" he asked.

She shook her head. "Computers are rational machines, and they expect people to behave in a rational manner." She chuckled. "Poor things."

"Where would you like me to wait for you?"

"That won't be necessary. I've arranged for Suma to take you to Security."

"I'm happy to wait," he insisted.

"You don't realize what a favor I'm doing you, Harry. Half of our patrons would happily walk through fire to spend a few extra minutes alone with her."

"I never got along well with children," said Redwine.

"How flattering," said the Madonna.

"Especially very bright, very self-centered ones," he added.

"And how perceptive."

"So, if it's all the same to you . . ."

"Harry, this could take me two or three hours of delicate negotiating," she said firmly.

He sighed. "You're the boss."

"I'll try to catch up with you later," she said, heading off toward her office. "Suma should be here shortly."

He watched her walk away, and decided once again that she was a damned attractive woman. Cordial and self-controlled, too, especially since she was obviously convinced that he was here to usurp some of her authority at the behest of whoever ran the gambling concession.

He lit a cigar and let the smoke roll around on his tongue for a few seconds as his accountant's mind kept cataloguing: attractive, cordial, self-controlled, well-read, demonstrably successful at managing a huge operation like the *Velvet Comet*, doubtless skilled as all hell in bed.

He frowned. He wished he hadn't hit it off so well with her this morning, that he didn't feel a sensation of budding friendship toward her.

He was going to feel genuinely sorry when he brought her tidy, affluent little world crumbling down about her.

3

Suma arrived about five minutes later.

Her outfit was, to say the least, spectacular. She wore an elaborate golden slave collar, from which were suspended perhaps twenty strips of narrow cloth that hung down almost to the floor and were gathered in very loosely at the waist by a gold belt. The outside of the cloth was scarlet, the inside a metallic gold, and as she moved the strips opened and closed, presenting Redwine with the kind of peepshow he'd paid good money to see when he was a kid.

She wore huge golden earrings, covered by gold coins, that hung down to her shoulders and jingled when she walked. Her hair was piled high in another complicated hairdo that involved dozens of gold beads. Slave bracelets, an armband, and a pair of very high-heeled shoes, also all gold, completed the picture.

"Good morning, Mr. Redwine," she said with a feline smile of greeting.

"Hello, Suma. You're looking exceptionally lovely today."

"Do you like it?" she asked, extending her arms and turning around, to the delight of a trio of passing patrons.

"It's eye-catching, that's for sure," said Redwine.

"Have you enjoyed your tour so far?"

"It's been enlightening," he replied. "And it's taught me to keep away from the free-fall room."

"Oh? Why?"

"The Madonna explained just how awkward it is."

Suma looked puzzled, then shrugged her shoulders, a gesture that caused new expanses of smooth, creamy flesh to be temporarily revealed. "Well, *I* like it." She flashed him a roguish smile. "Maybe you should try it and make up your own mind."

"Right now?" he asked, startled.

She looked amused. "I'm afraid not, Mr. Redwine. I'm supposed to take you to Security."

"What a shame," he said with a secret sense of relief. "I guess my education will just have to wait."

"By the way," she said, leading him away from the restaurant, "why does a Syndicate accountant have to take a tour of Security?"

Good question, thought Redwine. "The Madonna seemed to think I'd find it interesting," he answered her.

She took him to an elevator, descended one level, and then led him out to the tram tunnel. There were a number of cars stationed there, and Suma walked over to the nearest of them. It scanned her retina briefly, and then its door unlocked and swung open.

Redwine followed her and took a seat, and a moment later the tram began speeding toward the Home.

"I didn't see any unescorted employees in the Mall," mentioned Redwine. "Is there some house rule that requires you to take the tram when you're not with a patron?"

She shook her head. "No, but two miles is a long way to walk, even on a slidewalk. This way it takes about eighty seconds."

They rode the brief remainder of the trip in silence, then got off when the tram came to a halt.

"What if a patron wanders down to the Home while he's shopping?" asked Redwine.

"Then he bumps into a wall," she said. "The security system won't let him in unless he's got a reason to be here."

She approached a door, again waited for the com-

puter to verify her retinagram, and then they walked
into an unfurnished entry hall which seemed to belong
to some other universe than that which housed the
huge, ornate public rooms of the Resort.

Suma led Redwine to a bank of elevators, took him
up to the top level, and stopped at the first door they
came to.

"Here we are, Mr. Redwine," she announced.

"Thanks," he said. "How do I get back?"

"The same way you got here," said Suma. "Someone
in Security will transfer your retinagram to the Home's
system so that you can use the trams and get in the
door."

"And how do I get *into* Security?" he asked, looking
futilely for a lock or buzzer on the plain, unmarked
door.

"They know we're here," she said calmly.

No sooner had the words left her mouth than the
door slid open, revealing a small, functional, but rather
plain reception room that caused Redwine to reflect
wryly on how little time it had taken him to grow
accustomed to opulent surroundings. A uniformed woman
sat behind a utilitarian chrome desk, and as he looked
in she nodded pleasantly to him.

"I take it you're not staying here with me," he remarked when he noticed that Suma had taken a few
steps down the hallway.

She turned to him. "My current partner should be
through swimming in about twenty minutes, and it
wouldn't do to keep him waiting. Some other time,
perhaps," she added, smiling invitingly if insincerely at
him.

He tried with equal insincerity to look hopeful, then
entered the room and walked to the desk.

"My name is Harry Redwine."

"We've been expecting you," replied the woman.
"Won't you have a seat?"

He walked over to a chair, looked around for some
reading matter, and finally settled for reading the sports

headline that appeared on a small screen to his left. A moment later a short, stocky, gray-haired man wearing a dark green uniform entered the room through another door and approached him.

"Mr. Redwine?" he said, extending his hand.

"Right. And you're . . . ?"

"Chief of Security. You can call me Rasputin."

"An interesting name for a Security chief," remarked Redwine.

"I chose it myself," replied Rasputin proudly. He turned to the woman at the desk. "Hold all my messages while I'm with Mr. Redwine." He walked to the door through which he had entered. "Follow me, Mr. Redwine—or may I call you Harry?"

"Harry's fine," said Redwine, falling into step behind him. They walked down a narrow corridor, past a number of closed doors, and finally entered a modestly-furnished office that would easily have fit into one of the Resort's bathrooms.

There was a small computer console on a plain metal desk, and right next to the control panel was a holograph of a rather pretty women and two small boys. There were a pair of rather uninspired prints on the wall, one an astronomical scene and the other an alien landscape of some distant chlorine world. A small shelf held a holograph of the two boys, another showed them as young men with their own families, and a glass case contained a trio of medals.

Redwine approached the medals and scrutinized them.

"New Rhodesia," he read. "Did you see much action there?"

"Just mopping-up stuff," said Rasputin. "Some nut named Bland set up a death camp there, and the Navy moved in and ran him off the planet."

"How long have you been out of the service?"

"About fifteen years. I signed on here when they activated the *Comet* twelve years ago."

"Your wife?" asked Redwine, indicating the woman in the holograph.

Rasputin nodded. "She's dead now. Spaceship wreck."

"I'm sorry."

The Security chief sighed. "It happens."

An awkward silence ensued as Redwine wondered what to say next.

"Have a seat, Harry," said Rasputin at last, indicating a chair. He walked over to a small, built-in bar. "Can I offer you something to drink—a Cygnian cognac, perhaps?"

"Just whiskey will do. Straight."

"You're an easy man to please," remarked Rasputin, pouring out a glass and handing it to him.

"You're not joining me?" asked Redwine, as the security man sat down behind his desk.

"Never when I'm on duty," he replied. "It's a holdover from my military days."

"Well, perhaps later, then," said Redwine. "If you're over at the Resort later tonight, hunt me up and I'll buy you one."

"I wish I could take you up on that, Harry," said Rasputin, "but I'm afraid I'm going to be working late tonight."

"Nothing serious, I hope."

Rasputin stared at him. "I won't know that until I can figure out what you did to the main computer last night."

Redwine almost choked on his drink.

"I'm afraid I don't follow you," he said, coughing.

"Oh, come off it, Harry," said Rasputin easily. "We both know what I'm talking about." He paused. "You're *good*, I'll give you that. I still don't know how you got into it or what you did to it."

"Then what makes you think I did anything at all?" asked Redwine, quickly recovering his composure.

"Because *I'm* good at *my* job, too," replied Rasputin. "That's why I thought we ought to have this little chat before I showed you around."

"If you really believe I did something to the computer, are you sure you *want* to show me around?"

"Well, that's something else I gave a lot of thought to. But I've already checked you out with headquarters. You really are a company accountant. Your retina checks, your identification checks, everything checks. Whatever else you are, you're not a ringer." He paused and sighed heavily. "The thing that bothers me is that you couldn't have done it without a skeleton card—and not just *any* skeleton card, either. It has to be one that can transmit a Priority Code to the computer. That means you've got an awfully high security clearance." Rasputin frowned. "What I want to know is why I wasn't told about you? I mean, hell, I'm the Chief of Security!"

"Have you ever considered the possibility that you might be mistaken?" suggested Redwine mildly.

"Not a chance, Harry."

"Have you told anyone about your suspicions yet?" asked Redwine.

"Not yet."

"Not even the Leather Madonna?"

"There's nothing to tell," admitted Rasputin. "If headquarters didn't see fit to inform me, they're sure as hell not going to own up to it now." He leaned back in his chair and clasped his hands behind his head. "But I'm a very persistent man, and like I said, I'm good at my job. If I don't find out what you did tonight, I'll work at it tomorrow night, and next week and next month if I have to. And once I know, you and I and the Madonna can all sit down and have a nice friendly little talk."

Redwine stared at him for a long moment, then took a deep breath and exhaled it slowly.

"It won't take you that long," he said at last. "Three or four days if you're as good as you think you are, a week if you're not."

"Then why not tell me now and make it easy on both of us?"

"Because it's none of your business."

"My business is the security of the ship," Rasputin pointed out. "And you breached that security, Harry."

"If the Vainmill Syndicate wanted you to know what I was here for, they'd have told you."

"I thought you were here to go over the books."

"I am."

"And what else?"

"Nothing else—and if there *was* anything else, it also wouldn't be any of your business."

"I don't know what you did last night," persisted Rasputin, "but I do know this much: you never called up the financial data banks."

"If I give you my word that what I did has nothing to do with the security of the *Velvet Comet*, will you back off and leave this alone?" asked Redwine.

Rasputin shook his head. "Look," he said reasonably, "you broke into a computer that was under my direct jurisdiction. Probably everything you just told me is true, and probably I'm going to regret finding whatever it is that you did. But this is my job, Harry, and you made a fool of me." He extended his hand across the desk. "Nothing personal."

Redwine stared at the outstretched hand, then shrugged and took it.

"Fair enough," he said. He downed the remainder of his drink. "Now how about that tour?"

"Glad to," said Rasputin, rising to his feet and walking to the door. "I like you, Harry, I really do. I sure as hell hope I don't have to clip your wings."

"Acountants don't fly that high, believe me," said Redwine, following him out into the antiseptic, tiled corridor.

Rasputin walked about forty feet to another door, then waited for Redwine to catch up to him. He uttered a five-digit code and the door slid back, revealing a very small room filled with a number of computer banks and readout screens, as well as a large hologram of the airlock. A single security technician, a tiny receptor in his ear and a miniaturized microphone affixed just in front of his mouth, was monitoring the equipment while simultaneously carrying on a conversation with someone at the other end the system. As Redwine looked at the hologram, he saw two well-dressed men presenting their credentials to a trio of security guards.

"This is where it all starts," explained Rasputin. "We let the wrong people through the airlock and we've really got our work cut out for us. These three machines"—he indicated a trio of computers—"check out their luggage. We've got a lot of patrons who like to flash their jewelry or their cash; it wouldn't do to have a guest bring along a weapon or any burglar tools. In fact, I'm surprised we missed your skeleton card, but I suppose they made it peep-proof before they gave it to you."

Redwine chose to ignore his last remark. "Why would someone who could afford to come here in the first place want to rob another patron?"

"If you were a big-game hunter, you wouldn't take an expedition to a lifeless planet, would you?" said Rasputin. "Well, if you were a jewel thief . . ."

"I get the picture."

Rasputin turned to another bank of computers. "Now, while those first three machines I showed you are checking out the baggage, this batch here is checking out the patrons themselves."

"You don't need this much equipment just to take retina scans," noted Redwine. "What else does it do?"

"Harry, there are more than three hundred venereal diseases currently known and cataloged, and more are cropping up every year. We can't have our prostitutes spreading them, so they undergo a daily scan at the infirmary. But that only takes care of half of the potential problem." He paused. "Now, a number of our customers would probably be offended if we asked them to produce health certificates, and it would spoil their vacations if we made them undergo thorough examinations once they arrived, so we scan them surreptitiously in the airlock, and if there's a possible problem, one of our personnel tactfully but firmly takes them over to the hospital for treatment." He smiled. "You'll be pleased to know that you're in perfect health, except for slightly high blood pressure and a little excess weight."

"How very gratifying," replied Redwine dryly.

Rasputin stepped back into the corridor. "Now, if you'll come next door . . ."

Redwine followed him to the next room, a claustrophobic cubicle where he found two uniformed young women intently studying an array of sixteen holographic screens.

"We call this place the Duke's Castle," commented Rasputin.

"I can see why," said Redwine, noting that each of the screens displayed a section of the casino.

Rasputin tapped one of the women on the shoulder. "Is my friend the Lady Toshimatu at her usual place?"

The woman checked a screen, then shook her head. "I think she's back in her room with a companion," she replied.

"Too bad," said Rasputin, turning back to Redwine. "I was going to show you the sharpest little old lady I've ever seen. She inherited a fortune that took ten generations to build, and practically doubled it in five years. She's got money she hasn't even counted yet."

"And?"

"Best goddamned card sharp I ever saw," said Rasputin, not without a touch of professional admiration. "We've barred her from the blackjack and baccarat tables, but we *still* haven't figured out how she's cheating at poker. I think she goes to bed with the prostitutes just so she'll have access to the casino."

"So what do you do about her?"

"Once we figure out how she's cheating, we bar her or change the rules on her. Given the clout she carries, probably the latter. And in the meantime, we subtly warn her opponents off. But the thing that fascinates me is that here is a woman who could buy the *Comet* with her pin money, and she still risks humiliation and possibly even arrest, just for the kick of getting away with cheating at cards when she knows we're watching her." He sighed. "One of these days I'll nail her." He turned back to Redwine. "She and you are my two special projects, Harry."

"Maybe you're wrong about *her*, too," suggested Redwine.

"Maybe hell has chilled champagne," answered Rasputin. "You've got to understand that I don't hold what you're doing against either of you, Harry. After all, if security was never breached, there wouldn't be any need for a Security chief, would there? But by the same token, I've got a job to do too, and nothing's going to stop me from doing it."

"I have some friends back on Deluros who could *order* you to stop," said Redwine.

"Call anyone you want," said Rasputin pleasantly. "Even your pal Victor Bonhomme."

"Victor Bonhomme?" repeated Redwine, struggling to conceal his surprise. "I've never heard of him."

Rasputin cocked an eyebrow in amusement. "You keep saying things like that, Harry, and you're going to make me wish you were a betting man."

Redwine decided that the Duke's Castle, with its two trained observers, was no place to embark upon a further discussion of the matter, so he walked out into the corridor.

"I didn't mean to embarrass you, Harry," said Rasputin, following him. "But these are *my* people. Nothing you say in front of them will go any farther."

"Maybe not," said Redwine with obvious disbelief. "But Mama Redwine didn't raise any children stupid enough to talk about their private business in front of the Chief of Security, two of his employees, and a batch of recording equipment."

Rasputin chuckled. "Yeah, I guess I can appreaciate your point of view. Shall we continue the tour?"

Redwine nodded. "Where to now?"

Rasputin spent the next two hours showing him the security system for the Mall, the tramway, and the Resort's public and fantasy rooms. By unspoken mutual consent, they sparred about the Security chief's interest in Redwine only when no one else was within earshot, though Redwine soon got the feeling that nothing that transpired aboard the *Comet*, even within the Security Department itself, was ever completely private.

"Well, does that about do it?" he asked after enduring a boring explanation and demonstration of how the *Comet's* life support systems and orbital engines were constantly monitored.

"Just one more room to go. Then maybe I'll bend a rule and have a drink with you after all."

"Is seeing this last room absolutely necessary?"

"No, but I think you might find it interesting," replied Rasputin.

He took Redwine across the hall and entered what was by far the largest room in the security complex. There were fewer computer terminals here, but the walls were covered from floor to ceiling with upward of four hundred holographic screens, about a third of them currently activated. A team of three men and six women, all in standard green security uniforms, were posted about the room, sitting on stools and monitoring the displays.

A huge pot of coffee, the first sign of any creature comfort he had seen since leaving Rasputin's office, sat on a small table, surrounded by a number of disposable cups. Other than that, the working conditions were as Spartan here as elsewhere in the complex.

Redwine found his gaze drawn to the screens, many of which displayed scenes of frenzied sexual activity.

"The Resort suites?" he asked.

Rasputin nodded. "The cameras are activated when the room is entered. If you can tear your eyes away from the fun parts, you'll notice that a number of the screens just show people sleeping."

"Do you have a similar display for the Home?" asked Redwine, trying not to appear too interested.

"After what our prostitutes go through day in and day out, they deserve *some* privacy."

Which wasn't exactly an answer, but Redwine decided not to push it. If they tried to observe him in the Leather Madonna's auxiliary office, he had ways of handling the situation.

"Do the patrons know they're being watched in their own rooms?"

"Not officially, but I'd be surprised if most of them didn't."

"And they don't mind it?"

"The ones who have figured out that we're doing it are bright enough to figure out the reasons for it," answered Rasputin. "We're not voyeurs, Harry. Hell, after two days on the job, it's all just that much meat on the hoof. But we get some pretty wild sado-masochist scenes from time to time, and we have to make sure that things don't get out of hand—and if a prostitute is going to swipe some jewelry or a wallet, it makes more sense to do it when the patron is undressed and maybe asleep."

"I'll be sure to smile into the camera tonight," said Redwine sardonically.

"Do you mean to say you're going to let us watch?" replied Rasputin with a disbelieving smile.

"How can I stop you?"

"Come on, Harry—we both know what you're carrying around with you." Rasputin paused. "If I frisked you right now, would I find it?"

"No," said Redwine calmly, trying to remember which shoe he had slipped the skeleton card into.

"I could have your room searched while you're at this end of the *Comet*," suggested Rasputin pleasantly.

"Just be sure to tidy things up when you're done," replied Redwine. He paused, then added seriously: "You know, if you find it, they're just going to send me another."

"I know," agreed Rasputin. "That's why I'm not going to make you take your shoes off."

"My shoes? What are you talking about?"

"Harry, the second I mentioned frisking you, you

looked down at your feet like they were on fire. Now, either you're afraid to meet my steely gaze, or you've got more inside those shoes than your feet."

"I'll take them off if it'll make you happy," said Redwine, forcing himself to look bored and deciding that Rasputin was a lot more formidable than he looked.

The Security chief shook his head. "Don't bother. If I find out you lied to me it'll spoil a beautiful relationship—and besides, you're probably cleared to carry the card. I just want to know what you're doing with it."

"I wish I could help you out," said Redwine sincerely. "You're the *friendliest* antagonist a man could ask for."

"I just never found that screaming and threatening did all that much good," answered Rasputin. "But the operative word in your statement is *antagonist.*" He shrugged, as if momentarily tired of the subject. "Is there anything I can show or explain to you before we go back to my office?"

"As a matter of fact, there is," said Redwine. "But first, how about answering a silly question?"

"I'll do my best."

"Calling the other two sections of the ship the Mall and the Resort makes sense—after all, that's what they are. But what idiot coined the term Home for this end of it?"

"You're looking at him," answered Rasputin. "And it made a lot more sense when you figure that the other end used to be called the House."

"As in, a house is not a . . . ?"

"Right. But when the Madonna took over a few years ago, she decided that it was too vulgar, and she changed it to the Resort." He paused. "I liked my term better."

"So do I," agreed Redwine, "It has a certain tasteless elegance to it."

"Well said," laughed Rasputin. "All right. What else can I show you?"

"I keep hearing about the Gemini Twins. They wouldn't happen to be hard at work right now, would they?"

"Let's find out," said Rasputin. He walked over to one
of the computers, called up a complicated schedule,
and studied it for a moment. "You just may be in luck,
Harry," he announced, walking directly to one of the
screens. "Yeah, there they are."

Redwine joined him and stared at the small holographic display. Two dark-haired young men were sitting on opposite sides of a huge bed composed entirely
of alternating layers of silks and furs. Between them sat
a rather pretty redhead, perhaps forty years old, clad in
a rather insubstantial nightgown. All three held long-
stemmed crystal glasses filled with some exotic concoction.

As Redwine watched them—and they appeared so
identical that he could differentiate them only as The
One on the Right and The One on the Left—first one
and then the other began gently stroking the woman's
arms and her legs. Occasionally one—though never
both together—paused to take a sip of his drink, or to
utter some comment which seemed to elicit a pleased
reaction from her. Gradually, so slowly that Redwine
was hardly aware of it, the intensity of their ministrations increased, and with no awkward pauses or cessa-
tion of their gentle touching and stroking, he noticed
that they had somehow removed the woman's gown,
and that her glass was now on the nightstand.

The tempo of their love-making increased almost
imperceptibly. The touches and kisses become more
intimate, and still they seemed unhurried, relaxed,
leisurely. Now one of the Twins, now the other, would
pause to say something, or simply to offer the woman
yet another sip of her drink, while the remaining Twin
would lower his lips to an erect nipple, or gently trace
little patterns on the inside of her thighs with his
fingertips.

Before long the woman began writhing sensually, and
the Twins shifted their positions with the precision and
timing of skilled athletes—which, decided Redwine,
was probably the closest analogy to what they actually

were. Intimate kisses and touches increased in speed and fervor, and still neither of them would mount and enter her until the posture of her trembling body made it clear that no other response would be acceptable. Then, by some predetermined game plan, one of the Twins swiftly and gracefully moved on top of her while the other, with no apparent effort, managed to move his body out of the way while still kissing and caressing those portions of her body that were available to him.

"Harry," announced Rasputin, an amused grin on his face, "I think you're undergoing just a touch of culture shock."

Startled, Redwine stepped back from the screen and wondered just how long he had been staring in rapt fascination. "You people are expected to watch this *objectively?*" he said at last.

"After a day or two, so could you."

"I've seen my share of pornography, and most of it is pretty grubby and sweaty. But those two guys—they make sex look like a ballet."

"That's why they're so popular," replied Rasputin. "Though *all* of our people are pretty skilled. You're welcome to check some of the other screens, if you like."

Redwine shook his head. "I'm feeling quite inadequate enough, thank you," he said with a wry smile.

Rasputin nodded knowingly. "Getting used to that aspect of it occasionally takes a little *more* than a day or two. Shall we go back to my office?"

"I think I'm about ready for that drink," agreed Redwine devoutly.

A moment later they were sitting down on opposite sides of Rasputin's desk, each with a glass of whiskey in his hand.

"Are you properly impressed with our security system?" asked Rasputin, after taking a small swallow of his drink.

"It looks absolutely foolproof to me," said Redwine.

"Wonderful!" laughed Rasputin. "You're a very amusing guy, Harry. I hope to hell whatever I discover isn't too damning." He paused. "That's one of my bad habits: I tend to like my enemies much better than my friends, and then I feel like shit when I have to bring them down. Ever hear of anything that stupid?"

"Every now and then," said Redwine, trying not to think of the Leather Madonna.

"So," continued Rasputin, downing his drink, "we might as well be friends while we can."

"Suits me."

A light suddenly flashed on Rasputin's desk.

"I'm afraid I have to get back to work, Harry. Do you want me to have someone take you to your new office, or would you rather wait for the Madonna?"

"She's probably still busy. I think maybe I'd better just set up shop and go to work."

"Whatever you say," replied Rasputin, rising and escorting him to the door. "We've already got your retinagram on file. We'll program it into the Home and tram computers so you can get in and out of here without an escort." He turned to Redwine as the door slid open. "Are you really going to make me do all that work finding out what you did to the computer, Harry?"

"I'm afraid so."

"Well," said Rasputin with a shrug, "if that's the way it's got to be." He extended his hand. "I'm sure I'll be seeing a lot more of you around the *Comet*."

"I never doubted it."

"If anyone else tries to hassle you, Harry, you let me know," added Rasputin. "You're *my* project from now on."

"I suppose I should thank you," remarked Redwine dryly, as Rasputin summoned a green-clad woman to take him to his new office.

"We'll just have to wait and see, won't we?" said Rasputin.

4

Redwine sat in the Leather Madonna's auxiliary office, surrounded by mementoes of the many worlds she had visited prior to coming to work aboard the *Velvet Comet*. Part of one wall was covered by a meticulously woven tapestry from Alioth XIV, a plastic case housed an incomprehensible Domarian artifact that bore a tenuous resemblance to a large ashtray, and a wall shelf just to the left of the door held a trio of Denebian stone carvings. The room itself didn't begin to approach the luxury of her office in the Resort, but it had a desk and swivel chair, a pair of tufted sofas, and a small kitchenette.

Suddenly the largest of the three holographic screens flickered to life, and Redwine leaned forward in his chair. A moment later the image of Victor Bonhomme, tall, well-groomed, and conservatively dressed, stared out at him.

"Harry, you know better than to contact me here," he said by way of greeting.

"This room is secure," Redwine assured him. "I've changed the code on the door lock, and the skeleton card will keep anyone from monitoring our conversation."

"All right," said Bonhomme. "Give me just a minute to make sure I'm okay at this end." He leaned over his computer console and began checking his security devices, and Redwine got a glimpse of the tall steel-and-glass towers of Deluros VIII through a window behind his head. Finally he straightened up, obscuring Redwine's view of the planet. "Everything checks out," he announced. "What's up, Harry?"

"I think we've got a problem," answered Redwine.

"Can't the skeleton card access the books?"

"I haven't tried it yet."

"Then what kind of problem are you talking about?"

"I want you to think very hard before you answer this," said Redwine. "Does anyone else know why I'm here?"

"Just one person."

"Who?"

Bonhomme looked annoyed. "You know I can't tell you that, Harry."

"Could this person have told anyone else?"

"Out of the question. Why?"

"Because the Chief of Security knows your name. He knows there's a connection between us."

"Not to worry. He probably got it from your personnel file."

Redwine shook his head. "I got into the main memory bank and changed the file last night."

"Last night?" repeated Bonhomme, looking mildly disturbed. "He's a damned good man if he's already found what you changed."

Redwine shook his head impatiently. "You weren't mentioned in the original file."

"Well, *that's* a relief."

"Don't you understand what I'm telling you?" demanded Redwine. "Somebody's put a plant on board."

"One of the whores?" asked Bonhomme.

"It could be anyone: a prostitute, a technician, even a customer."

Bonhomme lowered his head in thought for a moment, then looked up and smiled. "It doesn't make any difference," he said at last. "Whoever it is can't do a damned thing to stop you as long as you've got that card."

"I don't like it," said Redwine.

"I don't blame you," chuckled Bonhomme. "Still, what harm can it do?"

"I don't know, but I thought we'd better talk it over before the Security chief figures out how to listen in on us." He paused. "I think we should postpone the operation for the time being."

"No way, Harry," said Bonhomme. "You were sent there to cook the *Comet*'s books. You'd better start putting them in the oven today."

"What if I refuse?"

"You won't," answered Bonhomme, amused. "Oh, you'll *threaten* to quit, just like you've threatened to quit four or five other times. But we both know you won't, so why don't you save both of us a lot of aggravation and just go to work?"

"Damn it!" snapped Redwine. "I swear to you, Victor, this is the last time!"

"Until the next time." Bonhomme smiled at him. "Face it, Harry, this is what you're good at. You'd go crazy sitting around in an office just auditing records and finding still more tax breaks for the Syndicate. You may bitch like hell, but you *like* getting out in the field."

"Industrial espionage isn't exactly the usual definition of 'getting out in the field,' " muttered Redwine.

"Come off it, Harry. I think you even like the danger." Redwine snorted caustically.

"And I know you like the money," continued Bonhomme.

"I've got enough to retire on right now."

"You'd die of boredom in two years' time."

"You wouldn't care to bet on that, would you?" snapped Redwine.

"I already have. Nine different times, to be exact— and I've never lost."

"Yeah? Well, don't push your luck. I'm getting pretty fed up with you, and with whoever it is I'm really working for."

"But you'll keep working for us, just the same," said

Bonhomme. "We've got a lot of good accountants in the Syndicate, Harry. What makes you the best isn't the way you balance the books—it's the way you *fix* them. Sabotage is your forte, so why fight against it?"

"There's a hell of a lot of difference between sabotage and subversion," said Redwine. "If I'm such a great master spy, why don't you ever send me out to ruin the Bello Conglomerate or the Reeling Corporation? Why am I always undercutting Vainmill?"

"Because Vainmill's the biggest of them all, and that's the prize we're playing for. You know that, Harry." He paused. "We're working for a very bright, very ambitious person, you and I. Instead of feeling angry, you ought to be grateful. Look at where we were when we started; then look at how far we've come."

"Over the corpses of nine Vainmill subsidiaries," replied Redwine sullenly.

"Vainmill will survive," said Bonhomme patiently. "Look, you know the Old Woman is retiring next year. When the person we work for surveyed the situation, there were half a dozen likelier candidates for the job. Now there's only one: Rubikov of Entertainment and Leisure. He fought for the *Comet* when no one else wanted it, so all we have to do is do a job on the books and we've eliminated the last stepping stone."

"*Then* will I know who I'm working for?"

Bonhomme chuckled. "Then the whole fucking Republic will know who you're working for."

"I still don't like it."

"The artistic temperament," remarked Bonhomme sardonically.

"When this job is through, our man is definitely in?"

"Our *person* is definitely in," Bonhomme corrected him carefully.

"Then why do you think you're going to send me out to do more of this stuff?"

"Because our employer recognizes your true value, Harry. You don't belong cooped up in an office."

"Yeah? Well, that's my fee for putting our person of

indeterminate gender into the catbird's seat: I want an office of my own, I want the job I was trained to do, and I never want to hear from you again."

"You'll be pounding on my door two months later, begging me to rescue you from a life of boredom."

"Don't you be too goddamned sure of that!" snapped Redwine. "Maybe I'm getting a little older and a little more tired than you think. Maybe, just once in my career, I'd like to do something *con*structive."

"Maybe," agreed Bonhomme. "But I doubt it. Don't forget, Harry—you practically begged me for those first two assignments."

"I was hungrier then."

"It took us ten months to transfer you to Entertainment and Leisure and place you where we wanted you. How come I never heard a whisper about your moral qualms during all that time?"

"Because I wasn't working on a ship that had a plant who knew about us!"

"Don't carry on so, Harry. Even if they can connect us, so what? I've been an officer in four of Vainmill's five divisions. It would be decidedly odd if we *hadn't* run into each other somewhere along the way." He checked his chronometer. "You've wasted almost twenty minutes, Harry. Hadn't you better be getting back to work?"

"If they catch me I'll tell them everything I know about you," promised Redwine.

Bonhomme chuckled. "If they catch you, you'll bluff and lie and bluster your way out of it. That's why you're the only man I trust."

"Well, you'd better find someone else after this job is over."

"Come to Deluros when you're through, and we'll talk about it, Harry," said Bonhomme, touching a section of his desk with a long forefinger and breaking the connection.

Redwine stalked over to the kitchenette, found a bottle of Alphard brandy, looked for something stronger, couldn't find it, filled up a glass with the brandy, and downed it in a single swallow. He poured another glass, then walked over to the sofa and sat down.

The frustrating thing was that Bonhomme was right: he'd probably go stark staring crazy if he had to go back to working full-time in an office. Espionage wasn't much—certainly no honor or pride of accomplishment accrued to it—but it was all he had.

He sipped his drink, more slowly this time, and wondered if this emptiness he felt was unique to him, or if it was common to everyone. Many times he had wanted to ask someone about it, but part of the emptiness was caused by the fact that he had never found anyone he could really talk to. Certainly not his ex-wife, though their parting had been relatively amicable. Not his three daughters, who were pleasant and cordial enough, but whom he understood about as well as he understood a six-legged chlorine-breathing native of far Teron. Not his fellow employees, who felt that the Good Life consisted of a portfolio, two homes, three mistresses, and four pension funds.

The funny part was that he had really *tried*. He had worked hard at being a good husband and a good father and a good accountant, and he still didn't know what had gone wrong, or why he had jumped at the chance to start working for Bonhomme. Certainly it wasn't from any sense of moral commitment; he didn't even know who his employer was. He had told himself originally that he was doing it for the money, but that wasn't true: his needs and tastes were simple, his only luxury was his book collection, and he had been well-paid long before Bonhomme ever came along.

He guessed that it was the excitement and the danger, which provided him with the certain knowledge that he was alive when he had been absolutely sure that he was just passing time, alone and isolated, from the womb to the grave. And because he cherished the knowledge that he *mattered*, even if only to someone whose identity was a mystery to him. So he mastered his new craft of destroying companies as competently as he had mastered his old craft of auditing them. Better, even.

Which led to still another question that he had nobody to ask: was *everyone* better at destroying things than fixing them, or was it just him?

He had the sinking feeling that he was unique, and he had a strong suspicion that those people who would think of him as a dashing and romantic figure if they knew what he really did were the same ones who currently considered him to be a fulfilled and successful man. Redwine sighed. He would be happy to settle for either description, instead of the one that was true: a hollow man, who had been lonely and empty for so long that he was half-convinced that this was the natural order of things.

He looked down at the pin he always wore, tried to envision the bright, hopeful young man who had earned the right to wear it, and wondered exactly how he had come all the way from *there* to *here*.

He stared at the pin for a long time. Finally he shrugged, finished his drink, and walked over to the computer.

"Activate," he said wearily, and a moment later he was going through the financial data banks of the *Velvet Comet*, hard at work at the only thing in his life at which he seemed able to excel.

Redwine was leaning back in his fur-covered contour chair that evening, reading his copy of *The Inferno*, when his computer came to life. A moment later he was confronting a full-sized holograph of the Leather Madonna.

"Harry, is this some kind of joke?"

"Absolutely not," he assured her. "I'm just following your instructions."

"*My* instructions?" she repeated.

He nodded, amused. "You're the one who said I should just activate the intercom and put in my request for a companion, aren't you?"

"Yes, but—"

"I don't think this particular companion has been reserved for the night—or could I be mistaken?" he asked with a smile.

"This particular companion isn't in the companion business any longer."

"Nonsense," said Redwine. "You're in *charge* of the damned business. Besides, didn't you tell me that you still . . . ah . . . met with an occasional customer?"

"*Patron*," she corrected him. "And you aren't a patron; you're an employee. Now stop playing games and request a suitable companion."

"You're the one I want," said Redwine, pleasantly but stubbornly.

"You're serious, aren't you?"

"Absolutely."

He shook his head. "Maybe this'll grow on me." He took another sip and tried very hard not to make a face. "Stop hovering like a worried mother."

She shrugged and sat down on a small loveseat. "Well, is the office acceptable to you?"

"Just fine."

"And you were able to access the material you needed?"

"No problem." He took another sip, and liked it better this time. "Look, I didn't ask you here to talk business."

"Just why *did* you ask me, Harry?"

"I'm lonely."

"You should have let me select a companion for you."

"I said lonely, not horny." He paused. "Well, maybe a little of each."

"Just a little?" she asked, arching an eyebrow.

"Accounting isn't exactly a universal aphrodisiac," he said. "Otherwise I would have propositioned you already."

"And why am *I* so blessed?"

"I don't know any of the others," he answered.

"And you only go to bed with people you know?" She laughed. "That's contrary to the whole purpose of a brothel."

"Maybe that's why this is the first one I've ever been to."

"Well, I can see that I'm going to have to introduce you to some of the others if I'm to get any rest at all."

"Do *they* read poetry?"

"They have other attributes," the Madonna pointed out.

"I prefer yours."

She smiled. "That's the kind of lie I could listen to all night."

"Well, if lying is what it takes to convince you to spend the night, I'm just the guy who can do it," said Redwine. He took another sip of his drink, then held the glass up in front of him. "Great stuff."

"It lacks the conviction of your other lies," she laughed.

"True," he admitted. "But you have to understand that my entire training as a liar has been directed at tax collectors."

"I didn't know that deceit and falsehood went hand-in-glove with accounting."

"They go hand-in-glove with everything," answered Redwine seriously.

"You don't really believe that, Harry."

"When was the last time Suma told a fat, balding, 73-year-old man that the only reason she's going to bed with him is because he's paying her?"

"You picked a bad example," said the Madonna. "I think Suma has a better time than the patrons."

"I didn't realize that prostitutes enjoyed themselves."

"Most of us do every once in a while, when conditions are right."

"And Suma?"

"She hasn't found any wrong conditions yet that I know of," said the Madonna. She smiled. "You know, I had to remove her from our teaching rotation."

"Teaching rotation?" he repeated. "What's that?"

"You don't think we just hire our prostitutes and put them right to work, do you?"

"I must confess that I hadn't thought about it at all," admitted Redwine.

"Well, we don't. We're very selective about who works for us: I'd say we reject more than 98 percent of our applicants. Those we hire are given an intensive training course in which they learn every sexual variation and refinement. All of our experienced prostitutes are expected to donate some of their time working with our newcomers. All except Suma, that is. She got so enthused in her work that her pupils needed a couple of days off to recuperate."

"Just your everyday teenaged girl," commented Redwine wryly.

"She's the ideal prostitute," replied the Madonna. "That's all I care about."

"I wouldn't turn my back on her, or you might find that she's the ideal madam, too."

"I'm aware of her ambition, but she'd make a lousy madam. She's much better handling patrons than problems." She paused. "How about you, Harry?"

"What about me?"

"Can I turn my back on *you*?"

"Without getting pounced on, you mean?"

"I'm being serious" she said. "I tried to contact you this afternoon to tell you why I was detained, and I couldn't get through to my own auxiliary office. So I tried to route the call through Security, and they couldn't get through either. But after you left everything was working fine again."

"I rigged the computer so that nobody could bother me while I was working," said Redwine.

"Can you do that?" she asked dubiously.

"First thing they teach you in accounting school," he said easily. "A good accountant can find money where none exists, but time is the one commodity that can't be replaced." He paused. "If you'd rather I didn't do it again, just say the word."

She stared at him for a moment, then shook her head. "Set it up any way that makes you comfortable."

"Thanks."

There was an awkward pause, and he was suddenly afraid that she might get up and leave.

"Have I told you how nice you look tonight?" he asked lamely.

"At length."

"Is that why you're called the Leather Madonna?" he asked. "Because you always wear leather outfits?"

"They came *after* the name."

"I don't quite understand," he said.

Another pause.

"I *still* don't understand," he persisted.

"Harry, if I wanted to tell you, I would."

"How are we going to be friends if we don't tell each

other our deepest, darkest secrets?" he said with an attempt at levity.

She looked at him, then exhaled deeply. "What the hell," she said at last. "If *I* don't tell you, someone else probably will. There are still a few people aboard who remember." She paused. "But you'd better not laugh."

"I promise," he said, and suddenly he had an urge to chuckle.

"It was ten years ago," she said. "I had been working here less then a month, and one of our, ah, specialists got sick. So, since I wanted to make a good impression, I volunteered to take her place. I got dressed up in a leather waist-cincher and a spiked collar and studded gloves and boots and spurs, and went down to service a very good patron who had brought his own cat-o'-nine-tails all the way out to the *Comet* and wanted nothing more than for me to whip the hell out of him."

She paused. "I had done some pretty kinky things as a prostitute, and I figured that as long as I was on the right end of the whip, this wouldn't be any more bothersome than the others. But when that poor, defenseless old man took his clothes off and I could see a batch of old scars plus some wounds that still hadn't healed properly from his last visit, I just couldn't make myself bring that whip down on his flesh."

"So what happened?" asked Redwine.

"He got on his knees and begged me to whip him, blubbering like a big, overgrown baby. I was afraid for my job and afraid of the damage I might do to him. Finally I just walked out of the room, and ten seconds later he followed me out into the corridor." She laughed. "It must have been quite a sight, me all done up in kink and being chased all over the *Velvet Comet* by a huge, overweight, naked man who kept screaming at the top of his lungs for me to whip him."

"Did he catch you?"

She shook her head. "You'd be surprised how fast you can run in five-inch heels if you're properly motivated. I've never lost my self-control with a customer before or since, but I was so upset and embarrassed that I couldn't think straight."

"Obviously you kept your job," remarked Redwine.

"That was the wild part. You know that old definition about a sadist—that he's a man who won't beat a masochist? Well, it seems that we had a really peculiar masochist on our hands. When he finally calmed down he told everyone who would listen that he had undergone the most moving and exciting encounter of his life, almost a religious experience, and that I was some kind of madonna dressed in leather. So I took his description for my name."

"That's a hell of a story," said Redwine. "It must have been quite a sight—a fetishist's dream being chased all over the ship by a fat, naked billionaire."

"Everyone who's ever heard it thinks it's hilarious."

"I don't know why," he replied. "I'd probably cry like a baby if you left *my* room, too."

"Harry, if you're not careful, you're actually going to make me blush," said the Madonna.

"Fate forfend!" he said, getting to his feet and walking to the wet bar. "Can I make you another Purple Polaris?" he asked, pouring himself a whiskey.

"That's *Blue* Polaris, and you don't know how to make one."

"True," he said, turning to her. "But if you were really going to blush, I thought the least I could do was turn my back."

"The crisis has passed," she laughed. "You know, Harry, you're really a very nice man."

"Thank you."

"It seems a pity that you spend all your time in an office somewhere, counting up columns of figures."

"Oh, I don't know," he said softly. "I suppose there's worse things for an accountant to do."

"What would you be if you could be anything at all?" she asked.

"Happy."

"That's what I mean. What would make you happy?"

"I really don't know," he replied. "I wish I did." He paused. "What would *you* do if you could do anything you chose?"

"Just what I'm doing."

"I didn't realize that prostitution was so addictive."

"It isn't," said the Madonna. "But I'm not a prostitute any more. I'm in charge of the most luxurious resort in the Republic, which just happens to offer prostitution among its services."

"And that's all you ever wanted to be?"

"It's *more* than I ever wanted to be. Hundreds of people work for me, billions of credits pass through my hands, an entire space station has been placed in my keeping. I took over a good business and made it even better. I enjoy my work, I enjoy my surroundings, I enjoy my power. Why should I want to do or be anything else?"

"But you make all this money for the Syndicate. Haven't you ever wanted to work for yourself?"

"Harry, I get a piece of the gross—and around here, I get more than my share of good financial advice. Over the years I've made a lot of sound investments."

"I imagine you have." He paused. "What are you going to do with all your money when you retire?"

She shrugged. "I haven't thought that far ahead. I like what I'm doing; why should I retire?"

"Who knows?" he said. "Conditions change."

"I own a farm on Pollux IV," she said. "Maybe someday I'll move there."

"I find it a little difficult to envision you traipsing through piles of manure in those thousand-credit boots," he said with a smile.

"Me too," she agreed. "That's why I plan to stay right where I am."

They both fell silent for a moment. Then Redwine walked over, picked up the book she had brought with her, and began thumbing through it.

"Your friend Tanblixt isn't very interested in rhyme or meter, is he?" he commented.

"You missed the translator's note at the beginning," the Madonna pointed out. "She says that she preferred to remain true to the eroticism rather than keep the meter and lose the things that mattered." She paused, as Redwine started reading one of the poems more carefully. "I think she was right."

He looked up, strangely moved by the few brief stanzas he had read. "I think she was right, too. I wonder what he would have produced if he'd had a real woman to write about."

"Probably not very much. Tanblixt was a Canphorite."

"The poor bastard never knew what he was missing."

"The poor bastard was an *it*, not a *he*."

"I don't know," said Redwine. "Put the author of this aboard the *Velvet Comet* for a few hours and I'll bet he'd find some use for the facilities."

"The inhabitants of Canphor VI reproduce by budding," she noted.

"Have I commented about your romantic soul?" he asked with a wry smile.

She nodded. "Yes. It seems to me that I also made some small mention of your hard-headed realism."

"Maybe we ought to change jobs," he suggested.

"Are you trying to save me from a life of sin?" she smiled.

"Just the opposite, I think."

"I wasn't aware that accounting was all that sinful."

"It has it ups and downs," he said. "Now, how about that Blue Polaris?"

"All right," she said, getting up and following him to the wet bar. "Let me show you how it's done."

He tried to concentrate, but got completely lost somewhere between the Alphard brandy and the blue liqueur from distant Binder, and by the time she poured the concoction over a ball of crushed ice he was once again seated on his contour chair.

"I guess it's an acquired taste," she said, indicating her glass as she rejoined him.

"What's wrong with that?" he replied. "I gather the *Comet* caters to a lot of specialized tastes."

"Well, then," she said, holding up her glass to him. "To sin—in both our professions."

"I hope that's a mandate."

"An invitation, anyway."

"Accepted without a moment's hesitation," he said.

"You do understand, though, that this can't be a regular arrangement?"

"I understand that it won't be," replied Redwine. "I don't understand why it *can't* be."

"First, because I'm a full-time madam and only a very occasional prostitute; and second, because I have a feeling that I could grow very fond of you, and that's a serious detriment in my line of work."

And in mine, Redwine agreed silently. Aloud, he said: "A point well taken. Maybe we ought to begin before you make *me* blush."

"Let me finish my drink," she said, sipping it slowly.

He watched her, and suddenly felt like a schoolboy, unable to sit without fidgeting, not quite knowing what to do with his hands, afraid to get up too soon or to appear too relaxed. Finally he picked up the book and began thumbing through the pages again.

After what seemed like an eon and was probably closer to a minute, the Leather Madonna put her empty glass down on the table and stood up.

"How about a whirlpool first?" she suggested.

"Fine," he agreed, starting after her as she walked toward the bathroom, then remembering to return and place the book back down on the table.

"Help me with my zippers, won't you?" she said when he finally arrived.

"Where are they?" he asked.

"You'll find them," she said, removing her boots and uttering a command that started a flow of hot water into the huge, circular tub.

And, after a bit of fumbling, he *did* find them. A moment later the Madonna stepped unselfconsciously out of her jumpsuit, and began unfastening Redwine's tunic.

"I can do it," he said, stepping back uneasily.

"Suit yourself," she replied, and climbed carefully into the tub. "Aren't you joining me?" she asked as he stood a few feet away, staring at her.

"Sure. You want me to dim the lights or anything?"

She laughed. "You never struck me as a conservative."

"When it comes to putting my middle-aged body on display in this place, I can be downright reactionary," he said, removing his clothes slowly and entering the tub.

"I've seen worse," she said.

"How comforting," he replied wryly.

"Well, if it's comforting you want, let's see what we can do about that."

Then she was hard at work at the business of pleasure. At first Redwine felt ungainly and awkward, but as she began doing things to him with her hands, her mouth, and her body, things he had never experienced before, things he had never quite hoped for in his wildest fantasies, he found himself responding with more grace and assurance than he had known he possessed. She was, he concluded during those few brief instants that he could think rationally at all, like the best kind of athlete or actress: she made everyone around her look good, too.

When the ecstasy became so intense that it almost turned into pain she slowed her pace, teasing and titillating him until he was almost out of his mind with desire and pleasure—and finally, when he was certain that there was nothing further she could do to heighten the sensations he was feeling, she found new things to do, things that made his every nerve end scream for release. And when at last release came, it came with an intensity he had not believed possible.

Exhausted and drained—as much emotionally as physically—he finally climbed out of the tub and began drying himself off. He shot an occasional glance at the

Madonna, who lay back languorously in the tub, only her face above the surface but all of her visible beneath the swirling water, and tried very hard to convince himself that she was just a piece of meat, a whore with neither emotions nor loyalties, who would find work somewhere else after he completed his mission aboard the *Comet*.

It didn't ring true then, and it didn't ring true a few hours later, beneath the satin covers of his circular bed, when she made love to him as if she meant it, slowly, tenderly, with softly whispered words and gentle caresses, as delicate and yielding now as she had been forceful and aggressive before. He told himself that nobody this skilled at the art of sex was worth feeling pity or friendship or anything but lust for. He reiterated to himself, as he buried his face between her breasts, that nobody in either of their professions could afford to care about anyone except themselves. He knew, as their bodies joined together with a pulsating rhythm, that saboteurs never felt compassion for their victims, that *nobody* ever felt compassion for a whore.

It was, he decided when they were through and lying in each other's arms, an easy litany to reel off in one's mind. Believing it was another matter altogether.

6

Redwine sat in the Leather Madonna's auxiliary office, a cup of coffee on the table next to him, and stared at the computer as it flashed row after row of financial data from the restaurants' operation on the screen. Now and then he would order it to pause, make a minuscule change or insertion, and then have it continue scanning the books.

Finally he checked his chronometer, realized that he had been hard at work for the better part of three hours, and decided to take a break. He went into the bathroom, rinsed his face off, walked back to the computer, and began scanning the entertainment channels. There was the usual abundance of pornography, and this time he found that he could recognize a number of the participants. He idly wondered if the Madonna herself would appear in any of the displays, then decided that if she did he didn't want to see it, and changed quickly to one of the news channels.

After finding out that nobody important had gone to war during the night, he decided to place a call to Deluros VIII. He waited impatiently for the computers to hook up, and for the elderly man he sought to be summoned to a receiving station.

"Oh, it's you, Harry," said the old man, squinting at Redwine's holograph. "What can I do for you? Another book?"

"Not this time," said Redwine.

"A magazine?" said the old man, surprised. "I haven't got an awful lot in stock—maybe two dozen at most."

Redwine shook his head. "A chess set."

"Harry, I don't handle things like that."

"Then find someone who does," said Redwine. "I'll make it worth your while."

"Just any old chess set at all?"

"I want the best, the most elegant, chess set you can find."

"Antique?"

"If that's what fills the bill."

"I don't know much about that stuff, Harry, but I have a feeling you're talking an awful lot of money."

"I know. Just get me the best."

"Any particular style?" asked the old man.

Redwine shrugged. "I don't know anything about chess sets."

"Then why do you want one?"

"Look," said Redwine. "Are you going to do this for me or not?"

"I don't know. What's in it for me?"

"A ten percent finder's fee."

"Ten percent of the purchase price? You've got yourself a deal." He paused. "You know how much money you could be spending on this thing, Harry?"

"Yeah, I know."

"I mean, I'm sure I can hunt up a platinum set studded with diamonds, if I try real hard."

"The key word was *elegant*, not garish."

"Maybe you'd better put a top on it anyway, just so we don't have a misunderstanding later on."

Redwine wondered what the going price of a conscience was, but named a figure that seemed to hover just between the top end of Reasonable and the bottom of Ostentatious.

"You're the boss, Harry. How soon do you need it?"

"Yesterday."

"I'll see what I can do. You want it sent to your home or your office?"

"Neither," said Redwine. "Send it to the *Velvet Comet* and mark it to my attention."

The old man grinned. "You're on the *Velvet Comet*?"

"Yeah."

"That must be one hell of a bimbo you've got yourself. Don't they charge enough without making you give 'em gifts?"

"Just do it!" snapped Redwine.

"That's by Charlemagne, in the Beta Sigma system, right?"

"Right. You're going to need my account number to pay for it." Redwine had the computer transmit his banking code. "If there's any problem, have the bank contact me here."

"There won't be. I've done favors for lots of people with no problems. I think banks like to keep their money in circulation." He paused. "Harry, I'll take nine percent if you'll give me a blow-by-blow description of what this girl did to you."

"Do you need anything else?" asked Redwine, ignoring the offer.

"No, I guess that'll do it."

Redwine broke the connection, then finished his coffee. He was about to go back to work when there was a knock at the door. He adjusted his skeleton card and commanded the door to slide open.

"Hi, Harry," said Rasputin, stepping into the office. "Hard at work?"

"Taking a break, actually."

"Good," said the Security chief. "I was afraid I might be disturbing you, since the door wouldn't open."

"No. I just like my privacy. Did you come here for any reason in particular?"

"As a matter of fact, I did," replied Rasputin, walking slowly around the room and scrutinizing it carefully. "You've been here for five days and haven't left this damned office except to go back to the Resort. I thought you might like to take a *real* break and come down to the gym with me."

"The crew's gym?" asked Redwine, and Rasputin nodded. "Why?"

"There's going to be an interesting little entertainment there in a few minutes, and I figured nobody had bothered to tell you about it."

"What kind of entertainment?"

"Ever hear of Gamble DeWitt?" asked Rasputin.

"I saw him the day after I got here."

"Ever see him fight?"

"Once, a few years ago."

"Think you might like to see him in action again?"

"Sure," said Redwine. "How much does a seat go for?"

"It's free."

"Seems kind of silly," commented Redwine. "You ought to be holding this over at the Resort and charging the patrons to watch it."

Rasputin shook his head. "This is a private grudge match."

Redwine chuckled. "It'll be a private slaughter. "Who's crazy enough to go into the ring with DeWitt?"

"The Duke."

"The pit boss? I remember him being kind of muscular, but still . . ."

"It'll be more even than you think. The Duke used to fight as an amateur, maybe twenty years ago, and he's kept in pretty good shape. It seems that he and DeWitt got into some kind of argument in the casino the night before last, and DeWitt said he could tear him apart with one hand tied behind his back and lead weights on his feet." Rasputin grinned. "So the Duke took him up on it. They're due to go at it at 1300 ship's time." He checked the time. "That's only about twenty minutes from now."

"Then what are we standing around *here* for?" said Redwine.

"No reason that I can think of," replied Rasputin with

a smile. He walked out the door, and Redwine fell into step behind him. The gymnasium was two decks down from the auxiliary office, and they arrived there a minute later.

Redwine had never seen the facility before, and while it fell far short of the luxurious accommodations provided for the Resort's guests, it was nonetheless quite spacious and well-equipped. There were a number of advanced exercise machines, and numerous sets of weights, both of which he assumed were used almost exclusively by the prostitutes for keeping their bodies in shape. But there were also racketball courts, a raised wooden jogging track, a small swimming pool, a row of trampolines, and a heavily-padded free-fall room for those reckless enough to indulge in a little null-gravity wrestling.

There were perhaps fifty people in the gym, and all but a handful were crowded around a ring that had been assembled in a large open area near the trampolines. Rasputin headed toward it, and Redwine followed him, intrigued at the notion of seeing the fabled DeWitt in action once again.

When they reached ringside, an absolutely breathtaking redhead approached them.

"You're Mr. Redwine, aren't you?" she said, extending a long, elegant hand.

"Harry," Redwine replied. "And you are . . . ?"

"Flaming Lorelei," she said. "You can call me Lori. I've been wanting to meet you."

"Oh?"

"Yes. You see, I'm one of the Resort's accountants . . ."

"With no offense intended, I would have sworn you were one of the more popular prostitutes."

"I've retired from the ranks," she replied. "Anyway, I was just wondering why you were here? I mean, if the Syndicate feels there have been any improprieties . . ."

He shook his head. "The only reason I'm here is

because I'm cheaper than an outside auditor. It's standard operating procedure."

"*That's* a relief," she said earnestly. "If there's anything I can explain to you, please feel free to ask."

"You'll be the first one I call for help," said Redwine. "So far, though, everything seems to be in perfect order."

"By the way, I saw Charlie from the casino setting up a handbook in the mess hall," interjected Rasputin. "You wouldn't happen to know the line, would you?"

"Six-to-five, pick 'em," said Lori.

"You're kidding!" exclaimed Redwine. "Gamble DeWitt was the champion of the whole damned Republic!"

"I don't make the odds," she said. "I just report them."

"Is an outsider allowed to lay a bet?" continued Redwine.

"No—but you're not an outsider, are you?"

"Fine. I once spent seven hundred credits to watch DeWitt fight. I'd like to put seven hundred on him to win." He paused. "Maybe I can come out even on him yet. Where can I find this Charlie person?"

"I'll cover it myself," offered Rasputin.

"You're not even going to give the house its percentage?" asked Lori with mock severity.

"I can give him even money," replied Rasputin. "Why should I give the casino six-to-five? Besides, Security chiefs don't make as much money as high-priced prostitutes. I've got to conserve my resources."

"Shall we grab some chairs?" suggested Redwine, noticing that most of the people had taken their seats, except for two young women who were playing racketball, oblivious to all the excitement being generated at ringside.

"Why not?" agreed Rasputin. He turned to Lori. "Are you joining us, or will you be in Gamble's corner?"

"Why should I be in Gamble's corner?" she asked.

"You're his trainer, aren't you?" grinned Rasputin.

"You're terrible!" she laughed. "Besides, the person hasn't been born yet who can train him."

Rasputin turned to Redwine. "You look confused, Harry."

"I assume it's a private joke," replied Redwine.

"The only joke is Gamble DeWitt," said Lori, leading them around a number of parallel bars and vaulting horses and over to a trio of folded chairs, which they carried to ringside. They set the chairs up, and she seated herself between the two men.

"I still feel I'm missing something," remarked Redwine, who had been dwelling on her last remark.

"How can I put it?" said the Security chief. "Lori isn't a working prostitute any more, but she still helps train a problem case from time to time."

"It's a way to make a little extra money and put some old skills to use before they atrophy," she explained with a smile. "Although calling Gamble a problem is like calling the Vainmill Syndicate a thriving little company."

"You see," said Rasputin, "Gamble approaches everything in life as if he were back in the ring. Finesse just isn't one of his strong points."

"Neither is endurance," added Lori caustically.

"So your job is to make him a better lover?" asked Redwine.

She laughed. "I'll settle for making him a barely adequate lover. He's got ten thumbs, two left feet, and the personality of a fern."

"Then why is he here?"

"The Madonna thought he could draw a crowd, so to speak, and for the first couple of weeks he did. Then word got out, and he's been a pretty lonely young man ever since. Usually the only time he works is when we're packed, or when some sports groupie asks for him—and believe me, they never ask for him twice."

"I assume you're rooting for the Duke, then," said Redwine.

"Of course not," she replied.

"But—"

"Look," she said. "After all the days and weeks I've spent in bed with that body, I'll be damned if I want to see somebody smash it to pieces. You're an accountant, Harry—you ought to understand the concept of protecting your investment."

He smiled. "Well, when you put it that way . . ."

Suddenly all the ringsiders fell silent, and Redwine saw that the Duke was approaching the ring. The pit boss stopped beneath a high bar, leaped up, chinned himself five or six quick times, and then continued his approach. When he reached the ring he climbed the stairs, bent over, and stepped through the ropes. He was a burly man, built along the lines of Rasputin, though about four inches taller. He wore nothing but a pair of sweat pants, and his muscular body glistened with perspiration. He nodded to a couple of people in the small audience—Redwine recognized them as casino employees—and began dancing around, shadow boxing and lashing out with an occasional kick.

DeWitt entered the ring perhaps two minutes later, the physical personification of a Greek god. He wore brief bathing trunks, his left arm was strapped securely behind his back, and he had lead weights taped to his Achilles' tendons, where they wouldn't come into contact with his opponent if he landed a kick. He looked rather bored, especially in contrast to the Duke, and his torso and legs were absolutely dry.

"Idiot!" muttered Lori. She rose from her chair, climbed up to the ring, and had DeWitt deposit a huge wad of gum in her hand.

"If there's another guy aboard the *Comet* who chews gum, I've never met him," she muttered as she rejoined Redwine and Rasputin.

"He looks reasonably fit," commented Redwine. "No more than five or ten pounds over the weight he fought at."

"He looks *beautiful*," she replied earnestly. "You

ought to see him with his clothes off!" She paused. "What a goddamned pity that he has to move!"

A young man stepped into the ring, called the two antagonists together, and quietly explained the ground rules to them.

"Is he the referee?" asked Redwine.

Rasputin shook his head. "There isn't any referee," he answered. "I told you—this is a grudge match."

"Then what's he doing there?"

"Explaining that if Gamble gets his left hand free and uses it, all the bets are off. It won't stop the fight, of course—I mean, who the hell is going to get in there and try to separate them?—but the casino will return all the money."

The young man directed the two fighters to their corners and then clambered out of the ring. They stood, staring at one another, until the young man took his seat and yelled "Time!"

The Duke bounded out to the middle of the ring with a speed that belied his years, and DeWitt slowly moved out to meet him. They circled each other for a moment, and then the Duke, head low, bobbing and weaving, blocked a short blow from DeWitt and landed a quick three-punch combination, spinning away quickly and delivering a powerful kick when DeWitt pursued him.

"He's rusty," said Redwine. "His timing's off."

"He's wearing ten pounds on each foot," replied Rasputin, as DeWitt plodded slowly after the jabbing, kicking pit boss.

The next three minutes were pretty much like the first, with DeWitt landing an occasional blow but taking six or seven in the process.

"You want your money now or later?" whispered Redwine.

"I'll trust you for it," grinned Rasputin. "Ten minutes from now will be fine."

Redwine shook his head. "He used to be such a damned fine ring general. If he could just get him in a corner where he could land a kick or two . . ."

"Not today, Harry," said the Security chief. "Three of his four weapons aren't firing."

"Sounds familiar," commented Lori wryly.

The Duke gained in confidence with each passing second. No longer did he strike and run; instead, he closed with DeWitt, as if the strain of carrying the weights around the ring had sapped most of his opponent's strength. Finally a whirling kick to the side of the neck dropped DeWitt to the floor.

"Get up, you big oaf!" panted the Duke, standing over him, fists clenched. Suddenly he grinned. "Oh—I forgot! Getting things up isn't exactly your specialty, is it?"

DeWitt's expression turned ugly, and he was on his feet in an instant.

The Duke landed two quick left jabs, then closed with him again.

"Low blow!" cried someone from the other side of the ring.

Lori leaped to her feet.

"Don't you hit him in the balls after all the work I've done!" she yelled furiously.

"I tried," laughed the Duke, "but he doesn't have any!"

Everyone in the audience laughed—and suddenly Gamble DeWitt went crazy. He lumbered across the ring and hurled himself, feet first, at the Duke. He didn't hit his target dead center, but the very suddenness of his actions froze the Duke for an instant, and a lead-weighted foot caught the pit boss on the shoulder and spun him into the ring post. He bounced off groggily, and then DeWitt was all over him, pummeling him with sledgehammer blows. Finally he grabbed the Duke's arm and hurled him against the ropes. The Duke came flying off, and DeWitt cracked him across the throat with a karate chop, and as quickly as that the fight was over.

While one of the men from the casino jumped into the ring to revive the Duke, Lori climbed the stairs and began unwrapping DeWitt's left arm. As soon as it was free she knelt down and took the weights off his feet.

"I'd have bought out of my bet for five hundred credits about a minute and a half ago," confessed Redwine.

"I wouldn't have sold it to you for six and a half," replied Rasputin. "Damn! If he'd just kept his mouth shut!"

The Duke was awake now, and he was led, groggy and rasping, back to the locker room. Once the crowd saw that he was all right, they began to disperse, and Redwine walked over to DeWitt's corner.

"Gamble?" he said.

"Yeah?" said DeWitt, looking down at him.

"My name is Harry Redwine, and this is the second time I've had the pleasure of watching you work. I made seven hundred credits off you this afternoon, so the least I can do is invite you by for a drink."

"Were you one of the ones who laughed at me?" DeWitt demanded.

"Not me. I was cheering the whole time."

The fighter's face lit up. "Yeah?"

"Absolutely."

"For just a minute there, it felt like the old days," said DeWitt wistfully. "Not like . . . well . . ." His voice trailed off.

"I'll be in the Madonna's auxiliary office all afternoon," continued Redwine. "Come on by after you've showered and rested."

Suddenly DeWitt's expression changed. "I don't go to *her* office, not even for a drink. I'll catch you some other time."

He stepped through the ropes, jumped down to the floor, and headed off toward the shower room.

"You said a wrong thing, Harry," remarked Lori.

"So I gather."

"He blames the Leather Madonna for his being here, and he isn't very happy with his new occupation." She paused. "Not that anybody twisted his arm to get him

to sign his contract. It's just that he didn't know quite
what was going to be expected of him."

"Well, not everyone's cut out to be a prostitute," said
Redwine.

"True enough," she agreed. "I had a good four-year
run of it, and then I figured I'd better learn to do
something else before they told me I had to."

Redwine watched DeWitt walk across the gym. "He's
as strong as an elephant!" he said admiringly.

"I read about elephants, Harry," said Lori. "They
could tear down trees, kill lions, carry a dozen men on
their backs." She smiled sadly. "But they couldn't peel
a grape."

"Maybe that's why they died out," suggested Redwine.

"That's why *this* one's dying out, that's for sure," she
said. "I suppose I could put up with what we euphemis-
tically term his technique if I didn't have to hear a
blow-by-blow account of his career." She sighed. "And
now he's got another one to add to the list. Sometimes I
wonder if the extra money is worth it."

Redwine chuckled. "I think I offered the wrong one
of you a drink."

"I was wondering how long it would take you to
figure that out. I'll be by in a couple of hours."

She turned and left, and Redwine rejoined Rasputin.

"Well, back to work," said the Security chief. "I'll
drop you at your office."

"Sounds good to me," said Redwine. "And thanks for
letting me know about this."

"My pleasure," said Rasputin. "Now, before I forget
. . ." He withdrew a billfold and handed over a wad of
credits.

"My pleasure," said Rasputin. "Now, before I forget . . ." He withdrew a billfold and handed over a wad
of credits.

"Invite me in for a minute, Harry," said Rasputin as
Redwine commanded his door to open.

"Won't you please come in?" he said sardonically.

"Thanks. I think I will." Rasputin walked to a sofa

and sat down. "We've got a couple of things to talk about."

"About the fight?"

Rasputin shook his head. "About you."

"I thought I asked you to back off," said Redwine.

"You did."

"Well?"

Rasputin smiled. "I thought I asked you to tell me why you were here."

"I assume my being here is what you want to talk about?"

"Right."

"I don't know how to tell you this," said Redwine, "but I'm really not interested in your speculations."

"Then you'd better *get* interested in them," answered Rasputin easily. "Especially considering how you've been spending your nights—and with whom."

"You don't have any idea what I've been doing at night," replied Redwine. "I've jammed the security system in my suite."

"Have you jammed it anywhere else?" asked Rasputin.

"No."

"Now, if you were me, and you couldn't find the Madonna anywhere else on the ship, what conclusion would you draw from that?"

"My conclusion, like my free time, is none of your business," said Redwine testily.

"True," admitted Rasputin. "But *my* conclusion may affect *your* business, and I think it's about time I laid my cards on the table."

"I don't know what you're talking about."

"Look, Harry, let me be as honest as I can," said the Security chief. "As near as I can figure it, the reason you're here is because they think someone is fixing the books. I'm a little upset that they didn't let me in on it, but they probably figured that since no one in Security is an accountant, there was no need for it. Anyway, my feelings aren't important. The main thing is that I'm happy working for the Syndicate, and I'd like to keep working for it for quite some time to come."

"You *are* going to get to the point sooner or later, aren't you?" asked Redwine.

Rasputin nodded. "I just want you to know where I stand on this. But there are also two other possibilities, neither of them very likely, but both worth considering. One is that you're either a thief or a saboteur from one of our competitors."

"And the other?"

"That this is just some kind of crazy test to see what Security will do."

"That's the first really stupid thing I've heard you say," commented Redwine.

"It doesn't make much sense," agreed Rasputin. "But I'm just trying to clear the air. Either you're a very high-powered troubleshooter, in which case I don't want to offend you or whoever sent you here, or else you're someone that I have to expose." He paused. "I'm asking you once more: who are you, and why are you aboard the *Comet?*"

"And I'm telling you once more: it's none of your business."

"Harry," said Rasputin almost pleadingly, "I'm not playing verbal games anymore. I've got to know."

"Have it your way," shrugged Redwine. "I'm a troubleshooter."

"Can you prove it?"

"Yes."

"Well?"

"There's a hell of a lot of difference between being able to and being willing to," said Redwine.

Rasputin was silent for a moment. "You're forcing me to do something I really don't want to do."

"Then don't do it."

"I don't have any choice." He paused again. "I finally brought up the stuff you changed on the computer."

"I didn't change anything," said Redwine, looking him squarely in the eye.

"You sure as hell didn't change *much*," agreed Rasputin. "You're still Harry Redwine, and you're still an accountant for Vainmill. Your identification checks out, your tenure checks out, there's nothing damaging there at all."

"So?"

"Damn it, Harry! If you can't give me a reason to stop, I'm going to have to keep digging!"

"It would make me very happy if you'd stop," said Redwine.

Rasputin uttered a humorless laugh. "I'll need a better reason than that." He fidgeted uneasily. "And if you don't give me one by the time I leave this office, I'm going to have to tell the Madonna what I know."

Redwine felt a hollowness in the pit of his stomach. "You don't *know* anything."

"I know you lied to us," said Rasputin stubbornly. "I don't know why, and I don't know about what, but I know you lied and I know that you're sleeping with the most important person on the *Velvet Comet*. That makes you a threat to the ship's security."

"You could make this a very unpleasant situation for all three of us," said Redwine slowly.

"I know. I'm asking you one last time: give me a reason not to."

Redwine shook his head.

Rasputin sighed and got to his feet. "Okay, if that's the way it's got to be."

"That's the way it is."

The Security chief walked to the door, then turned to Redwine. "I hope to hell you're a troubleshooter or a test."

I wish to hell I was, agreed Redwine silently, as he watched Rasputin walk out into the corridor and ordered the door to slide shut behind him.

7

Redwine watched the holograph as it flickered and took form.

"I was expecting you a couple of hours ago," he said. "Is anything the matter?"

The image of the Leather Madonna looked out at him.

"Yes," she replied. "I'm afraid I won't be able to make it tonight."

He frowned. "Is there anything I can do to help?" he asked. "I mean, it's not as if I've got any pressing business that's keeping me here in the suite."

"Yes, there *is* something you can do to help," said the Madonna. "But I don't think you're going to want to."

"Oh?"

She stared directly at him. "Tell me who you are."

He was silent for a moment. "What do you mean by that?"

"Damn it, Harry!" she said, and he couldn't tell if she was mad or unhappy. "Why did you lie to me?"

"I didn't lie," he answered her. "I'm Harry Redwine, I'm an accountant for the Entertainment and Leisure Division of the Vainmill Syndicate, and I'm here on business."

"You know exactly what I mean," she persisted. "Why did you sneak into the computer and change your dossier?"

"I take it you've been talking to Rasputin."

"I have."

"Did you find anything harmful in my original dossier?" he asked.

"That's not the point. Why did you change it?"

"That's precisely the point," said Redwine. "There's nothing damaging there. I'm not a murderer or a rapist or a fugitive."

"There's *something* there or you wouldn't have changed it," said the Madonna adamantly.

"I just didn't see why my entire personnel profile should be available to anyone on the *Velvet Comet*, so I deleted some of the details and left in the pertinent facts: who I am, who I work for, what I do."

"How were you able to get into the computer in the first place?" she demanded. "Rasputin says you made the changes the day you arrived."

He paused to consider his answer just a little too long before uttering it. "All the Syndicate's top accountants have pretty high security clearances."

"Then why did you pretend you couldn't access the material without my permission?"

"I had every intention of going through normal channels unless they were closed to me—and the day I got here, everyone gave me a runaround."

"You're lying again, Harry," she said. "You never asked me for permission to change, or even see, your dossier."

"I was curious," he answered. "And then, when I saw all the data you had on me, even my salary, I was upset. So I changed it. Maybe I shouldn't have." He paused. "Look. You're the last person in the universe that I want mad at me. Can't you come on down here so we can discuss it?"

"No."

"But this is silly! I want to be with you, and I know you want to be with me."

"It's my own fault," she said. "The first thing a prostitute learns is that you can't get involved with a patron.

I broke my own rule. I'm actually more upset with myself than with you, Harry."

"Well, *I've* got no such rule," he lied. "Can't we get together and discuss it?"

The Madonna shook her head. "I thought you were different." She sighed. "You put on a good act, Harry."

"I care for you. *That's* not an act."

"Then that's *your* misfortune," she replied.

"What if I came up to your office?" he asked. "I mean, if you feel talking to me in my own suite puts you at a disadvantage . . ."

"If you come, the door will be locked."

"That won't stop me."

"Are you threatening to break it down, or have you some other talent you haven't told me about yet?" she asked caustically, and he realized that he had blundered again.

"Look," he said at last. "You're the first person I've met in more years than I care to think about that I actually care for. Whether I behaved badly or not, you have your hands on the original dossier and there's nothing damaging or unsavory in it. I've offended you, and I'm deeply sorry—but how the hell can I make amends if you won't see me?"

"You can make amends by telling me who you are and why you're really here—and I don't mean your name and your damned accountant's job."

"But that's who and what I am," he said doggedly.

"Then we've nothing further to say, have we?" replied the Madonna, reaching for the disconnect square on her console.

"Wait!" he said with such urgency that she froze. "You won't come here. Okay. And you won't let me come to your office. Okay. But can't we at least talk this out via our holographs?"

"I have nothing to talk out, Harry. When *you're* ready to tell the truth, call me back. In the meantime, who would you like me to send down to your room tonight? I understand that you met Flaming Lorelei this afternoon and had a drink with her; I can see if she's willing to stop by."

"I don't *want* anyone else!" he said desperately. "I just want you."

"Good night, Harry," she said, and broke the connection.

So he spent that night alone, and the next night as well. The Leather Madonna would answer his intership calls just long enough to ascertain his identity and then break the connection. He haunted the restaurants and the casino, but she didn't come out of her office.

He tried to tell himself that he was acting like a lovesick schoolboy, or at least a very guilty one, rather than a romantic and dashing saboteur; that the last thing he needed to do was form an attachment to the woman he was out to break; that the Madonna was neither the loveliest nor, very likely, the most skilled woman aboard the *Comet* and that if he *had* to establish some kind of relationship with one of the prostitutes, any of the others would be preferable under the current circumstances. He would listen very carefully and thoughtfully to his own advice; then a memory of the Madonna, talking, laughing, or just lying in his arms, would appear somewhere in the cinema of his mind, and the advice was forgotten.

By the time he finished work the third day he was feeling so isolated and unhappy that he didn't even stop by the public rooms hoping for a glimpse of her, but instead went straight to his suite, determined to find some way to utilize his skeleton card so that she couldn't break the computer connection. He stalked into the bathroom, spent half an hour in the sauna trying to relax so that his loneliness and misery weren't quite so broadly displayed on his face, and finally showered, dressed, and returned to the parlor, still not quite sure what to do with the skeleton card but determined to make some attempt, however futile, to speak to the Madonna once again.

"Hi, Harry," said a soft, feminine voice coming from

the bedroom. "I was starting to wonder if you were *ever* coming out of that damned steambath."

Startled, he walked to the doorway and saw Suma, wearing the sheerest and flimsiest of negligees, lying on his bed.

"What the hell are you doing here?" he demanded.

She flashed him a sultry smile. "Charity work. The Madonna thinks you're feeling a little lonely, so here I am to the rescue."

"Well, you can just go right back!" he snapped.

Suma looked puzzled, and a little irritated. "Nobody's ever turned me down before, Harry."

"View it as a learning experience."

"What makes *her* so special?" demanded Suma.

"I don't know what you're talking about," replied Redwine.

"Then you're the only person aboard the *Comet* who doesn't!" she shot back. "Everybody knows you were sleeping with the Madonna, and everyone's seen you moping around after she threw you out."

"She didn't throw me out," lied Redwine, wondering just how foolish he had appeared during the past few days.

"Why did you even want to get *in*?" asked Suma, honestly curious.

"You wouldn't understand."

"I certainly don't." She stood up and turned slowly around. "Is she as pretty as this?" she asked, striking a pose that accentuated the fullness of her breasts and the strikingly smooth curve of her hips.

"No," he said honestly. "She isn't."

"Well, then?" she asked.

"That's just not very important."

"Maybe you think she's better in bed?"

Redwine shrugged. "I hadn't thought about it."

"Well, she's not," said Suma defensively. "There are things I can do that she's never even heard of."

"I don't doubt it," replied Redwine. "So what?"

"So why is she the only one on the whole ship that you want?"

"I have a feeling that it wouldn't make any sense to you."

"Try me," she said, smiling invitingly and looking inordinately pleased with her double entendre.

"I'd rather not." He paused. "Why the hell do you care?" he asked her. "You don't even like me."

"Call it professional pride. No one's ever refused me before, and no one has preferred the Madonna to me."

"Well, it's a cross you'll just have to bear."

A look of fury flashed across her face, and then, suddenly, she was smiling again. "You're presenting me with a challenge I can't resist, Harry."

"Force yourself."

She slipped out of her negligee and lay back down on the bed, undulating sensuously.

"*You* force me, Harry," she grinned.

"Forget it," he said, trying to sound uninterested while wondering if he had ever seen such a perfect body.

"You don't know what you're missing, Harry," she whispered, running her tongue over her moist lips. "Would you like me to tell you?"

"What I'd like is for you to leave," he said, knowing that he should walk out of the suite, or at least go back to the parlor, but unable to take his eyes off of her.

"*She's* never coming back. You'd better take what you can get." She turned onto her belly and stretched languorously. She noticed him staring at her, and arched her back and raised her buttocks provocatively. "Do you *really* want to be faithful to a whore who doesn't want any part of you?"

"She told you that?" demanded Redwine.

Suma smiled like a kitten. "*I* want a part of you, Harry. Want me to show you which part?"

"What exactly did she tell you?"

"That as soon as I had a couple of spare hours I should stop by here." She paused. "That was almost two days ago, Harry. You really don't know how generous she's being to you. I don't have many spare hours."

"She knew I'd tell you to leave," said Redwine.

"But I don't have to," replied Suma, turning onto her back again. "Just say the word and Sesame will open so wide you can see all the way through to next month."

Suddenly Redwine felt himself getting mad. "She *knew* I'd tell you to leave!" he repeated. "That's the only reason you're here."

"I've got about twenty other reasons," purred Suma. "Would you like me to whisper them all in your ear?"

"She counted on it!" he continued, feeling a growing sense of outrage building within him. "Well, screw her!"

"Oh, no, Harry," said Suma. "Screw *me*."

"You bet I will!" he said savagely. "This is supposed to be a whorehouse, isn't it?"

He began unfastening his tunic, but Suma was at his side an instant later, pulling his hand away.

"Let me do it," she whispered. "Your job is just to relax and let me do all the work."

"Fine," he aid. "But let me do one thing first."

"Will I like it?" she asked with a sly smile.

"*I* will," he replied, walking into the parlor. He got out his skeleton card and re-activated the security system. "I hope to hell you're watching!" he muttered under his breath, too softly for Suma to hear.

Then he returned to the bedroom.

"I'm all yours," he said, still staring at the computer in the next room. "I've got just one request."

"You just name it, Harry," she said, starting to unfasten his tunic and kissing each new section of his torso as it was revealed.

"I don't want you just to be good," he said savagely. "I want you to be *great!* You got that?"

"Oh, I will be, Harry," she promised him. "I'll be the best you ever had, the best you ever dreamed of having."

"I want this to be memorable, damn it!" he continued. He walked over to the bed and ripped the satin covers off, throwing them into a corner of the room. "And leave the goddamned lights on!"

"That's the spirit, Harry," she grinned. "I'll show you things you never thought you'd see."

And a moment later, after she had finished undressing him, she pulled him down onto the bed and began keeping her promise. Not a single orifice went unused, not a position remained unattempted, not a variation went untried, and with surprising suddenness Redwine felt his anger and outrage seep away from him, to be replaced by a hitherto unsuspected animal lust.

As he lay on the bed, alternately watching Suma and her mirrored reflection on the ceiling going to work with a vengeance, he found himself wondering how she could throw herself into her sexual encounters like this day in and day out. And even as his body responded to her kisses and caresses, her natural inclinations and her unnatural ones, a section of his mind seemed to hover dispassionately above their intertwining bodies, coldly surveying the situation, cataloging what was happening for the ease of his future recollection.

It puzzled and disturbed him. He had never found himself doing this with the Madonna. He couldn't even remember who did what to whom, let alone what order they did it in.

He forced himself to concentrate on the sensations he was feeling again. Nothing in his experience had ever felt this strange and unique and wickedly exciting—not with the Madonna, not with his ex-wife, not with any of the other women he had known. If there was a sexual heaven, this *had* to be it. There was no greater pleasure to be had anywhere in the universe, and if there *was*, the human body wouldn't stand it: it would go stark raving mad.

But he didn't feel stark raving mad, or anything like it. He felt aloof, withdrawn—*alone*. He was so stunned by the realization that he momentarily lost his concen-

tration on what Suma was doing to him. She noticed—
given where *he* was and where *she* was, she couldn't
help but notice—and after a quick glance at him to
make sure he wasn't in the throes of a sudden coronary,
she went back to her ministrations with renewed vigor.
As she did do, he tried to cope with the discovery that
since his first night with the Madonna he hadn't felt the
emptiness that had become second nature to him.

He knew with a grim certainty that it wasn't solely
the sex he had had with her that he cherished. Certainly those encounters, gratifying and fulfilling as they
were, didn't measure up to what he was experiencing at
this moment as Suma whirled about the bed like some
incredibly soft, smooth, insatiable dervish, touching,
kissing, massaging, stroking, pulsating, using sections of
her body, familiar and unfamiliar, in ways that he was
sure no one else had ever conceived.

He stared up into the mirror and watched her,
fascinated, as she climbed atop him, did something
with her legs that even a contortionist would view with
professional envy, and began rocking and swaying with
a primal, sensual rhythm. The sensations were almost
unbearable, and yet he felt no closeness, no sense of
joining emotionally as well as physically. She was just a
stranger, albeit an incredibly talented one, doing a job.
Even as he finally succumbed to the inevitability of his
orgasm, he knew that while he may have responded to
her physically—indeed, that he couldn't help responding to her physically—he didn't really like her. He was
equally sure this entire episode would vanish from her
mind the instant she left his room, nor did he especially
want her to think about him once this encounter was
over. After all, her job was to please *him*; if she enjoyed
her work, as she seemed to be doing, so much the
better, but it was a job and nothing more.

And then he realized the *real* reason for the emptiness that had once again fallen upon him. The Madonna's
pleasure *mattered* to him; Suma's did not. More, it
mattered to him not as an affirmation of his own sexual

prowess, but because it was important to him that she feel what he felt, that he know he was giving as well as receiving. It was simply another way of *caring*, a way of reaffirming their closeness when even words proved inadequate. The only bond he had with Suma would diminish and then break in a matter of half a minute or so; sex with the Madonna merely reaffirmed a bond that already existed.

At least, he decided unhappily as he finally separated from Suma and lay on his back, panting heavily, *half* of a bond existed. His half.

Smart, Harry, he told himself ironically. *After forty-three years of being alone, of ruining a decent woman's happiness and siring three girls whose names you still get confused, who do you finally fall in love with? A whore. And not just any whore, but a whore who won't even talk to you. Shrewd move, King of the Saboteurs!*

Suma turned to him, grinning triumphantly. "Well?" she said expectantly.

"You kept your promise," he replied.

"Want to do it again before I leave?" she asked.

"You're kidding, right?"

"It's good for the muscle tone," she said seriously. "Besides, I might not be able to get back here for a few more days."

"Give me a raincheck," he said. "I feel ten years older than when we started."

"Was it memorable enough for you?"

"It was memorable."

"I'd like to see that Madonna do *that*!" she said proudly.

"So would I," he answered sincerely.

Her mask dropped again for an instant. Then she was on her feet and slipping back into her negligee.

"If I hurry, I think I've got time to change into my clothes and grab a meal before my next appointment—if you have no objections?"

"None."

She walked into the parlor, then paused and turned to him.

"You're a fool, Harry."

"I know," he said softly.

"That doesn't make you any less of one," she replied. Then she was gone, and Redwine, after lying on the bed and sorting out his emotions for another few minutes, got up and slowly began putting his clothes on.

He pulled a cigar out of his pocket, stared at it for a moment, then shrugged and put it back. As he walked into the parlor he was suddenly aware of the security system. There were more than a dozen cameras hidden throughout the suite, all of which he had located his first night aboard the *Comet*, but now he walked up to the one that transmitted his image on the ship's intercom system.

He stared into it for a long, uncomfortable moment, then sighed deeply, and hoped Rasputin wasn't monitoring him at this precise instant.

"I think I love you," he said softly.

He continued to stare at the camera, his face a battlefield of conflicting emotions.

"I'm sorry," he added. "For what I just did, for what I feel, for everything."

And for what I'm still doing to you every time I go to your office.

Then he jammed the security system again, sat down heavily on the contour chair, and tried very hard not to think of the Madonna doing with her handsome, loincloth-wearing servant what he had done with Suma.

8

Redwine spent most of the next morning and early afternoon locked in his office, staring at the Madonna's alien tapestry and feeling very confused. He was so steeped in his own thoughts that he didn't hear Rasputin pounding on the door for almost a minute.

When the insistent rapping finally broke through into his consciousness, he jumped to his feet, startled, and then adjusted the skeleton card to let the Security chief in.

"This just came for you," said Rasputin, entering the office and handing him a rather heavy package. "I didn't know you played chess."

"I do, from time to time," said Redwine, taking the package and setting it down gingerly on a table. Suddenly he turned back to Rasputin. "Who told you you could open it?" he demanded.

"I didn't. But we *did* scan it. That's part of our job." He shifted his weight uneasily. "Harry?"

"Yes?"

"I *had* to tell the Madonna what I found out. I hope I haven't caused you too many problems."

"More than you can imagine," said Redwine bitterly. "And you didn't find out a goddamned thing."

"I think I should warn you that I'm finding out more all the time."

"There's nothing *to* find out," Redwine replied mechanically.

Rasputin shrugged. "Have it your way. I just hope we can still be friends."

Redwine stared at him. "I don't know if we ever were." He sighed. "When I met you, I thought you were a pretty nice guy."

Rasputin shook his head. "I'm a pretty nice Security chief. There's a difference."

"I know." He paused again. "Did you monitor my room last night?"

"No. I figured that if you were willing to let the signal go through, there was nothing worth watching."

"Do you know if the Madonna did?"

"I can find out."

Redwine considered it for a moment, then shrugged "No. Don't bother."

"Whatever you say," replied Rasputin. He began to leave, then stopped in the doorway and turned back to Redwine. "Protect your ass, Harry. I'm getting close."

"There's nothing to protect."

Rasputin stared at him, genuinely concerned. Finally he turned and left the office, and Redwine instructed the computer to lock the door behind him.

Then he picked up the package, sat down on a sofa, and began unwrapping it. It took about three minutes to remove all the protective substances, and when he was through what remained was a large, ornately carved wooden box made of what seemed like mahogany from Earth itself.

He opened it gingerly and found that all thirty-two pieces had been individually swathed in protective coverings. He removed one of the larger pieces, unwrapped it, and held it up to the light. It was a castle, complete with tiny moat and drawbridge, each brick clearly discernable, with a tiny pennant flying atop it. It had been created from a piece of milky translucent quartz, which acted as a prism when he held it up to the light, reflecting all the colors of the spectrum, changing its delicate patterns every time he moved his hand. He examined it closely, seeking the name or mark of the artisan who had so meticulously and lovingly crafted it, but could find no trace of a sign or signature.

He rewrapped the piece carefully, then examined two more, a knight and a queen, before he came to the first opposing piece, a regal, full-breasted, absolutely beautiful queen wearing a gown right out of Elizabethan England. Every stitch, every pattern, every button, every piece of jewelry seemed to have a reality of its own. At first he thought it was made of onyx, but it too seemed to glow and take on a life of its own when he held it up to the light, and he decided that it must have been carved from some form of volcanic glass with which he was unfamiliar.

He spent the next hour examining each of the pieces, and then gingerly replaced them in their box. Finally he closed and latched it, and placed it back on the table.

Then he sat down at the computer, but instead of going back to work he found himself staring wistfully at the box. He fantasized about sitting down to play a game with the Madonna, not here aboard the *Comet*, but somewhere else, perhaps her farm on Pollux IV, possibly in his apartment back on Deluros VIII. The background details were blurred, but he knew that they had been together for a long time, and that they were happy, and that the terrible aching loneliness he had lived with for so long was no longer there.

Then he remembered that the Madonna didn't play games that she couldn't win, and he decided that he'd have to let her see him losing a few games so she would know she could beat him, and then he remembered that she wasn't even talking to him, and he sighed and activated the computer.

He worked for about two hours, then picked up the box, shut down the office, and took the tram back to the Resort. He went straight to his room, poured himself a whiskey, and tried to figure out how to get the chess set to her. He didn't know how much it had cost, but he knew it was too valuable to ask one of the prostitutes to deliver it for him. The only person he felt he could trust to act as a messenger was Rasputin, but it was Rasputin who was responsible for the fact that he needed a messenger in the first place, and he stubbornly refused to ask the Security chief for a favor.

He found himself wondering if the Madonna had heard what he said to her last night. Even if she hadn't been watching at the time, she should have been curious enough to review the video disks that had automatically been activated when he unjammed the room. His little tryst with Suma shouldn't have upset her; after all, *she* had been with literally thousands of men and he had made his adjustment to it easily enough. But if she had heard him, had seen how sincere and troubled he was, why didn't she acknowledge it?

His unhappy conclusion was that she hadn't yet reviewed the discs, that no one except maybe Rasputin knew of his feelings for her, that she probably hadn't even thought about him since ordering Suma to visit him. Except that he couldn't believe the last part of it: she had made him feel so complete that it was inconceivable to him that she had felt nothing at all. Love and empathy were not exactly his greatest areas of personal experience, but he was absolutely certain that no one who was able to banish his emptiness after all these years could not be similarly affected. At least, he *thought* he was absolutely certain, but in the back of his mind was a tiny germ of fear, an unacknowledged suspicion that maybe emptiness *was* the natural state of things, and that far from being unique before, he was unique now. It was too painful a thought to bear, and he pushed it back into the bottomless abyss of fears and anxieties from which it had come.

Finally he decided to try the ship's intercom once more. This time, instead of her activating her end of it, seeing who was calling, and breaking the connection, there was no response at all, and he decided that she must be in one of the public rooms, ironing out one of the dozens of problems and misunderstandings that occurred on a daily basis. He toyed with going out in search of her, but decided against it; it was not that he didn't want to see her, but that he was afraid he would make a fool of himself in front of everyone, employees and guests alike. He could picture the Madonna, years from now, visiting another patron or auditor, and telling the story of how a middle-aged accountant chased her all over the *Velvet Comet*, begging her not to whip him but to accept his gift. Redwine shuddered at the thought.

And then a more devastating mental picture flashed across his mind. Years from now he was sitting at home, alone and miserable, and wondering why the hell he *hadn't* chased her all over the ship. If she wasn't worth a little embarrassment, why did he feel so empty in the first place?

His mind made up, he got to his feet and walked over to the chess set. He leaned down to pick it up, then straightened up again, empty-handed. If she refused it, it might be difficult to offer it to her again. Better to talk to her first, smooth over their differences, convince her that he truly cared for her. Her table had been without pieces for seven years; another few days wouldn't hurt.

He stared at the door for a long minute, trying to summon the courage to walk out of his suite in search of her, when suddenly he heard a pounding on the other side of it. He frowned; why the hell did Rasputin have to come *now*, now that he had decided not to enlist him as a John Alden after all?

He adjusted his security card, faced the door, and muttered "Open!"—and an instant later the door slid back to reveal the Leather Madonna.

"I was just coming to look for you," said Redwine, furious with himself for not being able to come up with a more eloquent greeting.

She stepped into the room.

"Lock the door and jam the security system," she

said. "We've got a lot to talk about, and I don't want anyone listening in."

Redwine did as she told him. "Did you see the disk from last night?" he asked, trying futilely to remember what he may have said to Suma while in bed.

She ignored his question and began pacing back and forth.

"Please sit down," said Redwine, wondering if she had stopped watching when Suma left.

"I'd rather stand."

"I love you!" he blurted out, and suddenly felt like a foolish schoolboy.

"Harry, you son of a bitch, you don't love anyone or anything!" she snapped. "You're a goddamned, double-dealing back-stabbing bastard!"

He stared at her, unable to come up with a reply.

"I'm so mad I could nail you to a wall and vivisect you!" she continued. "You're the most despicable form of slime I've ever met! And the worst part of it is I really liked you!"

"Look. If it's what I did with Suma . . ." he began lamely, but he knew that it wasn't.

"It's what you did with *me*, damn you! It's what you're still doing to me!"

"Rasputin," he said dully.

"Don't blame Rasputin, Harry. *He* isn't trying to destroy everything I've built!"

She walked to the wet bar and poured herself a glass of whiskey, then took a large swallow and turned to him.

"He showed me your original dossier. We couldn't see anything wrong with it, but he decided to check with all the Vainmill subsidiaries you had worked for. I thought you were probably just hiding some black mark on your record that wouldn't matter to anyone else, and I wanted so badly to trust you that I told him to go ahead." She paused for breath. "Do you know what he found?"

"You tell me," said Redwine grimly.

"Nothing. And do you know why he found nothing?" She glared at him. "Because every company you audited was out of business within six months!" She hurled her half-full glass against a wall. "You're a goddamned Typhoid Mary! Everywhere you go, things die!"

"Not quite everywhere," he said.

"Oh, you were clever, I'll give you that. What you did was well-hidden. Even after Rasputin had all the facts, it took him almost two days to put them together in the right order." She paused. "And now you're *here,* trying to kill my ship. *Why?*"

"It's what I get paid to do."

"To betray someone you say you love?" she demanded.

"That wasn't part of the bargain," he admitted.

"Damn you, Harry!" she said, fighting back tears of anger. "Don't you think *I* ever get lonely too? Everyone on this ship is either a patron or an underling. You were one of the few people I could meet on equal footing, you and your clumsy schoolboy earnestness. I was lonely and I was fond of you—and you took advantage of it!"

He shook his head. "I took fulfillment from it."

"Don't hand me that shit, Harry! You were using me!"

"I wasn't then, and I'm not now. I love you."

"You've got a hell of a way of showing it!" she snapped. Suddenly she saw the wooden box. "What's that—more espionage gear?"

"No," he answered her. "It's a present."

"For who?"

"For you."

"I may be a whore, but I'm sure as hell not a *cheap* whore! Go buy someone else with it!"

"I don't want anyone else," he replied.

"I've heard that before!"

He took a deep breath and released it slowly. "Sit down," he said at last.

"I told you—I don't want to!"

"Do it anyway!" he said harshly. She stared at him

for a moment, then walked over to the loveseat. Redwine sat down a few feet away from her.

"We've got a lot to talk about," he said.

"I'm through talking to you, Harry," she said. "Now I'm going to stop you."

He sighed, feeling a thousand years old. "You already have."

"How?"

"I've already told you."

"Told me what?" she demanded. "That you love me? You don't even know me!"

"I know that I've been unhappy for forty-three years, and that I'm happy when I'm with you." He stared at her. "That's the truth."

"You wouldn't know the truth if it jumped up and spat in your eye!"

"The truth is that all I want to do right this instant is take two steps over to you and put my arms around you," he said in strained tones. "But what I'm going to do instead is tell you the truth that you want to hear."

"That you're a goddamned saboteur?"

He nodded. "That I'm a goddamned saboteur."

"But why?"

"Because it's the only thing I do well," he answered her. "Because when I'm through with a job, I can see that I made a difference. Maybe it's not a very positive difference, but I caused someting to *happen*. I'm not just a clerk counting up other people's money—if I recall your description correctly."

"Who do you work for?"

"Vainmill."

"But that's crazy! Why does the Vainmill Syndicate want to sabotage its own companies?"

"Why does one politician try to discredit a colleague when theoretically they both want what's best for the people?" he replied. "Vainmill has assets of more than one hundred trillion credits, and the Chairwoman is due to retire in a year or two. That's going to put a mighty big prize up for grabs."

"You mean that all this is interoffice politics, that your boss is trying to destroy the *Velvet Comet* just to get a jump on his rivals?"

He nodded. "Or *her* rivals."

"You're working for a woman?"

He shrugged helplessly. "I don't know."

"You don't even know who you're working for?" she demanded incredulously.

"That's right."

"All I can think is that I must look awfully dumb to you, Harry. How can you not know who's ordering you to destroy all these businesses? And, more to the point, after the way you've lied to me and tried to destroy me, why should I believe anything at all that you tell me?"

"Because before you leave here, I'm going to call up the financial data banks I've been working on and show you exactly what I've done and how I've done it."

"Why?"

"Because I love you, and I'm all through hurting you."

She stared at him long and hard. "Oh God, Harry, you're such a damned good liar, how am I ever going to know when you're telling the truth?"

"You'll know," he said. "I'm going to give you enough details to lock me away for a long, long time."

"I may just use them," she said ominously.

"You won't," he replied. "*I'm* not your enemy, not any more. But that doesn't mean you don't *have* an enemy."

"What are you talking about?"

"There's a plant on board the ship."

"You mean a spy?" she asked, trying to absorb what he was telling her.

He nodded. "I don't know who my ultimate employer is, but I get my assignments from a man named Victor Bonhomme."

"I've never heard of him."

"Nobody on this ship should have heard of him. His

name wasn't in my dossier, and he doesn't work for the
Entertainment and Leisure Division."

"So?"

"So Rasputin knew that I was somehow connected
with him."

"Maybe someone mentioned it when he was following up on your dossier," suggested the Madonna.

He shook his head. "He knew it the day after I
arrived."

"Could *he* be the plant?"

"I doubt it. I can't imagine why he'd have mentioned
Bonhomme if he was." Redwine paused. "But it means
that I can't just walk away from the *Comet*. The plant
will know I didn't finish my job, and they'll simply send
in someone else."

"So what are you going to do, Harry?" she asked
cautiously, wanting to believe him but still not quite
sure that she could.

"I'm not sure," he replied seriously. "But we've got
some decisions to make."

"*We?*"

"We," he repeated.

"What kind of decisions?" she asked suspiciously.

"First I've got to ask you something."

"What?"

"I've spent the better part of three days telling myself I couldn't care for you this much if you didn't care
for me, too. I've repeated it and repeated it and repeated it—" a worried, uneasy smile flashed across his
face "—but I still don't know if it's *true*." He hesitated
awkwardly. "I know it sounds ridiculous on the surface
of it. People, *mature* people, just don't fall in love on
such short notice, at least not with total strangers—and
certainly a woman like you couldn't feel anything for an
overweight, middle-aged accountant who's starting to
lose his hair . . ."

"You're not overweight," she said quietly.

"But, damn it, I've got to *know!*"

She was silent for a long time, staring at her intertwined fingers. Finally she looked up at him. "Oh, shit, Harry—of course I care for you. I just don't know if I can trust you. You hurt me very deeply."

"I know."

"I don't think you *do* know," she replied. "This is a business of very fleeting, ephemeral relationships. For someone in my position to find a person she can feel comfortable with, whose company she can enjoy—well, it doesn't happen very often." She paused. "There have been an awful lot of men who have paid tens of thousands of credits to spend a night or a weekend with me, who truly thought they were attracted to me when we were in bed, and who never thought of me again once they left. You've got to be *so* careful before you let your guard down, before you let yourself start to care."

"It's not limited to *your* business," he interjected softly. "That's why I always keep to myself on a job. You can't let yourself care about the people you're doing this to." He smiled wanly. "Only I broke my own rule."

"So did I," she replied. "Now I just hope you can convince me I was right to." She sat erect, suddenly more businesslike. "All right," she said. "What kind of decisions are we talking about?"

"I think we have only two alternatives. The first of them is the easy one."

"Go public right now?" she asked.

"Nobody would believe me. Don't forget—I haven't done anything to go public *about*."

"Then what's the easy alternative?"

"You've got a lot of money socked away. So do I. I could do what they're paying me to do, and we can both pack it in when I'm through—just quit our jobs and get the hell out of here. To Pollux IV, maybe, or anywhere else you want to go."

She shook her head slowly. "This ship has been my life for ten years, Harry. I made it what it is, and I'm not going to stand by and let some nameless executive destroy all the work I've put into it, just so he can make five billion credits a years instead of four."

"I had a feeling that would be your answer," he said grimly.

"What's the other alternative?"

"It's a little trickier. As long as we know there's a plant on board, I've got to keep doctoring the books."

"That doesn't sound a hell of a lot different," she said.

"*This* is the difference," he answered, withdrawing the skeleton card and holding it up. "I can rig the computer to remember the original entries and put them back in whenever we tell it to."

"That little card can make the computer do *that?*" she asked skeptically.

He nodded.

"All right," she said, still looking for loopholes. "So you can tell it to put the books back the way they were. So what? Like you said, they'll just send in another saboteur."

"They won't know what I've done until it's too late. We'll activate it two or three months before the Board elects the new Chairman, and I'll make the records available to all of them. Once they get their hands on the data and Victor's name, a couple of them have *got* to figure out who my employer is and blow him right out of the race."

"*If* you're telling the truth, these people are playing for awfully high stakes. What makes you think they won't just kill you first?"

"Because when the plant checks the books after I've finished, he'll see that the *Comet* has been hiding some enormous losses. By the time we change back to the original entries, he won't have time to do anything about it."

"You're playing with fire, Harry," she said dubiously. "Somebody's going to be awfully eager to show you what happens to double-crossers."

"Somebody is going to be much too busy protecting

his own ass to worry about it," he replied with more confidence than he felt. "Besides, whoever benefits from this ought to be willing to offer the *Comet* whatever protection it needs in exchange for our giving him the goods on his chief rival."

"Do you know how many patrons come up here every day?" she asked him. "Hundreds! How can you spot one assassin?"

"I told you: this is the one job I'm good at. Nobody is going to know I'm responsible for it."

"Who else could they blame?"

"The plant. One of the ship's accountants. Someone in Security. They won't know, and they're sure as hell not going to kill them all."

"They'll blame *you*," she said adamantly.

He shook his head. "I'm the guy with everything to lose if the books aren't rigged. I'll have bet on the wrong horse."

"How will you release the real data? Surely they'll be able to trace it."

"Even *they* can't trace some of the things I can do with this," he said, indicating the skeleton card.

She looked at him and frowned. "I just wish I knew that this wasn't simply one more lie."

"You *will* know," he said. "I'm going to show you how to work the card. I'll turn over the pertinent priority codes to you and you can monitor everything I do. You can keep possession of the damned thing whenever I'm not working."

"When?"

"Right now, if you like. I'll show you how to rig the books, and I'll show you how to un-rig them, too."

She shook her head. "Tomorrow will be fine. I've already got too much to assimilate tonight."

He shrugged. "Whatever you say."

She stood up. "I think I'll have another drink—and I promise not to share this one with your wall. How about you?"

"I could use one."

"Sit," she said as he got up to join her. "I can do it."

She walked to the wet bar, poured him a straight whiskey, and spent a moment fixing herself a Blue Polaris. Then she returned to the loveseat, handing him his drink on the way.

"You really don't like these things, do you?" she said, indicating the concoction within her long-stemmed glass.

"I never said that."

"I thought we were starting a new era of honesty."

He grinned. "They're pretty awful."

"That's better," she said. "Wrong, but better." Suddenly her face became serious. "What are we going to do about Rasputin? He knows about you now."

"That's right," said Redwine, surprised the thought hadn't occurred to him already. He considered the Security chief for a moment. "I guess we're going to have to take him into our confidence, and hope he's not the plant."

"And if he is?"

"Then we're in big trouble." He shook his head. "He can't be. Why would he have mentioned Victor's name to me?"

"A friendly warning?"

"I don't think so."

"Are you willing to bet your future on it?" she asked him seriously.

"No," he said at last. "This is the first time I've ever liked my future. I don't think I feel like entrusting it to a stranger."

"Then what do you want to do about him?" asked the Madonna, declining to point out that she, too, was a stranger.

He sighed. "I suppose I can have Victor call him off."

"It won't work. Rasputin is the most loyal and incorruptible man I've ever met."

"Wouldn't a loyal and incorruptible man follow a direct order from a superior?" asked Redwine.

"Not if he thought your friend was in collusion with us to breach the security of the *Velvet Comet*."

"I suppose I could pull a couple of strings and get him transferred," suggested Redwine. "He couldn't very well refuse to go."

"He'd go—but he'd blow every whistle he could get his hands on first, and this place would be swarming with *real* troubleshooters. He'd make so much of a commotion that even your employer couldn't afford to ignore it."

"Then I'll just have to play it by ear," said Redwine. "I'll talk to him tomorrow."

The Madonna finished her drink. "Can I get you a refill?" she asked.

"I haven't touched *this* one yet," he pointed out.

She smiled awkwardly. "I guess I'm still a little more tense than I thought."

"It's been a long couple of days," replied Redwine. "By the way, there's a price for all this."

"Oh?"

Redwine nodded. "Get rid of the guy in the loincloth."

"His name is Adonis."

"*That* figures."

"And you think I'm sleeping with him?"

"Training him, maybe?" suggested Redwine.

She looked amused. "Harry, I'm the wrong sex for him."

"He's a homosexual?" said Redwine, surprised.

She chuckled. "You think only heterosexuals frequent the *Comet*?"

"I never thought about it at all," he admitted.

"I'd guess that almost a quarter of our patrons have only a passing interest in the opposite sex."

"And you have homosexuals who service them?" he asked.

"We *all* service them," she replied. "We just happen to have a few people who specialize in it."

"You've . . . ah . . . ?"

"Of course. With patrons, and with other prostitutes."

"Other prostitutes?" he repeated.

"A lot of patrons like to watch. Especially men."

"I think you get a cynical delight out of telling me these things," he said wryly.

"No. But I'm not ashamed of them."

"Well, whatever his sexual preferences, Adonis goes."

"I like to have someone around to talk to," she said, "and Adonis also likes poetry." She paused. "As soon as I'm convinced that you've been telling me the truth, I'll have him move back into the Home."

"I assume that means you don't want me to move in with you tonight."

"Not yet, Harry. You'd better have your talk with Rasputin first . . . and I want to monitor it. I think you owe me that much before we set up housckeeping together."

"I guess I do, at that."

He looked his disappointment for a moment. Then he noticed the chess set. "Are you ready for your present now?"

"What present?"

"The one in the box."

She looked first at the box and then at Redwine. "I don't think so, Harry. Not tonight."

"I've done something wrong again, haven't I?" he asked.

"No."

"Then I wish you'd let me give it to you. I think you'll like it. At least, I hope you will."

"I'm sure I will, Harry. You're a very thoughtful man."

"But not tonight?"

"No."

"When?"

"After you show me how to work the skeleton card and give me its priority codes."

"I suppose I deserve that." He sighed deeply. "Shall I shake your hand good-night?"

"I'm a prostitute, Harry. It's my affection and my confidence you have to win. If you want my body you can have it before I leave."

He stared at her for a very long moment.

"I think I'll wait until I can have all three," he said at last.

"Jesus, Harry!" she said, walking over and kissing him. "If your timing was any better I could put you to work here!"

Then she was out the door and into the corridor, while Redwine walked over to the wooden box and began examining the chess pieces once again.

It *had* been a good line; he had known it the instant he uttered it. The funny part, he thought with a rare feeling of serenity, was that it was also the truth.

9

The gymnasium was almost empty when Redwine arrived there the next morning. The Gemini Twins were working out with weights, three of the female prostitutes were using the exercise machines, and eight off-duty chefs and technicians were playing a vigorous if sloppy game of volleyball. He passed the pool, where the Duke, his face still puffy and bruised, was mechanically swimming laps with grim determination rather than any enthusiasm, and finally he came to the enclosed handball courts. He looked in the first two, found them empty, and then commanded the door of the third to open.

"Good morning, Harry," said Rasputin, who was wearing nothing but gym shoes and a pair of shorts.

"They told me in Security that I could find you down here," said Redwine, stepping into the enclosure and ordering the door to slide shut behind him.

"Yeah," said Rasputin, grabbing a towel and mopping the sweat off his glistening body. "I try to get down here three or four times a week."

"Am I interrupting a game?"

"Just with myself, if you'll pardon the connotation," replied the Security chief. "I never could get interested in weights or running laps, so I was just hanging around here, warming up, until I could con someone into a match. Are you interested?"

"It's been a long time since I've played," said Redwine.

"I'll go easy on you," answered Rasputin. He paused, then smiled. "What am I talking about? You didn't come down here to play handball."

"No, I didn't." Redwine looked around him. "Is this court secure?"

Rasputin shook his head. "No. If you want to speak in private, we'd better go to either your office or mine."

"That's all right. I *want* this thing to be broadcast."

The Security Chief looked puzzled. "To the whole ship?" he asked dubiously.

"No. Just to the Madonna."

Rasputin walked over to a sweatsuit that was folded neatly in a corner and withdrew a small communicator. "I'll tell my people to route it through."

"Will they be able to see and hear us too?"

"Of course."

"Is there any way you can bypass them, so nobody but the Madonna receives it?"

"I suppose so," said Rasputin unenthusiastically. "I just don't know if I want to."

"That's the only way I'll talk to you—and after what you learned yesterday, I have a feeling that you want to talk to me."

Rasputin considered it for a moment. "Okay. It'll take about five minutes to set up."

"Good."

"Why don't you change into a gym suit while we're getting ready?" suggested Rasputin. "Who knows? You might want to play a little handball when we're done."

"You're *that* anxious to make me look foolish?" asked Redwine with a smile.

"Harry, after what I told the Madonna yesterday, I figured you'd either try to have me fired or come looking for me with blood in your eye. Since you haven't done either one, I think it's pretty safe to say that I haven't made you look foolish yet. Why should this morning be any different?"

Redwine laughed. "All right. Where's the dressing room?"

Rasputin commanded the door to open, led Redwine out into the gym, and pointed to a door near the swimming pool. "Just find an empty locker," he said. "You'll see how to set your own code into the lock."

"And where do I get the gym suit?"

"There's a whole batch of different outfits in the locker room. You'll spot them the second you enter it. Just pick out something that fits, and toss it in the laundry tube when you're done with it."

"Okay. I'll see you in a few minutes."

Redwine crossed the gym and entered the locker room. Flaming Lorelei and two other women, both of whom he recognized from the computer's pornographic entertainments, were just coming out of the shower, wet, glistening, and nude.

"Excuse me," muttered Redwine. "I must have come in the wrong door."

"Hello, Harry," said Lori, walking over to a pile of clean, folded towels that sat on a small counter. "There's *only* one door."

"I meant the door to the *men's* locker room," he explained awkwardly.

"Your provincialism is showing, Harry," said Lori, amused. "This is the only locker room we've got. After all, no one on the *Comet* is exactly ashamed of their bodies."

"What about the technicians and the security crew?" he asked.

"They learn to adjust." She began drying herself off as the other two women, huge smiles on their faces, walked to their lockers.

"Then I guess I'll have to learn, too," he said resignedly. "How can I tell which locker is empty?"

"If it's not locked, it's empty," she said, facing him and drying her back with a vigorous motion that momentarily caused Redwine to forget exactly what he was doing in the locker room in the first place. Suddenly he became aware of the fact that he was staring at her, offered a brief and embarrassed apology, and went looking for an empty locker. He came upon one almost immediately, became uncomfortably aware of the presence of the three women, and decided to pick up some kind of gym suit before undressing. He walked over to the supply area, spent as long as he dared without feeling too foolish while choosing a pair of shorts, a jersey, and some rubber-soled shoes, and then returned to his locker.

Under other circumstances, and before he had met the Madonna, he'd have been happy to climb into bed with any of them; nudity in proximity didn't bother him in the least. But he was painfully aware of their youth and slimness, and his own rather slack muscles and excess poundage, and he hated the thought of undressing in front of them under the bright, artificial light of the locker room.

Finally he decided that he'd better get moving before Rasputin came looking for him, so he took a deep breath and began getting out of his clothes as quickly as he could. As he stepped into his white gym shorts he cast a furtive glance down the aisle and found, to his relief, that one of the women had left and that Lori and the other woman were engaged in an animated conversation, paying him no attention at all.

He slipped on his jersey, got into his shoes, set the code on his locker, and, forcing himself to nod pleasantly to Lori, walked back out to join Rasputin.

"Harry," said the Security chief, staring at him as he reentered the handball court, "you're going to have to spot me five points."

"I told you—I haven't played in years."

Rasputin grinned. "Anyone who can play handball without a jockstrap is too goddamned sure of himself not to give me a spot."

Redwine turned bright red. "I was in a hurry," he stammered.

"I hope you feel it was worth it by the time we're through," chuckled Rasputin.

Redwine struggled to regain his composure. "Has the connection been made?"

"About two minutes ago."

"How do I know you're telling the truth?"

"Because, unlike some Vainmill employees I could name, I don't lie," replied Rasputin pointedly.

Redwine stared at him for a moment, then nodded.

"All right, Harry," said Rasputin, lobbing the hard rubber ball against the far wall. "What's it all about?"

"I can't tell you," replied Redwine, slapping the ball back.

Rasputin caught the ball as it came to him and held it.

"I thought we were going to *talk*," he said.

"We are."

"Sounds to me like we're *avoiding* talking," said Rasputin, slamming the ball against the wall.

Redwine raced across the court and barely got his fingers on the ball. It fluttered back toward the wall and struck the floor first.

"We'll talk," said Redwine, surprised that he was already starting to sweat. "But why don't you let *me* begin?"

"Go ahead," said Rasputin, lobbing the ball once again.

Redwine raced forward and slammed his hand against the ball. It took off, hit the wall with a sharp angle, and sped toward the far side of the room. He stood back and relaxed, only to see the Security chief dive through the air and send the ball back toward the wall. Caught flat-footed, he merely stood and watched as it went by him.

"Two to nothing," grinned Rasputin. "You were saying?"

"Everything you found out about me is true, at least on the surface of it," said Redwine.

"*Just* the surface?"

"I'm on *your* side."

"I find that just a little hard to believe, Harry,"

replied Rasputin. He lobbed the ball up to the wall again.

"It's true," said Redwine, taking two quick steps to his left and hitting the ball back.

"Harry, you do to Vainmill companies what predators do to prey!" said Rasputin, taking a vigorous whack at the ball.

It came off the wall with surprising force and Redwine tried to hit it back with equal strength. He misjudged its height and yelled in pain and surprise an instant later as it caromed off the tips of his fingers.

"Are you all right?" asked Rasputin. walking over and looking at Redwine's hand. The fingers were already starting to change color.

"I'll be fine," he grated. "But I think I've just retired from the ranks of the ship's handball players."

"I can get you some ice," offered Rasputin.

"I'm all right," responded Redwine irritably, trying to shake some life back into the fingers.

"I guess I should have believed you when you said you hadn't played in a while."

"It's my own fault," said Redwine, finally spotting the security camera and staring straight at it. "I was trying to impress my audience."

He leaned his back against a wall, then slid down until he was sitting on the floor, still tenderly massaging his fingers. "Well, let's get on with it," he said.

"I'm still listening," replied Rasputin, sitting down cross-legged a few feet away.

"Last night I had a long talk with the Madonna. I told her what my orders are, I gave her a way to check out my story and my actions, and I gave her enough information about my past to cause me a great deal of trouble should she decide at any time in the future that I'm trying to deceive you. That's why she's monitoring this conversation—so that she can confirm that I'm telling you the truth."

"And just what *are* your orders?" persisted Rasputin.

"I've told your superior, and she's satisfied with my

answers," said Redwine. "That should be enough for you."

"Harry, you've got to be kidding," said the Security chief. "First of all, you're a proven liar and a demonstrable saboteur. Second, if I don't know how she's checking out what you do, I don't know whether you gave her the means to do it properly. And third—and I'm sorry, Madonna—I can't be sure of anyone's loyalty to the *Velvet Comet* except my own. Maybe you've bribed her; there's certainly enough money behind you to afford it. Maybe you've scared or threatened her off. Or maybe you've taken her into partnership." He looked up at the camera. "I apologize, Madonna, but it's my job to consider these things."

"All right," said Redwine wearily. "What do *you* think I'm doing?"

"Based on what I've learned about you, my guess is that you're tampering with the books to defraud the *Comet*."

"Then why don't you report me?"

"Harry, I'd be reporting you to the guys who authorized you to *do* the tampering."

"Look," said Redwine. "If I allow Flaming Lorelei and your other accountants complete access to all the ship's financial records, dating back to its inception, will that satisfy you?"

"I don't know if it will satisfy me," answered Rasputin, "but it'll make me a lot happier."

"It's a deal," said Redwine, absolutely confident that no one who didn't know exactly what they were looking for could uncover the minute, careful changes he had made. Lori and the rest would spend all their time on the two biggest-ticket items, the brothel and the casino, and he hadn't even begun working on them yet. They'd probably give up long before they got to the restaurants, the concessions, the fuel that powered the life support systems, all the unlikely places he had hidden the *Comet*'s mythical losses. "They can audit *me* while I'm auditing *them*."

"And will you turn over your card to me?" asked Rasputin.

"Not a chance," said Redwine. "I have clearance to carry that card, and I intend to do so."

"*That's* what troubles me," admitted Rasputin.

"The card?"

"No. Your clearance." He paused uneasily. "Harry" —he looked toward the camera again—"Madonna—I like my job. I like working on the *Comet* and I'm very grateful to be working for Vainmill. They pay me well, they treat me well, they've been very good to me. I wouldn't want to do anything to jeopardize my relationship with them."

"Then just back off, and if you won't trust *me*, trust *her*."

"I'd like to," he said earnestly. "But this could still just be a test of Security, or of me."

"It isn't."

"Would you say otherwise if it was?" asked Rasputin with a smile. "Harry, you're a nice guy and I enjoy your company, but you're corrupt through and through. I can't take your word about anything."

"Then take the Madonna's."

He shook his head. "Corruption is like a disease; it tends to spread to everyone who comes into contact with it. I hope to hell the Madonna is telling the truth when she confirms your story, but I can't count on it."

Redwine shrugged. "Then we're at an impasse. You want more details; I can't give them to you. I want you to believe me; you don't." He paused. "What comes next?"

"I don't know," admitted Rasputin. "But I'll go this far: I'll keep my doubts and my suspicions to myself until I know for sure that you're out to sabotage the *Comet*."

"Fair enough," said Redwine.

Rasputin got to his feet. "That's it, then?"

"Not quite," replied Redwine, also rising.

"Oh?"

"You're right about one thing: there's a saboteur on board the *Comet*."

"I assume you're referring to someone other than yourself?" remarked Rasputin dryly.

Redwine nodded.

"I don't suppose you'd care to tell me who it is?"

"I don't know," answered Redwine. "But *you* do."

"Me?"

Redwine nodded. "Who told you that I knew Victor Bonhomme?"

Rasputin stared at him distrustfully. "That person is a saboteur?"

"A spy for the *Comet*'s enemies, anyway."

"What makes you think so?" asked Rasputin.

"Only a spy would know of my connection with Bonhomme."

"Why?"

"I can't tell you."

"Can the Madonna?" asked Rasputin.

"She can, but she won't."

"Well, I'll keep it in mind, Harry."

"You remember who it was?"

"Yes."

"Will you tell me?"

Rasputin smiled. "I guess we all have our secrets, Harry."

"Don't keep this one too long," said Redwine seriously. "This person can cause all of us an awful lot of damage."

"How much damage?"

"As long as I don't know who it is, I think my life will be in increasing danger."

"Well, a guy who works at espionage ought to be used to that, Harry," said the Security chief. "It goes with the territory." He paused. "What other damage do you think this spy can do?"

"Put the *Comet* out of business," said Redwine.

"I thought that was *your* department."

"You thought wrong."

"I hope you're right," answered Rasputin seriously. "Anything else?"

"No, I guess that's it."

"Then let's go shower."

"Sounds good to me," replied Redwine. He smiled at the camera. "No peeking. I'm not at my best in the light."

They crossed the gym and entered the locker room. Redwine went directly to his locker, muttered his code, and the door opened. He reached in, fumbled around for his skeleton card, touched four small areas in order, and walked over to Rasputin.

"I've jammed the security for a minute," he announced softly.

"Why?"

"Because I didn't want the Madonna to hear what I'm about to tell you."

The Security chief stared intently at him. "And what is that?"

"That she's in as much danger as I am."

"You're sure?"

Redwine nodded. "The longer I don't know who's keeping tabs on me, the worse it's going to get."

"She's a fine woman, Harry," said Rasputin. "If you're telling the truth, getting her involved in this was a shitty thing to do."

"I couldn't help it," said Redwine. "But that's why I don't want you to wait too long before giving me the name I need."

"I've got to think about it," said the Security chief, a troubled expression on his face.

"Think all you want," said Redwine seriously. "Just remember this: I don't give a damn what happens to the *Comet*, and I don't give a damn what happens to me—but if any harm comes to the Madonna because you wouldn't tell me what I need to know, and I live through it, you're a dead man."

He returned to his locker and reactivated the security system.

"How's your hand?" asked Rasputin, aware that they were being monitored once again.

Redwine examined his swollen fingers. "Well, I probably won't perform any piano concertos for a few days."

"You shouldn't let yourself get so far out of shape."

"I was never *in* shape," grimaced Redwine.

They slipped out of their clothes and dropped them off at the laundry tube on the way to the showers. The Gemini Twins were leaving just as they entered.

"I'm going to have to work out and shower at the Resort's gym from now on," remarked Redwine, staring after them. "I don't just feel fat and ugly around here, I feel like a whole different species."

"I saw you with Suma the night before last," grinned Rasputin. "*That'll* take weight off you!"

"Lock someone in a room with her and I'll bet he dies of old age within a week!" said Redwine devoutly.

"Let's hope so."

"What do you mean?"

"Lori told me this morning that she's Gamble's new instructor."

"She? You mean Suma?"

"Right."

"The poor son of a bitch. I have a feeling that she can be pretty demanding."

"Maybe not. She's so busy she'll probably only get to work with him once or twice a week."

Suddenly Redwine became aware of another presence, and turned to see a tall, statuesque black woman, her body moist and glistening, entering the shower area.

"Hi, guys," she said pleasantly, as Redwine began edging behind the Security chief. "Anyone want to scrub my back?"

"What the hell," said Rasputin with a smile and a shrug. "Why not?"

Redwine grabbed his arm as he started to walk over to her.

"Remember what I told you!" he whispered.

"Like I said—I'll have to think about it. As soon as

I'm convinced you're telling the truth, I'll give you what you need to know." Suddenly Rasputin grinned. "Did anyone ever tell you that you look a lot more formidable with your clothes on?"

Redwine forced himself to laugh, waited until the Security chief was diligently scrubbing his companion, and left the shower. He dried himself off, dressed quickly, and was soon back at work in his office.

He knocked off in early afternoon and returned to his rooms, only to find that they had been emptied out. He then took the elevator up to the public room level and made his way to the Madonna's office.

She was sitting in her metal lounge chair, reading the *Inferno*. When she heard him enter she looked up and smiled.

"I've sent Adonis back to the Home," she said. "He was heartbroken."

"Better him than me," replied Redwine, returning her smile.

"How's your hand?" she asked.

"I don't think we'll have to amputate. You saw the whole thing?"

"You're a good liar, Harry, but you're an absolutely terrible handball player."

"Did I handle Rasputin okay?"

She nodded. "You did fine."

He saw that the chess table was still empty.

"That wooden box I had in the suite last night—where is it?"

"In my bedroom, along with your other things," answered the Madonna. She paused. "Sit down, Harry. I've got a question to ask you."

He walked over to one of the sofas that flanked her computer/table. "Just how long a question is it?" he asked lightly.

"That depends on your answer. This morning you told Rasputin that your life might be in danger. Last night you assured me that it wasn't." She stared directly at him. "Which of us were you lying to?"

"I never denied that the course of action we've chosen is more dangerous than cutting and running," he replied seriously. "I told you last night that I thought I could keep it under control. I still think so." He paused. "But the danger is there. I won't deny it."

"And you think it will come from the plant?" she persisted.

"Directly?" He shook his head. "I doubt it. But the plant has got to be acting as a conduit. He can precipitate the danger based on what he reports. I think I can hide what we're doing—but I'll be honest: I'd feel a lot better about it if I knew who was keeping tabs on me."

"Are you sure he's keeping tabs on *you*?" she asked. "Couldn't he be here on another assignment?"

"Not a chance. He knows about Victor and me."

"And before long he'll know about you and *me*," she added thoughtfully.

"It won't matter," he said with more conviction than he felt. "He'll never know what I'm planning to do to the books. And besides, aren't prostitutes supposed to sleep with patrons?"

"You're not a patron, Harry. He'll know."

"He'll know we've set up housekeeping together, and that's *all* he'll know. Probably he'll think I'm doing it to gain your confidence."

"Are you?"

"If you believe that, I'm sure as hell not succeeding, am I?" he asked in pained tones.

"The last thing I want to do is hurt you, Harry, but there are questions I have to ask." She paused. "How much danger am *I* in?"

"More than if you change your mind and decide to leave the ship with me," he said. "Less than me if we stay here." He exhaled deeply. "The danger's not going to come now. It's going to come when we revert the books and expose what's been going on. Hopefully I'll have found a couple of protectors on the Vainmill board of directors by then—and even if I haven't, I still think I can cover our tracks. The one thing they'll never figure is that I'm willing not just to cut down my own employer but to take a fall myself."

"I hope you're right," she said.

"Well, you've got company. I hope so too." He paused. "Now *I* have a question to ask."

"What is it?"

"I thought I wasn't moving in until I showed you how to work the card and rig the books."

"I did a lot of thinking about that, Harry," replied the Madonna. "It boils down to this: either I'm going to have to start trusting you or I'm not. I don't know anything about accounting or skeleton cards; nothing you show me might work when the time comes. So either I'm with you from the start of this enterprise, or I'm not." She sighed. "I don't know if I've decided to trust you because I want so badly to believe in you, or because you've convinced me you're telling the truth." She stared at him and shrugged. "I suppose it doesn't really make any difference in the long run. I want to be with you, and I want to protect my ship, and if it turns out you're lying again I'll just have to face that when I come to it."

There was a long silence.

"Would you like me to get you your present now?" he asked at last.

"In a little while," she said. "Would you like to look around first, now that you're going to be living here?"

"I assumed it was just like all the other suites."

She smiled. "The madam gets special privileges."

"How many rooms do you have?"

"Five. Six, counting this one."

"What do you do with them all?" he asked.

"I live in them. I haven't set foot off the *Comet* in more than five years." They stood up, and she walked over and took his arm. "Which room would you like to see first?"

"The bedroom."

"Not the library?" she asked with a smile.

"Later."

"Or the dining room?"

"Some other time."

"But bedrooms all look pretty much alike."

"This one won't," he said. "*You'll* be in it."

She led him through a door at the back of the office, down a corridor, and into her bedroom, a huge room that was decorated with opulent, if traditional, furniture, and filled with some of her more valuable *objets d'art*.

"Welcome home, Harry," she said, as he began unfastening his tunic.

10

When Redwine awoke, the Leather Madonna was no longer in bed with him. He tried three closets before he found the one that held his clothes. He pulled out one of his gray business outfits, then changed his mind and decided to wear something a little more colorful instead, and discovered to his surprise that he didn't *own* any colorful clothing. He made a mental note to stop by one of the shops in the Mall and purchase something that would put a little life in his wardrobe, then set his chosen outfit on the bed while he shaved and showered.

After getting dressed he made a quick tour of the apartment, and wasn't especially surprised to find that the Madonna was gone, probably off solving another of the daily problems that never seemed to diminish in frequency. He found a container of coffee warming in the kitchen, poured himself a cup, and finally went to the office to see if he could discover her whereabouts with the computer, and possibly join her.

He was four steps into the room when he noticed the chess set. He had given it to her just before they had gone to sleep, and she had seemed quite overwhelmed by it—but it wasn't until now, when he saw that she had actually taken the opposing forces out of their ornate container and set them up on the table, that he was convinced that she liked them as much as she had said she did. She had re-polished each piece before leaving the apartment—though they certainly didn't need it—and he had to admit to himself that they looked *right* in their new setting.

He walked over to the table, sat down on one of the chairs, and spent the next few minutes once again admiring the thirty-two pieces. He still didn't know what they had cost him, but if they made her happy they were worth it, whatever the price.

He was still sitting there, sipping his coffee and re-examining one of the knights, an intricate sculpture of an armored warrior on a charging stallion, lance at the ready, the horse's mane and tail whipping in an imaginary wind, when a beeping sound told him someone was at the door. He commanded it to open.

"Where's the Madonna?" asked Suma, entering the office as the door slid shut behind her.

Redwine shrugged. "I haven't the slightest idea."

"Then what are *you* doing here?"

"Drinking coffee," he replied. "What about you?"

"I have to talk to her." Suma stared at him for a moment, then grinned. "You've moved in with her, haven't you?"

"Yes, I have."

"Your taste hasn't improved any," she said with barely concealed contempt. "Of all the whores on the *Comet*, why *her?*"

"I don't see that it's any of your business," replied Redwine irritably.

"Is it because she's the madam?" persisted Suma.

Redwine merely stared at her without answering.

"It sure as hell isn't because she's the best in bed—or have you forgotten already?"

"She's good enough for me," said Redwine, surprised that he felt as defensive as he sounded.

"You're a stupid man, Harry."

"Perhaps."

"You're not a very attractive one, either," continued Suma. "So why did she *let* you move in?"

"Maybe *I'm* good enough for *her.*"

Suma shook her head. "Swans swim with swans; ducks swim with ducks."

"Why don't you just let *us* worry about it?" suggested Redwine, hoping to change the subject.

"Because I don't trust anything that runs contrary to my experience," she answered.

"Your experience is limited to staring at every ceiling on this ship."

"It has to be that she's the madam," said Suma, ignoring his remark. "That was dumb, Harry. She's not going to be the madam forever . . . and *then* what will you do?"

"Who's going to replace her?" asked Redwine with a harsh smile. "*You?*"

"Eventually," was her confident answer.

"You're sure of that, are you?"

"I'm the best there is, so why shouldn't I have the best job?"

"Modest, too," commented Redwine dryly.

"The next modest whore you meet will be the first," replied Suma. She paused. "I'm the only one who ever outlasted the Demolition Team."

"Is that good?"

"Your Madonna couldn't have done it," said Suma proudly.

"I sincerely hope not," agreed Redwine.

Suma looked at him and sighed. "You're a fool, Harry."

"So you've told me."

"You probably even think she does a good job running the *Comet*."

"You don't?" he said, cocking an eyebrow.

"Of course not. She's got no imagination, no flair."

"What would you do differently?" he asked, curious in spite of himself.

Suma walked over to the metal lounge chair and sat down.

"Do you really want to know?"

"I wouldn't have asked if I didn't."

"All right," she said. "First of all, I'd double the rent

of every shop in the Mall as quick as their leases came up for renewal."

"That's a lot of money," commented Redwine.

"Our business has tripled in the last five years, and their rents have only gone up sixty percent. They'll pay." She paused. "Next, I'd get rid of the blackjack tables. They only give the house a three percent break. I'd replace them with some alien game, probably *jabob* that the Dabihs play out on the frontier worlds. I'd get rid of half the fantasy rooms, replace them with more suites, and triple the price on the fantasy rooms that remain."

"I thought they were pretty popular," said Redwine, fascinated and just a little uneasy about all the thought she had obviously put into this.

"They are—but we have too many of them. Anyone who spends a weekend here is likely to be able to use one. If we make them harder to come by, we can charge more, and do more business in the extra suites. I'd start selling drugs—which the Madonna absolutely refuses to do, despite the fact that anyone who wants them can get them in the Mall; that costs us perhaps two hundred thousand credits a week."

"It sounds like you've given it a lot of consideration," commented Redwine noncommittally.

"This ship is my life, Harry," she replied seriously. "And someday I'm going to run it. I plan to know what to do when that time comes. You want more?"

"Absolutely."

"I'd get rid of the tramway."

"You were the one who told me how convenient it is," noted Redwine.

"It is—but it means most of the prostitutes don't walk by the Mall very often. The whores on this ship make good money, Harry—based on what they tell me, the lowest contract we've got is for a third of a million credits a year."

"You're not paid—uh—piecework?"

"I thought you were auditing the books," she said, looking at him sharply. "How come you don't know?"

"I haven't gotten to the payroll yet," he replied.

"Well, we're not. Most of the people who work here have developed expensive tastes, and they've got very little to spend their money on. I'd make them take the slidewalk every day."

"Makes sense," he agreed.

"And there's one more thing." She paused. "You've seen the Gemini Twins?"

He nodded.

"*That's* what I would do!"

"I don't think I follow you."

"They were surgically altered to appear identical," she said, irritated that he seemed unable to jump to the proper conclusion.

"So what?" asked Redwine. "Are you saying that you would encourage more of the men to look like them?"

Suma shook her head impatiently. "Who's the most popular whore on the *Comet?*"

"Let me take a wild shot in the dark and say that you are."

"And the most beautiful?"

"You're suggesting that someone become a surgical twin of yourself?" he asked, puzzled. "That you want to work the way the Gemini Twins do?"

"No!" she almost shouted, her face taking on the glow of a fanatic as her mask finally dropped all the way off. "I'm talking about a whole ship filled with copies of myself! We'll call them the Suma Girls, and I'll select and train them myself. No more Gemini Twins, no more male whores at all. We wouldn't need them. Men would come from all over the galaxy to sample the Suma Girls."

"Have I already mentioned that modesty isn't among your strong points?" inquired Redwine wryly.

"You think it won't work?"

"What about the man who craves a little variety?"

"He won't—not once he's had the best."

"*I* did."

"Yes, but you're not a man, Harry—you're a sniveling toad who thinks he can get special treatment by shacking up with the madam. We'll get along just fine without customers like you."

"From now on, you're going to have to—and the word is *patrons*."

"Are you telling me how to be a whore, Harry?" she asked with a smile.

"I don't think *anyone* could tell you how to be a whore," he replied truthfully. "But what are your female customers going to say when you bar the doors to them?"

"Not much. We'll start a sister ship for them. I've already chosen a name for it. Want to hear it?"

"I can't stand the suspense."

"The *Satin Comet*," she said proudly.

"Have you discussed any of these plans with the Madonna?" he asked her.

"She doesn't like them." She flashed him a smile. "Especially the part about the Suma Girls."

"I can't imagine why."

"Because it's in her best interest to keep the *status quo*," replied Suma. "After all, she's responsible for it."

"And just how are you going to get rid of her?"

Suma laughed. "You don't really think I'm going to tell you, do you, Harry?"

"Why not?" he persisted.

"You're her new houseboy." She paused. "I still don't know why, though. You're nowhere near as pretty as Adonis."

He shrugged. "Maybe I have other advantages."

She grinned. "I could straighten him out in two days."

"He's probably the way he is because he *spent* two days with someone like you."

"There *isn't* anyone like me."

"Yet," he said.

"Yet," she agreed. She paused. "You're not being very nice, Harry."

"I'm just a guy who's trying to drink his coffee and mind his own business."

"I thought your business was to audit the books, not to screw the Madonna."

"When *your* business is to tell me how to run my own, I'll take your opinion under advisement."

"It may not be that far off, Harry." Suddenly she smiled. "You were much nicer to me in bed. Perhaps I ought to seduce you again."

"I don't think that would be a very good idea."

"I could, you know," she said confidently, as she shifted her position on the chair to better display her jutting breasts. "What do you think the Madonna would say if she came in and saw us tumbling around together?"

"She's not going to, so your question is academic."

"This may be your last chance, Harry."

"I sure as hell hope so," he said devoutly.

"She'd never even have to know," persisted Suma, amused by his discomfort.

"Why would you want to, *except* to have her know?" he asked.

"I told you that the last time: I don't like being rejected."

"Then don't ask me, and you won't be."

She stared at him. "It's funny," she said at last. "You don't *look* dumber than Gamble."

"Ask Gamble if he can do double-entry bookkeeping sometime," replied Redwine.

"She's not keeping you around for your wit, that's for sure." Suma looked at the chess set. "Did you buy her that?"

"Yes."

"How much did it cost?"

"I'm afraid that's none of your business."

She walked over to get a closer look. "Ugly queen," she commented. "Skinny and flat-chested."

"Well, not everyone can look like you," he said. "Until you become the madam, anyway."

He stood up.

"Where are you going?"

"To get another cup of coffee, if you've no strenuous objections. Can I get you one?"

"No," she replied. "I really have to speak to the Madonna about a scheduling conflict tomorrow night." She picked up a bishop and examined it. "Maybe I'll take one of these pieces with me. The Madonna doesn't play anyway, and it would look nice in my room." She grinned at him and waited for a reaction.

"You do," he replied seriously, "and I'll come after you and break your arm."

"Can't you think of anything you'd rather do to me?" she asked with a seductive smile.

"Truthfully? Not at this minute," he replied, going to the kitchen. When he returned to the office she was gone.

The first thing he did was check the chess set to make sure all the pieces were there. The second thing he did was sit down on the lounge chair and allow himself to feel a moment of genuine pity for Gamble DeWitt. And the third thing he did was decide to take the morning off, since so much of it had been wasted already.

The Madonna returned half an hour later, walked over to where he was still sitting, and kissed him.

"Good morning, Harry."

"Hi," he said. "You had a visitor."

"I know," smiled the Madonna. "I met her in the reception foyer. She told me you tried to seduce her."

"She did *what*?" he said incredulously.

The Madonna laughed. "First of all, I can't believe you'd have the energy after last night. And second, as far as seducing Suma is concerned, I don't think *anyone* has ever tried and failed."

"She thinks she's going to replace you," said Redwine.

"I know. She's not exactly unambitious."

"She's given it a lot of thought," he continued. "She knows exactly how she's going to run things."

"Like raising the rents and changing the casino?" replied the Madonna.

"Yes."

"It won't work. Half of the stores will pull out; they're only here as prestige showcases anyway. And by the time you explained how one of those alien games works to a patron, his vacation would be over."

"Has she mentioned her Suma Girls to you?" he asked.

"They'd probably make a lot of money," commented the Madonna. "Still, one Suma at a time is about all I can keep tabs on."

"You know she's taken over Gamble DeWitt as her own personal project."

"Poor son of a bitch," she said. "He'll never be the same."

"I keep wondering if she hasn't got something special in mind for him."

"Such as?"

He shrugged. "A bodyguard?" he suggested.

The Madonna smiled. "Her body's never still long enough to guard it."

"A hit man, then?"

"You're letting your imagination run away with you, Harry."

"Maybe, but I think we should tell Rasputin to keep an eye on him."

"Rasputin's already keeping an eye on him. That's his job."

"Just the same . . ."

She sighed. "I already spoke to him about it yesterday."

"You did?" he said, surprised.

"Harry, I didn't get to this position because they drew my name out of a hat. You're good at protecting yourself when you're working; well, so am I."

"I guess you are at that," he said admiringly.

"Well, *that's* taken care of," she said briskly. "Now I have a special favor to ask."

He smiled. "I thought I wasn't supposed to have the energy."

"Oh, you'll have the energy for this," she replied, walking over to the table and seating herself at one of the chairs. "Show me how to play chess."

"You mean it?"

She nodded, picking up a bishop and holding it up to the light. "I've waited seven years for a chess set that was worthy of this table. It seems a shame not to know how to use it. Will you teach me?"

He got up, crossed the room, and sat down opposite her.

"I'd be honored," he replied.

11

The next three weeks were the happiest Redwine had ever spent. Thanks to Victor Bonhomme and his unknown employer he had occasionally felt needed, but this was the first time in his life that he actually felt *wanted*.

He woke up happy each morning, went off to the auxiliary office to continue going through the motions of rigging the books, began taking time off for some rather unambitious daily exercise in the gym, and even resolved to go on a diet, though he carefully placed the date for it sometime in the nebulous future. Each night he and the Madonna would eat at one of the *Comet*'s array of fabulous restaurants, and then would return to her apartment, where they would talk, or read, or play chess, or make love.

It was an idyllic twenty-one days. Flaming Lorelei had gone over his work and had been unable to spot what he was doing, Rasputin had stopped trying to pry the details of his mission from him, and the Madonna, after learning how to manipulate the skeleton card, finally believed that he was telling her the truth. Indeed, the only bad news came when he found out how much he had paid for the chess set, and even that didn't bother him very much, considering how much pleasure it gave the Madonna.

He slept late on the morning of the twenty-second day. On a ship where there were no days or nights, and even the official time was pretty much of an arbitrary convenience, he had taken to working in odd shifts, trying to match his hours to the Madonna's.

She was already dressed in a black, patent-leather jumpsuit and silver boots and gauntlets when he finally got out of bed. He shaved and showered, donned one of the flashy new outfits he had purchased in the Mall, and wandered into the kitchen to get some coffee. Then, cup in hand, he walked into the office.

"Good morning," he said, sitting down on one of the sofas.

"Aren't you running a little late today?" she asked him, looking up from the day's schedule, which was listed on the small computer inside her fruitwood cabinet.

"Let 'em take it out of my pay," he replied with a smile.

"The sooner you go, the sooner you can get back," she said in persuasive tones.

"Maybe I'll take the day off."

"Don't be silly, Harry," she said. "I'll see you later."

"You sound like you're trying to get rid of me."

"Of course not. I just have a lot of work to do."

He leaned back and put his feet up on the chrome table. "Let me just finish my coffee."

"Harry, I wish you wouldn't do that."

"Do what?"

"Your feet," she noted irritably. "They're on my computer's communications screen."

He took them off and stared at her. "Are you sure you're all right?" he asked. "You seem kind of touchy this morning."

"I'm fine," she responded with a smile. "I didn't mean to snap at you."

"Is there anything I can bring back from the Mall to cheer you up?"

"Just yourself."

The tabletop flickered to life, and a young man's face appeared.

"Madonna."

"Yes? What is it?"

"We've got a holograph problem in the ski lodge."

"Again?" She frowned. "All right. Close it up for the next two days and make sure that the techies fix it right this time." She paused. "And see that everyone who's scheduled for it gets a full refund."

"Ski lodge?" asked Redwine when the connection had been broken.

"One of our fantasy rooms," she explained. "It resembles a section of a huge ski lodge atop a mountain on Mirzam X. It has lovely oak and leather furniture, a roaring fireplace, a bar that specializes in hot buttered rum, and a fabulous view of the mountains—except that right now it looks like a storage room with a couple of chairs and a bar. The holograph projector keeps breaking down." She shook her head. "This is the fourth time this month. I don't know why the hell they can't fix it right the first time."

Redwine sipped his coffee thoughtfully. "Maybe I should take a look at it myself."

She laughed. "What do you know about holograms, Harry?"

"Not a damned thing," he admitted. "But I know a lot about how to make the ship's computer jump through hoops. Maybe I can get it to analyze the problem."

"That's just what *they* do," she pointed out.

"Yeah—but *I* do it better."

"All right, Harry," she said with a smile. "If they screw it up again, maybe I'll unleash you."

The screen lit up again.

"One of those mornings, huh?" he remarked.

"It's starting to look like it," she replied.

The face of the black woman Redwine had seen in the shower appeared.

"Yes?" said the Madonna.

"Peter Brennard is due to leave in about three hours," announced the woman. "He wants to say good-bye to you."

The Madonna glanced at Redwine, then looked at the screen again. "Where is he now?" she asked.

"In the casino," came the reply. "He says he'll be there for another twenty minutes or so."

"All right," said the Madonna, breaking the connection.

"What's *that* all about?" asked Redwine. "Have you taken to wishing godspeed to all your patrons?"

"No. Just some of our special ones."

"Well, if you'll excuse me, I think I can do with another cup of coffee."

He got up, walked to the kitchen, poured himself a cup, and returned to the office.

"Are you still here?" he said, surprised.

"Of course."

"But I thought this Brennard guy was only going to be in the casino for a few more minutes."

She turned to him.

"Harry, I'm not meeting him in the casino," she said softly.

He looked puzzled. "I thought you said—"

"I'm meeting him in his suite."

"*What?*" he exploded.

She sighed. "Do you remember the first day we were together, when I was showing you the ship, and you asked me if I still serviced any patrons?" She paused. "I explained to you that I occasionally serviced an old and cherished one. Well, Peter Brennard is one of the men I was talking about."

"That was before you met me, damn it!" he snapped.

"I know," she said soothingly. "But this is my job, Harry."

"Your job is running this damned place, not jumping in the sack with every guy who comes along!"

"That was crude, Harry," she replied severely. "Peter Brennard has been coming here since before I was hired, and he's spent over two hundred million credits on the brothel and the casino." She paused. "He's a very good, very old friend."

"If he's such a goddamned good friend, why did it

take him until just before he leaves to remember that he wants to sleep with you?" demanded Redwine.

"It didn't, Harry."

"You mean you've slept with him since I moved in?"

"He's been here eight days," she replied with a calm that seemed to enrage him further. "This is the third time he's requested me."

"You've been with him twice and didn't tell me?" he yelled, pacing back and forth.

"I knew it would upset you," she explained reasonably. "I had a feeling that he would ask for me again today. That's why I was trying to rush you out of here."

He muttered an obscenity. "And all this time I thought the onus of proving we could have an honest relationship was on *me!*"

"Harry, this is just a job," she said, her expression a cross between irritation and exasperation. "I don't feel anything toward him."

"Except that he's a cherished old friend!" Redwine shot back.

"I have many old friends," she continued, forcing herself to remain calm. "I only love one person."

"Well, you've got a funny way of showing it!" he snapped, still pacing.

"Harry, you came here to sabotage my ship and destroy me personally. If I didn't love you, why the hell would I have let you move in with me?" She shook her head wearily. "I should have *made* you leave before. I *knew* you were going to react like this."

"How the hell did you expect me to react? Be glad that the woman I love is hopping right our of *my* bed and into the bed of any old friend who asks?"

"Harry," she said patiently, "I've only known you for a month. I've been a prostitute for twenty years. Did you really expect me to tell a patron whose business we value that I'm no longer available?"

"I've only known *you* a month, and I'm putting my fucking life on the line for you! The least you can do is offend an occasional customer for me!"

"Patron," she said mechanically.

"Patron, customer, what the hell's the difference? It's what you're *doing* with him that's important!"

She stared silently at him for a moment. "It means that much to you?" she said at last.

"What do *you* think?"

She sighed. "All right. I'll tell him I can't make it."

"You will?"

"I never meant to hurt you, Harry," said the Madonna. "I hope you believe me."

"I know," he said, suddenly ashamed of his outburst. "I've been ranting like a jealous schoolboy—but damn it, I *feel* like a jealous schoolboy. I know sex is just a commodity to be bartered up here, but I can't get myself to look at it that way. Not with you."

They fell silent for a few minutes.

"Well, I'd better let him know before he gets back to his room," said the Madonna at last. She activated the screen. "Casino."

The computer scanned the huge casino until the Madonna ordered it to stop at the roulette table.

"*That's* Brennard?" asked Redwine. "The bald one with the six chins and the runny nose?"

"No," she replied. "The one standing just to his left."

"*Him?*" demanded Redwine, staring at a very handsome man in his early thirties. "*He's* your cherished old friend?"

"Yes."

"Damn it! He looks like a clone of Adonis!"

"Are you saying you wouldn't have minded it as much if I had gone to bed with the man standing next to him?" asked the Madonna, genuinely curious.

"I don't know," he muttered. "But I sure as hell didn't think you were sneaking off to screw a guy who looks like he ought to be working here!"

She smiled. "Harry, if all I cared about was how a man looked, do you really think I would have let you move in with me?"

"But he's not just good-looking," complained Redwine,

realizing that he sounded petulant but unable to stop himself. "He's got to be ten years younger than me and maybe fifty times richer."

"So what?" she said, still smiling. "I have aberrant tastes. I prefer *you*."

"I sure as hell can't imagine why."

"Well," replied the Madonna, "when you're like this, I have a little trouble remembering why, too."

"Look," he said, struggling to regain his composure. "I love you, and I don't like the thought of another man laying a finger on you. It's jealous and possessive, and given our present surroundings it's absolutely ridiculous, but I can't help the way that I feel."

She sighed. "Well, it's inconvenient as all hell, but I suppose I'd probably be upset if you *didn't* feel that way." She paused, amused. "I almost hate to tell you who's arriving tomorrow."

"I don't want to know."

"I'll just tell her I'm indisposed."

"*Her*?" he repeated.

"It's all right, Harry. From this moment on, I'm retired from the ranks for as long as we're together." She paged Brennard to an intercom screen, explained that a couple of unforeseen problems had come up and that she wouldn't be able to get away, and suggested another prostitute whom she knew was available. He accepted her story with good grace, smiled pleasantly, and went back to the roulette table.

"Shit!" muttered Redwine.

"Now what, Harry?"

"He's not just better-looking than I am, he's got better manners, too." He grimaced. "I can't even make myself hate him. Hell, I admire his taste."

She was about to reply when the door monitor chimed, and a moment later Suma, dressed in a translucent green and gold material, her hair laced with artificial vines and flowers, stormed into the office. "You've got to do something about the Duke!" she said furiously.

"What's the matter?" asked the Madonna.

"He's cheating my patrons because of what Gamble did to him."

"What makes you think so?"

"I don't *think* so, I *know* so!" responded Suma. "Ever since he found out that I had taken over Gamble's training, none of my patrons has been able to win at any of the games—and don't tell me it's just a string of bad luck. I can tell by the way that bastard grins at me that he's doing it on purpose!"

"You're sure?" asked the Madonna.

"Of course I'm sure! And it's got to stop!"

The Madonna sighed. "I'll have a talk with him."

"See that you do, because if he's still cheating tonight, I'll send Gamble over to have a talk with him, and I guarantee you're going to be looking for a new pit boss when he's done!"

"That sounds remarkably like a threat," put in Redwine.

Suma turned to him. "You keep your nose out of this, Harry!" she snapped. "This is between the Madonna and me."

"I said I'll look into it," replied the Madonna coldly.

"By tonight?" persisted Suma.

"By tonight," agreed the Madonna.

Suma stared at her for a moment. "I half hope you're lying," she said. "I'd love to turn Gamble loose on him."

"Gamble isn't yours to turn loose on *any*one."

"We'll see about that!" said Suma. Then she turned on her heel and left the office.

"Well," said Redwine after a moment. "What do you make of *that*?"

"She's probably telling the truth. The Duke isn't the kind of man who forgives and forgets, and I gather Gamble gave him a pretty sound thrashing. I suppose I'll have to speak to him."

Redwine shook his head. "That's not what I meant. I'm talking about Suma. She practically *dared* you not to talk to the Duke."

"Just bluster," replied the Madonna. "If Gamble attacks anyone outside of the Home's gymnasium, I'll see that he's off the *Comet* in five minutes' time."

"Who's going to throw Gamble DeWitt off the ship if he doesn't want to leave?"

"In case it's escaped your notice, Harry, we *do* have a security crew."

"Maybe," he said dubiously. "But if I were you I wouldn't turn my back on Gamble *or* Suma."

She smiled at him. "For a professional saboteur, you worry an awful lot."

He grinned. "Maybe that's why I'm still at large after all these years." He paused, then added seriously: "All I know is that when I look at her, I see a very ambitious girl who wants your job so bad she can almost taste it."

"Popular fantasies to the contrary, no one wants to be a whore forever," replied the Madonna. "*I* wanted to be a madam when I was in the ranks. What's wrong with that?"

"Nothing's wrong with that," said Redwine. "But I assume now that you're the madam you want to *stay* the madam?"

"Of course."

"Then don't make the mistake of underestimating her."

"I haven't underestimated her, Harry."

"If I were you, I'd get rid of her."

"She has a contract," the Madonna pointed out.

"Break it."

"She's the most popular whore on the ship."

"Still, I think—"

"The subject is closed, Harry," she said. "I don't tell you how to fix the books, and I don't think you should tell me how to run the *Comet*."

"I'm only doing it because I'm concerned about you," he replied.

"I know. That's the only reason I'm not mad at you." She activated the computer once more. "And now I think I'd better call the Duke in here for a little chat with him." She turned to him. "It would really be best if you weren't here for it, Harry. He can get pretty vituperative when he's on the defensive. It's just his manner, and he won't mean what he says, but I have a feeling that it will upset you."

"If you insist," he said reluctantly.

"Let's say that I strongly request it," replied the Madonna.

The Duke wasn't in his office, and she ordered the computer to scan the casino.

"He must be taking a break," she mused when the camera was unable to find him. "I'll give him an hour to get back to work, and if he's not back by then, I'll have to page him."

"The son of a bitch looks like he could even give DeWitt a tussle," muttered Redwine, glaring balefully at the screen, which once again showed Peter Brennard standing at the roulette table.

"It's possible," commented the Madonna. "I know he studied martial arts for a few years, and he seems to have kept in good shape."

"How does a guy who's so young get enough money to come up to the *Comet* in the first place?"

"He inherits it," she answered him with an amused laugh.

"All that, and martial arts too," he said. "Are you sure you didn't make the wrong choice?"

"I'm satisfied with what I have."

"But he's so goddamned good-looking!" persisted Redwine resentfully.

"True," admitted the Madonna. "But he's not really very thoughtful."

"What do you mean?"

She turned to him and smiled. "*He* would never purposely lose at chess just to make me happy."

"How long have you known?" he demanded, so surprised that he didn't even bother to deny it.

"Since the second or third game."

"Then why didn't you say something?"

"Because it made me happy," said the Madonna.

"To win?" he asked.

She shook her head. "No," she said gently. "To know that you were willing to lose. *That's* why you'll never have to worry about Peter Brennard or anyone else."

He frowned, puzzled. "Then do you want me to keep losing?"

She laughed. "No. The next time I beat you I want to know that it was because I was the better player."

"I'll accept that as a separate but equal right answer," he replied wryly. "Will you keep playing?"

"Of course."

"Even if you lose?"

"For a while, anyway."

"What the hell did I ever do before I met you?" he asked pensively.

"You sabotaged companies."

He grimaced. "Too bad I didn't hit one of Brennard's companies along the way."

"I'll make your a deal, Harry."

"Yeah?"

"I'll keep playing chess as long as you don't have any more jealous outbursts."

"Fair enough," he replied. "With one stipulation."

"What's that?"

"The future starts right now. I won't say a word about anything that happened up to this minute if you won't give me a reason to be jealous about anything that happens from this minute on. Deal?" he asked, extending his hand.

"Deal," she replied.

12

Redwine was sitting in the auxiliary office, going over the books, when suddenly he found himself staring at Victor Bonhomme's image.

"What the hell is going on here?" he demanded.

"Good afternoon, Harry," said Bonhomme, dressed and groomed in his usual meticulous fashion. "I thought we ought to have a little talk."

"I had this terminal sealed off," continued Redwine. "How did you get through to me?"

Bonhomme grinned. "*My* skeleton card is bigger than *your* skeleton card."

"Can anyone monitor us?"

"Not to worry, Harry," said Bonhomme easily. "Your terminal is still secure."

"All right," muttered Redwine. "What's up?"

"You've been there for over a month now, and I'm getting a little pressure about when you're going to finish up and come home."

"It'll be a few more weeks yet."

"Come off it, Harry. You and I both know that damned job shouldn't have taken more than twenty days, tops."

"It's trickier than I thought," lied Redwine. "They had a damned good accountant. Besides, you booked me in here for thirty days, not twenty."

"Those last ten days were in the nature of a bonus," said Bonhomme. "The Syndicate is picking up your tab. Which leads me to another question."

"Yeah?"

Bonhomme nodded. "Your department receives a weekly statement from the *Velvet Comet*, and I just happened to get my hands on it." He paused again. "It seems that they're no longer being charged for your room."

"They needed the suite, so I moved somewhere else."

"I hope you're not thinking of making any lasting friendships, Harry," said Bonhomme. "The *Comet*'s going down the tubes."

"What I do on my own time is my own business," responded Redwine.

"I never said it wasn't," agreed Bonhomme smoothly. "But an awful lot of people who work for the *Comet* are going to be very unhappy a few months from now, and I would hate to think that any of them might get the idea that you and I were in any way responsible for their condition."

"Cut the crap and get to the point, Victor."

"The point, Harry, is that I don't much care who you sleep with, but I think you'd better be very careful who you talk with."

"Have I ever blown my cover yet?" demanded Redwine.

"No, but you've never shacked up with the enemy before."

"I don't know what you mean."

"Harry, I'm not without my sources. I know you moved in with the ship's madam twenty-two days ago."

"Who told you that?" asked Redwine sharply.

"What difference does it make?" replied Bonhomme. "Just get all your fucking out of your system in the next few days, or I may have to come out there."

"I told you—it'll take another two weeks. The book-keeping system is so simplistic it's hard to hide what I'm doing."

"Bullshit," said Bonhomme. "This is Victor you're talking to, remember? Our employer is getting anxious, and I'd hate to tell him that you're messing up."

"Is that a threat?"

"Of course not. Why would I threaten you, Harry? Maybe you've been spending too much time in the sack and too little at your work, but you know where your best interests lie. I'm just suggesting as strongly as possible that you put your ass in gear and get the job done."

"I'm doing my best," said Redwine.

"Maybe," replied Bonhomme. "But this is the first time I've spoken to you in three years that you didn't threaten to quit. Don't enjoy yourself too much, Harry; we're playing for awfully high stakes."

"Have you got anything else to say, or do you think I might get back to work now?" said Redwine irritably.

"I'll be in touch," promised Bonhomme. He touched a small spot on his desk and broke the connection.

Redwine immediately left the office and took the tram back to the Resort.

"What is it, Harry?" asked the Madonna as he entered the apartment. "You look upset."

He used his skeleton card to seal off the room.

"I just heard from Victor Bonhomme."

"And?"

"I think I can stall him for another two or three weeks, but after that I'm going to have to leave the *Comet* until this thing comes to a head."

She frowned. "There's no way you can stay longer than that?"

He shook his head. "I doubt it. The man's a pro; he knows I've had time to do the job twice over already."

"Does he have any suspicions about what you're really doing?"

"Not yet," replied Redwine. "Right now he just thinks I'm like a kid turned loose in a candy shop."

"How long will you be gone?" she asked.

He walked over to where she was sitting. "As long as it takes," he replied, caressing the back of her neck. "Six months is a pretty fair guess."

She reached up and touched his cheek. "I'm going to miss you."

"I know," he agreed unhappily. "But it's got to be done. Besides, I have some business to take care of on Deluros."

"Like what?"

"I've got to take copies of what I've done and put them in a safe place—or, better still, two or three *different* safe places." He kissed her fingers as they passed near his lips. "These people play for keeps, and I've got to make sure we're protected."

"Did Victor threaten you?" she asked suddenly.

"No," he said, moving his hand to her shoulder and then gently down to a breast. "Who'd waste a bullet on a middle-aged accountant?" he added with a self-deprecating chuckle.

"Harry, I want you to tell me the truth," she persisted. "If you're in more trouble than you anticipated, I want to know about it." She turned and looked up into his eyes. "If you think your life may be in danger, I'll agree to your original plan and leave the ship with you."

"You'd really cut and run?"

"Yes, I think I would," she replied, looking quite surprised with herself.

He smiled. "You know, there was a time, and not so many days ago either, when I'd have lied and said there was a hit out on me, just to get you to come away and avoid all this trouble." He paused. "But I love you too, and I know how much the *Comet* means to you, so I'm going to have to tell you the truth—and the truth is that I'm in no more danger now than I ever was." He exhaled deeply. "It's just that talking to Victor finally brought home the reality of what we're doing. It's beyond the planning stage now."

"You're sure that's all that's bothering you?" she insisted.

"Yeah." He paused. "Well, we've got one other little problem, too."

"Oh?"

"Someone told him that I've moved in with you, so

I'm going to have to hunt up Rasputin and try to find out the name of the plant." He sighed. "Again."

"Maybe it was Rasputin himself," suggested the Madonna. "After all, it's his job."

"Maybe," said Redwine dubiously. "But whoever it was, I've got to find out who's spying on us for Victor so you'll know who to watch out for after I've left." He walked over to the computer. "And the sooner I do it, the better." He activated the screen. "Security."

The image of a young man clad in a green uniform suddenly materialized.

"Let me speak to Rasputin, please," said Redwine.

"I'm afraid he's not here just now, Mr. Redwine," came the reply.

"This is urgent. Where can I find him?"

The young man checked the duty roster on a nearby screen. "He's in one of the fantasy rooms."

"Alone?"

"Yes, sir. In the Fishbowl."

"The Fishbowl?" repeated Redwine, puzzled.

"I'll explain it," said the Madonna, and Redwine broke the connection.

"What the hell is the Fishbowl?" he asked.

"That's Rasputin's term for it, and now he's got everyone in Security using it," she explained. "It's the Ocean Bower."

"How do I find it?"

"It's on the same level as the Tropical Paradise," she said. "Two doors further down, on the opposite side of the corridor."

"Well, I might as well get on with it," he said, unjamming the security devices and walking to the door. "Wish me luck."

He took the elevator up to the fantasy rooms, walked down the long corridor to the Ocean Bower, and commanded the door to open.

The door remained shut, and suddenly he remembered that the fantasy rooms only responded to those who had been scheduled to use them, so he began pounding on the door. A moment later it slid silently into the wall, revealing Rasputin, an odd-looking machine slung over his shoulder, standing about six feet away. "Hello, Harry," he said. "What the hell are *you* doing up here?"

"Looking for you," said Redwine, entering the room just before the door slid shut again. He looked at his surroundings. "This is some place!"

"Pretty, isn't it?" agreed the Security chief.

The Ocean Bower was much the smallest of the fantasy rooms, no more than thirty feet square. Its sole piece of furniture was a huge, circular waterbed, carefully disguised as the bottom section of an enormous, open seashell that rested on a small spit of silvery sand. There was a transparent plastic dome surrounding the spit and the bed, and just beyond it was a holographic representation of an ocean, filled with mermaids, incredibly colorful schools of tropical fish, a Neptune figure astride a gigantic sea horse, nude men and women swimming amidst schools of dolphins, even a replica of Jules Verne's *Nautilus*.

"Beautiful," said Redwine at last. "And tranquil." He paused. "What's that thing you're carrying on your shoulder?"

"Kind of a sensor," replied Rasputin, activating it and pointing it at a section of the sand.

"Did somebody lose something?"

The Security chief smiled. "I sure as hell hope so."

"I don't understand."

"My old friend the Lady Toshimatu is back on the *Comet*," explained Rasputin.

"The one who cheats at cards?" asked Redwine.

"Right. She's been cleaning up for a couple of days, and she's due to leave tonight."

"So?"

"Well, like I said, she's one of my pet projects, and it seems that whenever she's through gambling she always takes a young man down here before going home. It's never the same man twice, but it's always the Fishbowl, so I got to thinking that maybe it wouldn't do any harm to check the place out. She just left it about half an hour ago, and I gave orders not to let anyone in until I had a chance to go over it myself."

"What do you expect to find?"

"Probably nothing—but this little gadget will tell me if there's anything here besides sand." He looked up from the machine's dials and meters. "You still haven't told me why *you're* here."

"I have to ask you a question."

"Go right ahead."

"Have you been in contact with Victor Bonhomme?"

"Not that it's any of your business, but no, I haven't," replied Rasputin.

"You're sure?"

"Harry, I don't even know him."

"Then I've got another question. It's the same one I asked you a month ago: who is Bonhomme's spy?"

"So we're back to *that* again," said Rasputin wearily.

"I'm getting a lot of pressure from Deluros," persisted Redwine. "I've *got* to have that name."

"Harry, you poor dumb bastard," replied Rasputin, not without a trace of sympathy in his voice. "You think just because you deal in espionage, *everyone* does? No one's spying on you."

"What are you talking about?" demanded Redwine.

"You've made that damned office absolutely bugproof, and you do the same every night when you go back to the Madonna's apartment. Who the hell could spy on you even if they wanted to?"

"Somebody told Bonhomme that I've moved in with the Madonna."

"That's not spying, Harry," laughed Rasputin. "That's common knowledge."

"But it means that he's got someone keeping track of me!"

"Well, maybe you're not bankrupting the *Comet* fast enough to suit him," said Rasputin pleasantly. He paused. "You know, Harry, if you didn't want people to know where you were spending your nights, you could have been a little more discreet about it."

"That's not the point!" snapped Redwine.

"Oh? And just what point are you trying to make?"

"That there *is* a spy on the ship!"

"I agree," said the Security chief. "But his name's Harry Redwine, and if he wanted to convince me that he was a poor innocent victim the first thing he'd do is stop jamming my security system every time he walks into a room."

"Look," said Redwine, feeling extremely frustrated. "I'm going to be leaving the ship in a couple of weeks. Will you give the name to the Madonna after I'm gone?"

"Harry, I don't know how you've convinced her that you're one of the good guys, and that you're going to tackle the big bad Syndicate all in the name of love, but you haven't convinced *me*—and until you do, I'm not going to give you what you want."

"Damn it, Rasputin!" yelled Redwine. "I'm trying to *help* her!"

"Everything I know about you makes me doubt that like all hell," replied Rasputin calmly.

"*She* knows I'm on her side," said Redwine defensively.

"Yeah. Well, with friends like you and Suma, she sure as hell doesn't need any enemies."

"What is *that* supposed to mean?"

"DeWitt told me this morning that if Suma's patrons kept losing in the casino, he was going to kill the Duke. You don't seriously believe it was *his* idea, do you?"

"I thought the Madonna put a stop to it," said Redwine, surprised.

"She did—but that little bitch has got herself a full-time enforcer now."

"What for?"

"Well, let me take a wild guess and say that it's not to

protect her from the patrons," said Rasputin caustically. He stared at Redwine. "The Madonna's got enough trouble, Harry. Why don't you do her a favor and leave her alone?"

Redwine sighed heavily. "You wouldn't believe me."

"If you're going to start spouting lyrical poetry about affairs of the heart, you're right," agreed Rasputin. "Look—why not be reasonable about this? If what you say is true, we're on the same goddamned side. Just for once, stop playing cloak and dagger games and give me enough facts so that I'll know you're telling the truth. Then I'll be happy to give you all the help you want."

Redwine stared at him thoughtfully for a moment. "You want the facts?" he said at last. "All right. I'll trade them to you for the name I need."

"All right," said the Security chief. "What are they?"

"The name first."

Rasputin chuckled humorlessly. "No chance, Harry. First the facts."

"I think this is what they used to call a Mexican standoff," said Redwine with a wry smile.

"Looks like," agreed Rasputin.

"You won't help me?"

"Harry, everyone has to live by some kind of code. Mine is simple and old-fashioned: you do your job, you honor the truth, and you don't betray a trust. You're asking me to disregard all three simply on your say-so—and to put it frankly, you're about as untrustworthy a man as I've ever met. The fact that you're a likeable guy doesn't matter, and the fact that you might even be telling the truth doesn't matter. Until you can prove to me that I won't be betraying my employer or failing in my job as Chief of Security by helping you, I just can't do it."

"You're making a very big mistake," said Redwine seriously.

"It's possible," conceded Rasputin. "I've been wrong before."

"You are this time, too," said Redwine. "Just remember what I told you would happen if any harm comes to the Madonna because you wouldn't give me the name."

"Answer me one question, Harry," said Rasputin. "Would the Madonna be facing any trouble if she hadn't hooked up with you?"

Redwine stared at him, started to say something, changed his mind, and walked out of the Ocean Bower. He took the elevator back down to the public room level and began wending his way back to the Madonna's apartment.

"Hey, Redwine!" a masculine voice called out as he was passing by one of the lounges.

He turned and saw Gamble DeWitt sitting alone at a small table.

"Yes?"

"You're almost a month late with that drink you promised to buy me."

Redwine shrugged, walked over, and sat down opposite DeWitt.

"What'll you have?"

"Anything that's wet," replied DeWitt with a grin.

Redwine signalled for a waitress, ordered two whiskeys, and turned back to DeWitt. "I don't think I've seen you since the fight," he said. "Believe me, if there's one person I don't break promises to, it's the heavyweight champion of the Republic."

"Former," DeWitt corrected him.

"You'll always be the champion to me," continued Redwine. "I was there the night you took the title away from Nkimo."

DeWitt's face brightened perceptibly. "You were?"

"I always wondered how either of you walked out of that ring on your own power."

"It *was* a hell of a fight, wasn't it?" said DeWitt wistfully. "God, I miss those days!"

"How many title defenses did you make?"

"Fourteen," DeWitt answered proudly. "I retired

undefeated. Well, undefeated as a champion, anyway. I lost a couple of fights real early on, before I changed managers." He paused. "Management makes the difference."

"Yeah, I suppose it does to a fighter."

"To *everyone*," said DeWitt firmly.

The drinks arrived, and Redwine signed for them.

"Well," said Redwine, holding his glass up, "here's to you. I never thought I'd be lucky enough to see you fight again."

"I'll drink to that," agreed DeWitt, downing his whiskey in a single gulp and signalling for another.

"By the way," said Redwine, "I hear on the grapevine that you and the Duke still aren't what one might call the best of friends."

"I've got nothing against him personally," replied DeWitt. "I mean, hell, we fought and I won and as far as I'm concerned that ended it." His face clouded over. "But he's cheating my Suma's patrons, and I can't let him get away with that."

"*Your* Suma?"

DeWitt nodded. "She's the only one on this whole goddamned ship who gives a damn about me, so the least I can do is make sure that nobody messes around with her."

"I get the feeling that you're not exactly thrilled with your new occupation," remarked Redwine.

"It's sure as hell not what I expected it to be," muttered DeWitt. "I figured I'd do a little serious fucking, a little serious drinking, and try to keep in shape in the gym, you know what I mean?"

"Sounds reasonable," said Redwine. "So what's the problem?"

"The problem is that damned Madonna!" said DeWitt unhappily. "She didn't play square with me."

"In what way?"

"I figured that this would be kind of an extended vacation, you know? Like I'd be getting the cream of the crop. I mean, hell, I'm Gamble DeWitt! So as soon as I start, she's wanting me to do it five, six times a day, and half of my patrons are goddamned grandmothers—and then, suddenly, it's like I don't exist. Nobody asks for me, and I'm stuck over in the Home while people like those mousy little Gemini bastards barely have time to eat and sleep they're so busy!"

"Little?" repeated Redwine.

"I could break them in half like dried twigs!"

"I suppose you could, at that," agreed Redwine hastily.

"Anyway, thank God for Suma!" he continued. "I was just about ready to hop the first ship out of here when she took me over." Suddenly his expression softened. "But she's not like the others."

"She certainly isn't."

"She *cares* about me. She can name all the opponents I fought, and she's been to my home world, and she knows how the Madonna lied to me. Hell, half the time she comes to my room we just sit around and talk."

"How often *does* she come?" asked Redwine.

"Every day. Sometimes twice a day."

Redwine frowned. "I had the impression that she was booked pretty heavily."

"She finds a way to make the time," replied DeWitt. "Like I said, she cares."

"It certainly sounds like it."

He nodded. "She wants me to keep working out, too. The others—the Madonna and Lori and the rest—they all thought it was a waste of time, but not Suma. She knows how important it is to me."

"It sounds like she's got plans for you," offered Redwine.

"I hope so," agreed DeWitt. "I'm not a goddamned studhorse. I just wasn't cut out for this damned line of work. Hell, just between you and me, Suma is about all I can handle."

"What other lines of work *are* there on the *Comet*?" asked Redwine.

DeWitt shrugged. "Security, maybe. Though what I'd really like to do is run the casino. Suma's been teaching me a couple of games they play out on the frontier worlds that would do real well here." He paused. "She's got lots of great ideas for the *Comet*," he added admiringly.

"It sounds like she's put a lot of thought into it."

"She has," agreed DeWitt.

"You know," said Redwine, "I can envisage the day that the *Comet* caters only to male customers."

"Yeah?" said DeWitt, surprised.

"Yeah. And I think when that day comes, there's a ready-made job for you. After all, who's going to get rough with one of the girls when he knows he's got to face Gamble DeWitt?"

"You know," said DeWitt, "that's exactly what *she* says!"

Redwine smiled. "Great minds think alike."

"You're okay, Redwine," said DeWitt. "I know you're shacking up with the iceberg, and I'm not going to apologize for anything I said about her, but you're all right. I'm sure you've got your reasons."

"I suppose I have," said Redwine noncommittally.

"Suma doesn't like you much, but I'll have a little talk with her."

"Thanks."

"Don't mention it. You're pretty high up with the Syndicate. Maybe someday she might want to have a friend there."

"You never can tell," agreed Redwine, getting to his feet. "I hate to run, but I've still got a lot of work to do."

"See you around," said DeWitt, as the waitress arrived with his next drink.

Redwine walked back to the apartment with a very bad feeling in the pit of his stomach. There were no visible signs of motion, but he had a feeling that things were moving very fast indeed. Bonhomme was unquestionably going to increase the pressure on him, Rasputin would be at best a bystander and at worst a hindrance—and now, after his little talk with DeWitt, he had a feeling that the biggest problem the Madonna faced was stopping Suma from stealing the *Velvet Comet* out from under her before she even had a chance to defend it from Redwine's unknown employer.

13

"Harry, are you *ever* coming to bed?"

Redwine looked up from the tabletop computer screen and saw the Leather Madonna, totally nude, standing in the doorway leading from the office to her apartment.

"Soon," he grunted, returning his attention to the screen.

"That's what you said an hour ago."

"It's taking a little longer than I thought."

"Harry, it's five o'clock in the morning," she persisted.

He looked at her and smiled. "I thought we didn't have days and nights up here." He paused. "By the way, have I told you how much I admire your outfit?"

"Then come into the bedroom and admire it close up," she said.

"In a few minutes."

She disappeared into the apartment, then emerged a moment later wrapped in a white satin robe trimmed with brilliant white plumes from one of the wild polar birds of Selica II.

"I thought you were going to bed," remarked Redwine.

"I thought *you* were," she replied, walking over and standing in front of him. "Harry, if I find out that you've been playing chess with the computer . . ."

He chuckled. "Store and hold in my priority file," he ordered the computer. Then he reached out, gently grabbed her arm, and pulled her down on his lap.

176

"Sorry," he said, kissing her lightly on her lips. "I got carried away."

"What was so important that it couldn't wait until morning?" she asked, putting her arms around his neck and kissing him back.

"Nothing," he answered, holding her tightly.

"Really," she continued. "I want to know."

He sighed. "No, you don't."

"Why not?"

"We'll just fight."

She straightened up and pulled back from him. "Does this have something to do with Suma?" she demanded.

"Yes."

"I thought we settled that at dinner, Harry."

"You were wrong."

"Harry, she's no more of a threat than anyone else on board the *Comet*," said the Madonna irritably. "They *all* want my job."

"Yeah, but they're not all convinced they're going to *have* your job in the immediate future. *She* is."

"We've been all through this half a dozen times, Harry," she said, getting up from his lap and walking to the bar, where she began mixing herself a Blue Polaris. "There's nothing wrong with being ambitious. *I* was."

"I know," he said. "But you didn't talk with DeWitt; *I* did."

"Five minutes after Gamble gets out of line he'll be off the ship."

"A lot can happen in five minutes," replied Redwine ominously.

"Don't be melodramatic, Harry. You spend five minutes with a girl who has delusions of grandeur and ten minutes with a dissatisfied athlete and suddenly you see conspiracies everywhere."

"Not everywhere," he said patiently. "And what I've been doing for the past couple of hours is making sure that it's a coup and *not* a conspiracy."

"It's a fantasy," scoffed the Madonna.

"I hope so," he said. "But in my line of work, you learn to listen to your instincts."

"Accountants listen to their instincts?" she said skeptically.

"No," he answered seriously. "But saboteurs do. And my instincts say that you're taking her too lightly."

"We've gone over this all before," she said, pouring her drink and walking over to sit down on the sofa next to him. "She's just another hungry prostitute who thinks she could do a better job of running the show than I can."

"She's too sure of herself," said Redwine.

"She's very young," replied the Madonna. "So far she's gotten everything she's ever wanted. Why *shouldn't* she be sure of herself?" She paused. "Harry, I control every facet of the Resort, including Security. What the hell can she do?"

"That's what I've been trying to find out."

"And?"

"Her dossier's not complete yet."

"Cut the crap, Harry. Have you found a single thing that substantiates your suspicions?"

"I don't know," he admitted.

"What do you mean, you don't know?" she persisted. "Either you've discovered something or you haven't."

"I'm not through yet."

She sighed deeply. "All right, Harry. I can see we're not going to get much sleep until this is over with." She took another sip of her drink and stared at him. "What *have* you got?"

"Not much."

"You've been talking to the computer for almost three hours," she pointed out. "Shouldn't *that* imply something?"

"Nine-tenths of the trick is knowing which questions to ask it," he responded. "I began by seeing how much time she's spent with DeWitt in the past month."

"And?"

He turned to the computer, activated it, and called up his priority file.

"Eighty-five hours, spread out over twenty-three days."

"That much?" she asked, mildly surprised.

He nodded.

"Still," she continued, "it doesn't mean anything, except that I can schedule her more heavily."

"The computer says that it was all done on her free time," noted Redwine.

"Then the computer's wrong," said the Madonna. "When she goes to bed with Gamble, she's working as a tutor—and when she's working, *I* decide where she works."

"I agree," said Redwine. "So I asked the computer how many times she's been to bed with him."

"And?"

"Fourteen times, totalling about twenty hours."

"Then what does she do the rest of the time?" asked the Madonna. "I mean, no one can spend sixty hours *talking* to him."

"Sure they can," said Redwine. "If they talk about a subject he knows."

"The only thing he knows is fighting."

"Computer," ordered Redwine, "bring up a list of all the tapes and disks Suma has called up from your library banks in the past month."

The screen displayed two biographies of DeWitt, both written while he was still champion, plus some fifty-seven news items, all concerning his career.

"All this means is that she's got some silly notion of using him as a bodyguard," said the Madonna firmly.

"Or an enforcer."

"Or an enforcer," she agreed. "I told you at dinnertime that I'd put a stop to it." She paused. "Is that the sum total of what you've got?" she asked sardonically.

"No," said Redwine. "The next thing I did was check and see if she'd been sleeping with anyone from the casino."

"The casino? Why?"

"Because what you said before wasn't exactly true. You control all facets of the Resort *except* the casino. That's why you were so suspicious of me when I first came aboard: you thought the Duke had somehow convinced the Syndicate to send me here so he could prove that the casino was more lucrative than the brothel and that he should be in charge."

"I never said that."

"You never had to," he replied with a smile. "I'm good at my job, remember? And part of that job is listening to what people say and figuring out what they mean."

"All right," she said with a shrug. "I was wrong."

"Half-wrong, anyway," said Redwine. "The Duke has been hinting that he should be in charge for years—but nobody in Entertainment and Leisure pays any attention to him. After all, they've got bigger gambling operations on half a dozen worlds; the brothel is what brings people to the *Comet*, except for an occasional oddball like the Lady Toshimatu." He paused. "Still, it made sense to check and see if there was any connection between Suma and the Duke—a pooling of dissatisfactions, so to speak."

"And was there?"

He shook his head. "No. She hasn't spent two minutes alone with anyone from the casino—but while I was checking it out, I made an interesting discovery."

"Oh?"

"She's been sleeping pretty regularly—once a week or so—with a member of the Security team."

"Who?"

"A woman named Lena Boatswain."

"Lena's a lesbian?" asked the Madonna, surprised.

"You're missing the point," said Redwine. "The fact that Lena is a lesbian isn't important. The fact that she's in Security *is*." He paused. "Suma is a very shrewd little girl, and I have a feeling that she doesn't give *anything* away for free. But just to make sure, I called up her contract, and I found out that it's got a bonus clause in it."

"That's standard in all our contracts," noted the Madonna.

"I know," said Redwine. "But since I haven't noticed a lack of patrons where Suma is concerned, I had to ask myself why she would go to bed for free with a member of Security when she could get paid for doing the same thing in the Resort?"

"And what's your answer?"

He shrugged. "I don't know."

"You're being paranoid, Harry," said the Madonna.

"Maybe."

"What else do you have?"

"That's it so far," he admitted. "I've been spending the last hour trying to figure out why she needs a friend in Security."

"Maybe she enjoys going to bed with her," suggested the Madonna dryly.

"I thought she enjoyed going to bed with *everyone*. Why should she sleep with Lena on a regular basis?"

"Maybe she's formed an emotional attachment to Lena."

He shook his head. "Up until the time she hooked up with DeWitt three weeks ago, she had an awful lot of free time on her hands. If they were emotionally attached, why were they only together for an hour or two per week?"

"You tell me."

"Because that was the minimum amount of time and effort required to keep Lena on the hook."

"For what?"

"I don't know."

"Harry, this is ridiculous!" snapped the Madonna.

"I don't think so," he replied. "This girl is a threat to you, even if you won't admit it, and I'm not going to stop until I've figured out exactly what she's doing."

"If I were you, I'd be more worried about Victor Bonhomme."

"I can handle Victor," said Redwine.

"Well, *I* can handle Suma."

He shook his head. "I can handle Victor because I know how his mind works, and I know everything he can and can't do. Until you know what Suma's got planned, she's going to remain a problem."

"And you're actually going to stay glued to this computer until you solve this mythical conspiracy?" she demanded.

"Yes."

She sighed deeply. "Well, let's get on with it."

" '*Let's*'?" he repeated.

"I probably shouldn't admit this to you, but I don't enjoy sleeping alone since I've met you. And I'm certainly not going to seduce your body if I know your mind is still working away on this paranoid fantasy." She paused. "So the sooner we get this over with, the sooner we can go back to behaving like normal adult human beings."

"Thank you," he said, placing his hand on her leg and squeezing it gently. "I get lonely out here, too."

"That's hardly *my* fault," she said, moving her leg away. "Now keep your mind on business, and let's get to work."

He nodded, activated the computer, and fed in his priority code.

"But if you're not through by eight o'clock, you'll have to finish up in the auxiliary office," added the Madonna. "That's when I'm on call again, and I can't let you keep the room sealed off."

"Fair enough," he said. Then he turned to the screen. "Computer, please bring up a list of Lena Boatswain's duties."

"Pretty standard rotation," commented the Madonna as the list appeared. "One week on observation, one week in the airlock, one week in the Resort."

"Computer, what is Lena Boatswain's security clearance?"

A number flashed across the screen.

"Nothing special," muttered Redwine.

He stared at the screen for a few minutes, absolutely motionless.

"Aren't you going to ask it anything else?" asked the Madonna at last.

"I'm thinking," he said.

"Well?"

"Nothing's coming."

"Have you called up her personal dossier and job history?"

"Of course," replied Redwine. "Absolutely ordinary."

"What did you expect?"

He shrugged. "I don't know."

"Then why persist with her?"

"Because there's *got* to be a reason."

"There is," said the Madonna. "Suma likes her."

"Suma doesn't like anyone but Suma," he said firmly. "There's something else here, if I can just get a handle on it."

"How long has this been going on?" asked the Madonna.

"An hour or so," he said grimly.

"No. I mean between Suma and Lena."

"Close to a year," he said, calling up the data and staring at it. "Well, forty-five weeks, anyway."

"Then it can't be connected to Gamble," she pointed out. "He hasn't been with us that long."

Redwine called up DeWitt's record. "Thirty weeks," he read. "You're right."

"Well, that was simple," she laughed. "Now that I've shown you there's no connection, are you willing to call it a night?"

"No. She still had to have some reason for seeing Lena."

"Since there can't be any connection between Lena and Gamble, are you at least willing to admit you were wrong about *him*?" persisted the Madonna.

"Maybe," said Redwine. "But first let me check back

and see if she was thinking about another enforcer before Gamble arrived."

He called up Suma's file again.

"Nothing," he said, frustrated. "Except for Lena and DeWitt she hasn't had a single liaison in the Home in more than a year." He muttered a curse. "There's *got* to be a connection! I'm missing a bet somewhere, and I can't spot it!"

He got up, walked over to the bar, and poured himself a whiskey. He downed it, poured another, returned to the couch, and stared at the screen as if the computer itself was an antagonist.

"Harry, try to relax," said the Madonna soothingly. "You look like you're about to have a stroke."

"What the hell can she need her for?" he repeated. "She's been keeping this damned thing going for almost a year; she's got to have a reason!" Suddenly he straightened up. "Wait a minute!" he said excitedly.

"What is it?"

"There's another way to approach this thing! It's got to be the timing!"

"I don't follow you."

"Forty-six weeks ago she didn't need a friend in Security, and one week later she did. Why? What happened during that week?"

"I give up—what?"

"Let's find out," he said, instructing the computer to bring up a list of Suma's daily activities during the week in question.

"What's going on here?" he demanded a minute later. "She wasn't on the ship."

"Even prostitutes get vacations, Harry," said the Madonna.

"Where did she go for it?"

"Deluros VIII, I think," replied the Madonna. "Ask the computer."

The computer confirmed her answer.

"Computer, give me a list of all locations Suma visited and all people she met during her trip to Deluros."

An INFORMATION UNAVAILABLE message appeared.

"I could have told you that," commented the Madonna. "After all, why should our computer know what she did on her vacation?"

Redwine ignored her answer. "Tie in to the Vainmill computer on Deluros VIII, feed in my priority code, and obtain the data."

"Why would *Vainmill* know?" asked the Madonna.

"She's an employee," he replied. "She had to register at customs, so maybe they kept tabs on her."

"And if not?"

He shrugged. "Then we'll have the Vainmill computer start checking around and talking to other computers until one of them finally tells us what we want to know."

He had another drink while waiting for the computer to send out a subspace tightbeam. It beeped twice to confirm that it had tapped into the Vainmill computer, then flashed a red CLASSIFIED light.

"Classified, not unavailable?" asked Redwine.

The machine answered in the affirmative.

"What security clearance is required to read the information?"

The computer flashed a figure on the screen.

"Shit!" muttered Redwine, a worried expression on his face. "All right, break the connection with Deluros."

"What does all this mean, Harry?" asked the Madonna.

"It means trouble," he said, downing his drink. "Computer, bring up a list of all Vainmill employees who visited the *Velvet Comet* and slept with Suma during the period six months prior to her most recent vacation."

A list of more than fifty names appeared.

"Which of them has the following security clearance?" He rattled off the figure the Vainmill computer had supplied.

Three names remained.

"What are the positions within Vainmill of these three people?"

The computer flashed the information on the screen.

"Well," said Redwine to the Madonna. "Take a good look: one of them is my employer."

"You're sure?" she said dubiously.

He nodded. "Eric Nogara, Director of Natural Resources and Manufacturing; Belinda Watson, Director of Finance; and Padani Makumbwa, Director of Acquisitions. They've all slept with Suma, they've all got a shot at the Chairmanship, and they've all got a high enough security clearance to keep the details of her trip to Deluros a secret from me."

The Madonna looked skeptical. "Just how rare *is* this security clearance, Harry? How many people can keep you from reading that file?"

"With my skeleton card? The Chairwoman, the five division heads, and that's it."

"How about Victor?" she asked.

"Not a chance. His card can't hide anything that my card can't find."

"And what's Suma's connection to all this? Are you trying to tell me she's the plant you've been looking for?"

"Right. Except *plant* is a pretty inadequate word. I thought Victor had a spy on the ship; she's playing so high above him she probably doesn't know he exists. She most likely reports straight to my boss, and he passes stuff on to Victor." He paused. "I don't know what kind of deal she cut, or why she needs a friend in Security, but she's so goddamned certain that she's going to become the madam that your job has got to be the payoff for whatever she's doing."

"You know, Harry," said the Madonna after a moment's silence, "you make it all sound very neat and pat and logical, but there are other equally valid explanations."

"What are you talking about?" he demanded.

"You began with the preconceived notion that Suma is a serious threat to me, and that there's a spy aboard the ship, so it colors your analysis of what you learned. It's as if you presuppose that because all spies breathe in and out and Suma breathes in and out, she must therefore be a spy."

"What other explanation have *you* got?" he insisted.

"I don't need one," she replied. "All I have to do is point out the fallacies in yours."

"Go ahead."

"Well, if Suma is really in league with the head of a Vainmill division, why does she need someone like Gamble?"

"Protection."

"Oh? Who's going to attack her?"

"How the hell do *I* know?" said Redwine. "Hell, if you wait until you're attacked, it's a little bit late to be thinking about a bodyguard—and like I said before, probably he's an enforcer rather than a protector."

"That's no better, Harry," said the Madonna. "If one of those three division heads issues an order, she won't need Gamble to enforce it."

He stared at her without answering.

"Then there's Lena," continued the Madonna. "Why does Suma need a friend in Security? Everything I do is recorded and filed."

"Not anymore, it isn't."

"She couldn't have known that forty-five weeks ago, Harry," the Madonna pointed out.

"Don't forget who she's working for," said Redwine stubbornly. "Maybe she *knew* I was coming forty-five weeks ago. *I* did, so why shouldn't she have, too?"

"Then she'd probably have known what you were going to do, and that you'd have a skeleton card that would make a contact in Security absolutely useless," said the Madonna. "And even if she didn't know about the card in advance, she surely knew about it a month ago—so why would she still be keeping Lena on a string?"

"Because if she knows what I'm here for, she knows I won't be around much longer, and *that* means she knows she's going to be able to keep tabs on you again after I take my skeleton card with me."

"So what?"

"Look," he said. "We both know that she plans to be the next madam, and we both know that she's aware of what I'm doing. Now what good is it to be the madam of a whorehouse that's been shut down because it's losing money?"

The Madonna looked puzzled. "I hadn't thought of that."

"I think at the right moment they're going to need a handy fall guy, and you're going to be accused of embezzlement," he continued. "It'll happen after my employer is the Chairman, so he'll have what *he* wants. And once he blames you for what I did to the books, he'll reactivate the ship—if they've even closed it down by then—and Suma will have what *she* wants. It'll be your word against theirs, and at the last moment I wouldn't be surprised to see them pull in a surprise witness named Lena Boatswain who will swear that she caught you messing with the books and you threatened to fire her if she ever told anyone."

"Damn!" she muttered. "I hate to admit it, but it makes sense the way you say it." She sighed. "Still, I can't just fire our biggest moneymaker without some more tangible proof."

"You're making a big mistake," he persisted. "We've got all our rotten eggs in one oversexed little basket. The only logical thing to do is get rid of her before she can do us any harm."

"What if you're wrong?" she asked dubiously.

"I'm not."

"But *if* you are?" she repeated.

"Then the *Comet* will have to get by with one less prostitute," he said.

"That's not a good enough answer," replied the Madonna. "Besides, even if I agree to fire her, I can't do it without cause. What grounds do I give—espionage? You can't prove that she's done anything wrong, and even if you could, do you really want to let your employer know that you've changed sides?"

"Where there's a will, there's a way," said Redwine, lowering his head in thought. Suddenly he looked up. "Does her contract permit her to accept direct payment for sexual services?"

"No."

He turned to the screen. "Computer, scan Suma's credit account and tell me if she paid for her trip to Deluros."

The answer was negative.

"Who did?"

The CLASSIFIED sign lit up.

"I didn't really think I could find out," he said with a shrug. "Well, there's your grounds for dismissal. My employer, who just happens to be one of her patrons, paid for her trip to Deluros."

"That's an awfully tenuous connection, Harry," said the Madonna. "I don't think we could win if she appealed it."

"She won't appeal it," he said confidently. "She'd have to claim that she went to Deluros on business, and my employer is never going to corroborate that, not after the pains he's gone to to keep this thing a secret." He paused. "Well, what do you say?"

The Madonna remained silent for a long moment. "I'll talk to Suma in the morning," she said at last.

"About Deluros?"

She nodded. "And other things." She stared long and hard at Redwine. "I'm not promising anything, but if I get the feeling talking to her that you're right, I'll probably fire her."

"That's all I ask."

"I just hope it doesn't become more than you bargained for," she said seriously.

14

The usual number of minor problems arose in the morning—two scheduling conflicts, an unanticipated patron who had to be detained in the airlock until his credit had been established, a shortage of wine in one of the restaurants, a holographic breakdown in one of the fantasy rooms—and it wasn't until slightly after noon that the Leather Madonna was able to send for Suma.

"She should be here in about twenty minutes, Harry," she announced to Redwine, who was seated on the metal lounge chair, sipping a cup of coffee. "She's just finishing up with a patron." She paused. "I don't want you here when she arrives."

"Why not?" he asked, surprised.

"Because if I decide to fire her and she appeals it, I don't want there to be any charges of collusion between us."

"She's not stupid," he replied. "She's *got* to know I had something to do with it."

"I'm sure she will. But I don't want her to be able to say that you were sitting in on this meeting, hurling accusations at her while she was trying to defend herself."

"You're sure?" he asked.

She nodded. "Yes, I am. And before you leave, unjam the security system. I want this meeting recorded, just in case we ever have to go to court over it."

"All right," he said, manipulating the skeleton card

190

and getting to his feet. "I might as well watch the fireworks from the auxiliary office."

"Will you be able to?"

He made a minor adjustment to her computer. "Just leave this channel open. I won't be able to talk to you, but I'll see and hear everything that goes on." He kissed her as he walked to the door. "Good luck."

"Let's hope I don't need it," replied the Madonna.

It took him about five minutes to get to the tramway terminal, and another five to reach the auxiliary office. Once there he activated the computer, pulled a cigar out of his pocket, lit it, and stared at the holographic image in front of him.

The Madonna was sitting on one of the couches, reading. After a few minutes had passed she walked over to the bar and began mixing herself a drink. She had just about finished making it when Suma arrived, dressed in one of the most exotic costumes Redwine had yet seen aboard the *Comet*.

She wore an elaborate rhinestone headdress which flared out some thirty inches in all directions, and was matched in brilliance by a rhinestone collar and long strands of pearls and rhinestones that draped her almost-nude body in swirling patterns. A diaphanous white veil, attached to her collar and wrists, flowed gracefully behind her. Her shoes, also covered with rhinestones, were so high that Redwine couldn't figure out how she kept from falling on her face.

"What a pleasure it is to get this damned headdress off!" said Suma, removing it and placing it down carefully on the couch.

"How are things in the Ice Castle?" asked the Madonna, pouring her drink into a long-stemmed glass.

"Active," replied Suma. "Mr. Lumbwa decided to be an errant Knight of the Round Table, and insisted that he had to have a genuine Fairy Princess." She made a face. "I just wish he knew how hard it is to fuck in this outfit."

"Can I fix you something to drink?" offered the Madonna.

"No," said Suma. "What was it you wanted me for?"

"I thought we might have a little talk," said the Madonna, walking over and sitting down on the opposite couch.

"About the Duke, I hope," said Suma. "When are you going to fire that bastard?"

"I thought your problem with him was all cleared up," remarked the Madonna.

"Until the next time," said Suma.

"*Will* there be a next time?"

"If there is, I know how to handle it."

"With Gamble?" asked the Madonna.

"Of course, with Gamble!" she shot back. "No goddamned pit boss is going to cheat *my* patrons!"

"Perhaps I haven't made my position on the matter clear," said the Madonna. "If that's the case, let me do so right now." She stared coldly at Suma. "If Gamble DeWitt strikes any patron or any member of the *Comet*'s crew, he's gone. No ifs, ands, or buts."

"He won't attack anyone without cause," said Suma defiantly. "*Your* job is to see that nobody gives him any cause."

"In fact, Gamble is getting to be a bit of an embarrassment to the *Comet*," continued the Madonna, ignoring her outburst. "I wonder if you have any suggestions about what to do with him."

"Is that what this is all about?"

"No, not really," said the Madonna. "But I'd appreciate any input you might care to offer."

"Just leave him alone and he'll be fine," said Suma. "I'm working with him every day."

"Are you?"

"What is *that* supposed to mean?"

"I had the impression that you were spending an inordinate amount of time with him *without* working."

"Well, whoever told you that lied."

"It's easy enough to check," said the Madonna. "Shall we ask the computer?"

"How I spend my time is my business!" said Suma defensively.

"I hate to correct you, but how you spend your time is *my* business," replied the Madonna. "And I think you're spending too much of it with Gamble."

"Not as much as you're spending with Harry Redwine!" snapped Suma.

"Let me further suggest that how I spend *my* time is not *your* business." She shrugged. "However, that's neither here nor there. I didn't ask you here to talk about Gamble."

"And what *did* you ask me here for?" demanded Suma suspiciously.

"You're sure I can't fix you a drink?" asked the Madonna pleasantly.

"Let's just get this over with."

"Well, as a matter of fact, I need your advice."

"My advice is to get rid of Harry," said Suma. "The sooner the better."

"I need your advice about a *different* subject," said the Madonna with a smile. "I have some vacation time accumulated, and I've been thinking of using it to take a trip to Deluros VIII. You've been there much more recently than I have, so I thought you might be able to recommend a good hotel—the one you stayed at, perhaps?"

"I didn't stay at a hotel."

"Possibly some restaurants, then, and perhaps a museum or two?"

"I don't go to museums," said Suma. "And I ate in."

"How dull," commented the Madonna. "I hope you at least made some new and interesting friends."

"A few."

"Well, perhaps you can give me their names. I'm sure that any friend of yours is a friend of mine."

"I doubt that very much," replied Suma with a sarcastic laugh.

"I wonder why," remarked the Madonna dryly.

"Harry lives on Deluros. Why don't you ask *him* about it?"

"Oh, Harry doesn't know any interesting people," said the Madonna.

"You'd be surprised."

"Well, he certainly doesn't know any of the Directors of the various Vainmill divisions," continued the Madonna.

"All right!" snapped Suma suddenly. "What's going on here?"

"Nothing at all," said the Madonna. "We're just having a pleasant little talk about your friends on Deluros."

"What I did on Deluros is none of your business!"

"I think it is."

"Well, you're wrong," said Suma decisively.

"Who paid for your trip there?"

"I don't think I'm going to tell you," said Suma with a confident smile.

"I didn't think you were, either," said the Madonna. She paused. "Let's change the subject."

"That's fine by me."

"Tell me about Lena Boatswain."

"She works in Security."

"I thought you might tell me a little more than that."

"Ask your computer," said Suma with an amused laugh.

"What's so funny?"

"You don't know a damned thing," responded Suma. "This is all guesswork."

"I know *one* thing," said the Madonna seriously. "I'm not ready to step down yet—and when I am, I won't be replaced by some avaricious teenaged girl who doesn't give a damn about anything except herself."

"You think not?" said Suma. "Well, let me tell you, *nobody* cares more about this ship than I do!"

"I sincerely doubt that."

"You think *you* do?" said Suma contemptuously. "You don't even know what's going on! You're so busy worrying about the decor and the cuisine and the ambience that you don't even see what's happening right under your nose!"

"What *is* happening right under my nose?" asked the Madonna calmly.

"Well, for one thing, you're shacking up with the man who was sent here to kill the *Comet*!"

"If you've known that all along, why haven't you told me before now?"

"Because I'm not saving it for *you*," said Suma. "I'm saving it for *me*. You're an obsolete old woman who's outlived her usefulness. You let Harry sweet-talk you into neglecting your duties, and you're going to pay the price for it."

"What duties do you think I've neglected?" asked the Madonna.

"How about the preservation of the *Comet*?" responded Suma. "Isn't *that* supposed to be your primary duty?"

"Yes, it is," agreed the Madonna. "And you've just convinced me that you're a bigger threat to the *Comet* than Harry is."

"A bigger threat to *you*, maybe."

"It comes to the same thing," said the Madonna.

"The hell it does. The *Comet* will be here long after you're gone and forogotten."

"I sincerely hope so," said the Madonna. She stared directly into Suma's eyes. "But *you* won't be."

"What are you talking about?"

"You heard me," replied the Madonna calmly. "I'm firing you."

"On what grounds?"

"Insubordination."

"Don't make me laugh."

"I wasn't trying to," said the Madonna. "Also, when you accepted a direct gratuity from a patron, in the form of a trip to Deluros, you were in violation of your contract."

"You think that'll hold up?" said Suma contemptuously.

"For a while, at least. Besides, it doesn't have to hold up forever; just until I choose my successor."

"Then you're quitting?"

"I'm thinking of it."

"When?" demanded Suma.

"When I'm ready," replied the Madonna noncommittally.

"This isn't going to work, you know," said Suma. "I'll be back."

"Probably you will," agreed the Madonna. "And hopefully you won't be able to do any more damage then than you did now."

"This is a really stupid thing for you to do. I'm the biggest earner you've got."

"Then we'll all just have to tighten our belts and make do as best we can."

"You're making a very big mistake," said Suma ominously.

"I don't think so."

"You don't think at all! Don't you know why Harry came out here in the first place?"

"Harry isn't the subject of this conversation," said the Madonna. "*You* are. How soon can you be ready to leave?"

"Thirty days."

"I'd prefer it to be sooner."

"What you prefer really doesn't interest me," said Suma. "My contract gives me thirty days." She paused. "Do you want me to keep working during that time?"

"If you wish."

"Will I be paid for it?"

"Yes."

"Then I'll work." Suma got to her feet, picked up her headdress, and walked to the door. "You're going to regret this," she promised.

"Perhaps," said the Madonna.

"There's no perhaps about it," said Suma coldly. "You're going to be very, very sorry that you did this to me—and sooner than you think."

Then she stepped out into the corridor, and the door slid shut behind her.

The Madonna walked to the bar and began mixing another drink.

"Harry?" she said. "Are you still there?"

Redwine activated his end of the intercom, and allowed his image to be transferred to her screen.

"Yes, I'm still here," he said. "I had a ringside seat for the whole show." He paused. "I just hope you haven't made a mistake."

"I thought firing her was *your* idea," said the Madonna ironically.

"Not about that," replied Redwine hastily. "But I sure as hell wish you hadn't agreed to give her thirty days to clear out."

"I didn't have any choice. It's a standard clause in our employment contract."

"Why? It doesn't make any sense to let someone stick around that long if you've already fired them. Why not just give them some severance pay and be done with it?"

"Because this isn't a planet, Harry; it's a spaceship. You can't go home to your apartment, lick your wounds, and start looking for a new job the next morning. Most of the people I've fired have needed all that time and more, just to find a new job and a new world to live on, and to make the necessary transportation arrangements."

"Well, I think I'd better keep tabs on Suma, just to be on the safe side. I hate to think of the mischief she can do in thirty days." He dumped a long ash off his cigar. "Enough about Suma. There's something more important I want to talk to you about."

"Oh?"

"You said something about quitting," continued Redwine. "Was that for her benefit, or did you mean it?"

"I talked about retiring, not quitting," replied the Madonna. "I won't cut and run under fire."

"To hell with semantics. Did you mean it?"

She stared at his image thoughtfully for a moment. "Yes, I did. I've had a good run at this business, and I've built it up into something to be proud of—but I've been working on the *Comet* for more than a third of my life. Maybe it's time I did something else."

"Like what?"

"Don't look so frightened, Harry," she said with a smile. "Whatever it is, I'll be doing it with you."

"You'll really come away with me when this situation is over?" he persisted.

"Who knows? *You* might come away with *me*. Have I ever shown you the holographs of my farm on Pollux IV?"

He shook his head. "You've talked about it, but I've never seen it."

"Remind me to show them to you tonight. It's very pretty. There's a stream running by the house, and a pond in back with the strangest-looking waterfowl you ever saw."

"There's a lot of things to see and do on Deluros," he said. "Maybe we could use the farm as kind of a retreat, when things get too hectic."

She laughed. "I'm not really anxious to move from one hectic environment to another." She paused and stared seriously at the screen. "We've never really spent much time discussing our future, have we?"

"No, we haven't."

"We've got the rest of our lives ahead of us. Maybe it's time we started making some plans."

"I've been making them since that first night we spent together," said Redwine.

"You, too?" she asked with a smile.

"Get those holographs out. I'll be with you in ten minutes."

Redwine deactivated the computer, left the auxiliary office, and took the tram to the Resort. Once there he went into the Mall just long enough to purchase a dozen roses imported from Earth itself; and then, idly wondering what the climate was like on Pollux IV, he hurried back to rejoin the Madonna.

15

Redwine spent the next three days alternately putting the final touches on the financial records and monitoring Suma's activities.

He had hoped that she might give away his employer's identity by placing a call to Deluros to complain about being fired, but he was totally unprepared for what she actually did. During the twenty-four hours following her meeting with the Madonna, Suma placed *twenty-six* calls to Deluros, each to a different executive of the Vainmill Syndicate, complaining about the Madonna's handling of the *Comet* without ever mentioning that she herself had been dismissed.

Redwine had the computer check out the list of names. All twenty-six of them—twenty-one men and five women—had been patrons of the *Comet* during the six months prior to Suma's trip to Deluros, and each had spent at least one evening in her company. His three potential employers—Eric Nogara, Belinda Watson, and Padani Makumbwa—were all on the list.

Which meant, he acknowledged grimly, that she was smarter than he had anticipated, or at least that she possessed better survival instincts. She still believed that he was loyal to the Syndicate and that he was doing his level best to subvert the books, and yet she had made certain that if he were spying on her, as indeed he was, he wouldn't be able to learn anything more than he already knew. Twenty-five of those messages would be ignored; one might not be—and he had no way of telling the one from the others.

He stared at the list again for a moment, then sighed and deactivated the computer. He lit a cigar, sat perfectly still while savoring the first few mouthfuls of the strongly-flavored tobacco that had been grown on the distant colony planet of Beta Hydri II, and then withdrew a small cube from his pocket. It contained a hologram of the farmhouse and the pond on Pollux IV, and a contemplative smile crossed his face as he stared at it once again, imagining himself and the Madonna sitting on the huge porch in the summer sun, or seated at her chess table, lost in concentration, as an icy winter wind whipped against the windows.

He had no idea how long he had sat, examining the cube for perhaps the hundredth time since she had given it to him, when he heard the door slide into the wall.

"Good afternoon, Harry," said a familiar voice, and he looked up to see Victor Bonhomme, as immaculately-tailored as ever, walk into the room.

"They told me I'd find you here," continued Bonhomme, "and since I assumed you were hard at work on the books and had the room sealed off, I decided to use my card so as not to disturb you." He smiled. "I was half-right, anyway. The room was sealed."

"Just taking a break," said Redwine, putting the cube back into his pocket. "Have a seat, Victor."

"Thank you," said Bonhomme, sitting down by the computer.

"What brings you here, as if I didn't know?" said Redwine.

"Oh, I just wanted to see how things are coming along," replied Bonhomme. "Also, I've never been out here before. I thought I might sample the services before we shut the place down." He withdrew a platinum container from a lapel pocket, pulled out a long, thin, blue-tinted cigarette, placed it in a diamond-studded holder, and lit up. "How soon do you think you'll be finished here, Harry?"

"Maybe a week," said Redwine. "Certainly less than two."

"Oh, I guarantee it'll be less than two weeks," said Bonhomme with a chuckle. "Now suppose you tell me why you weren't done twenty days ago?"

"I already explained it to you," replied Redwine.

"I know," nodded Bonhomme. "But this time I'd like the truth."

"I told you the truth."

"Let me ask it another way: how long would this job have taken you if you weren't spending all your time with the Leather Madonna?"

"Just the same. I put in seven hours a day, six days a week. Check Security's log if you don't believe me."

"Security just knows when you arrive and leave, Harry. They don't know what the hell you do once you seal off the room—and to be perfectly honest about it, neither do I."

"All right," said Redwine with a shrug. "I'm just pretending to rig the books so I can sink our boss and throw my career into a trash atomizer. Actually I watch pornographic entertainments all day long."

Bonhomme threw back his head and laughed. "You always had a good sense of humor, Harry, I'll give you that!" Suddenly his mirth vanished. "You've got four days to finish up."

"What will you do to me otherwise?" asked Redwine sardonically. "Fire me on the grounds that I'm not a fast enough saboteur?"

"No. We'll just replace you with someone else."

"You don't trust anyone else, remember?"

"Harry, I love repartee as much as the next man. I always have. But things have gotten serious in the past few days. I'm under a lot of pressure, and I've got to pass some of it along to you."

"Consider it done," said Redwine. He paused for a

moment. "Even if I finish up in four days, I want to stick around for a couple of weeks."

"Out of the question."

"You don't have to pay me," said Redwine. "I've got some vacation time coming, and this is where I want to spend it."

"Sorry, Harry, but we've got another job for you." He grinned. "I only wish it was in a monastery."

Redwine shook his head. "No way. I told you: this is my last job."

"You *always* tell me that, and you always go back to work."

"Not this time."

"I understand that you're temporarily infatuated," said Bonhomme, "but it'll pass. Hell, it always does for *me*."

"The answer is no."

"You'll be going to a nice little colony world out on the Rim. Hell, if it's your sex life that concerns you, we'll buy you another whore once you get there."

"Forget it," said Redwine, struggling to control his temper.

Bonhomme scrutinized him for a moment, then shrugged.

"We'll talk about it later," he said at last. "Maybe over a game of chess with your new set. I understand it's a beauty."

"What do you know about it?" demanded Redwine.

"Everything. Where you bought it, what you paid for it, when it was delivered to you." Bonhomme smiled. "You're a valuable member of the team, Harry, so naturally we take an interest in everything you do."

"Naturally," said Redwine wryly.

"Well," said Bonhomme, rising to his feet, "I'm absolutely famished! Which restaurant do you suggest?"

"They're all pretty good."

"I saw one in the brochure where the waiters are all dressed like Elizabethan Englishmen," remarked Bonhomme. "I think maybe I'll try that one."

"They're Revolutionary Americans," Redwine corrected him.

Bonhomme shrugged. "Six of one, half a dozen of the other. I'd ask you to join me, but you're obviously going to be much too busy working."

"That's right."

Bonhomme walked to the door, then turned to face Redwine. "Since I'm going to be here for a few days, I suppose I really should rely on your expertise."

"I thought that was what I was applying right here," commented Redwine.

"You are. But I thought you might recommend a few suitable companions for the duration of my stay."

"Ask for the Gemini Twins," said Redwine, managing to suppress a grin.

"The Gemini Twins? They sound intriguing."

Redwine nodded. "And you might ask for the Demolition Team, too."

"Thank you, Harry," said Bonhomme.

"My pleasure."

"What about Suma?"

"I don't know," said Redwine, aware that Bonhomme was watching him for a reaction. "What *about* Suma?"

"I was led to believe that she was something quite special."

"If that's your taste," replied Redwine with a show of indifference. "Who recommended her?"

"Just a friend."

"Do I know him?"

Bonhomme smiled. "I doubt it."

"Well, good luck. She's usally booked up months in advance."

"Oh, really? What a shame! I understand that she's an absolutely fascinating conversationalist."

"I wouldn't know about that," said Redwine with a shrug. "Do what you want—but I think you'll be happier with the Gemini Twins."

"I'll keep it in mind," said Bonhomme. "See you later, Harry." Then he stepped out into the corridor, in quest of his various pleasures, and the door slid shut behind him.

Redwine waited a moment to make sure Bonhomme wasn't coming back for any final words, then raised the Madonna on the intercom.

"What's the matter, Harry?" she asked, staring at his image. "You look upset."

"Victor's here."

"You mean he's aboard the *Comet*?"

"Right."

She lowered her head in thought for a moment, then looked up. "Well, that's really not much of a surprise, is it? We knew if Suma made enough calls, one of them would elicit a response. Victor is the response."

"He wants me off the *Comet* in four days," said Redwine.

"What did you tell him?"

"I said I wouldn't go."

"I think you may have to, Harry," said the Madonna. "Right now he's irritated with you, but nothing more. You fight to stay here and he might start figuring out what's really going on."

"Not Victor," said Redwine with conviction. "He'll never be able to conceive of my doing something he himself wouldn't do."

"Did he say anything about Suma?"

"Not really, but I imagine he'll be hunting her up sometime tonight."

"Well, I guess we'd better play it by ear," said the Madonna. "The next move is up to him." She paused. "Is there any way you can monitor him?"

Redwine nodded. "Yes, but it's not worth the risk. He's got a pretty powerful card, too—and since his security clearance is higher than mine, there's a chance it might be able to tell him that I'm spying on him. As long as he thinks I'm on his side, let's not disillusion him."

"If he checks your work, will he know what we plan to do?"

"Not a chance. That's hidden so deep in the computer's memory that he'd have to ask about two hundred unrelated questions to dredge it up, and then it's filed under *your* voice-print rather than mine."

"Then I can't see what harm he can do us," she said.

"Probably none—but I thought I ought to let you know he's arrived."

"Thank you, Harry," she replied. "I'll see you at dinnertime."

"Right," said Redwine, breaking the connection.

He re-lit his cigar, which had gone our sometime during his talk with Bonhomme, then stood up, walked over to the cabinet where he had stashed his liquor, and pulled out a bottle of whiskey. He was pouring himself a glass of it when he heard a pounding at the door. He checked his security screen, saw that it was Rasputin, and let him in.

"Hi, Harry," said the stocky Security chief.

"Good afternoon," responded Redwine. "Care for a drink?"

Rasputin shook his head. "Never when I'm on duty. Mind if I sit down?"

"Suit yourself," said Redwine, capping the bottle and putting it away. "You don't mind if I indulge?"

"It's your liver," said Rasputin with a shrug.

"Well," said Redwine, walking over to a couch and sitting down, "since you're not drinking, I assume this is a business call."

"I see that your boss has arrived," said Rasputin. "I was thinking you might want to talk about it."

"What did you want me to say?"

"Why he's come at this particular point in time, how close you are to finishing your espionage work, how long we've got before the *Comet* goes bankrupt, that sort of thing."

"It seems to me that I spent more than a month asking you for a single piece of information that you refused to relinquish," Redwine pointed out.

"True," admitted Rasputin. "But you figured it out

for yourself, so you really didn't need me. I watched the Madonna fire Suma a few days ago."

"That's beside the point."

"That's *precisely* the point," said Rasputin with an amused smile. "My job is to ferret out information, not dispense it. Besides, Suma really wasn't a spy or a plant in the normal sense of the word, was she?"

"She was the name I needed, and you wouldn't give it to me. Why should I help you?"

"Because I think you're in more trouble than you're willing to admit. I notice that Victor Bonhomme didn't show up until *after* Suma was fired. That tells me that someone on Deluros is very unhappy about this turn of events, and since they sent your immediate superior I have to assume that you're the one they're unhappy with."

"How thoughtful of you to care," said Redwine sardonically.

"Harry, I don't give a damn whether you sink or swim," said Rasputin seriously. "Everything you touch turns to shit, and as likeable as you are; we'd all be better off without you." He paused. "But I care about the Madonna, and you've gotten her involved in this somehow. And I care about the *Comet*."

"What does caring about the *Comet* have to do with anything?"

"Look," said Rasputin impatiently. "It's pretty damned obvious that someone is out to destroy it. Now, if you're at odds with your people on Deluros, it means that one of you might *not* be trying to destroy it. I mean, what the hell else could you be arguing about?"

"I thought we were arguing about Suma, remember?"

"Firing a nineteen-year-old whore shouldn't elicit this kind of response," said Rasputin firmly.

"You overestimate Victor's importance," replied Redwine.

"Harry, if Suma was the issue, Deluros would have slapped the *Madonna's* hand. Bonhomme is here to slap *yours*. The only thing you could possibly be in disagreement about is the fate of the *Comet*."

"This story would go over better in one of the fantasy rooms," said Redwine.

"Damn it! You've been swearing to me for more than a month that you're out to save the ship. If you meant it, and if you're in trouble, I'm the logical person to ask for help. My job is protecting the goddamned ship, for Christ's sake!" He paused for a moment while Redwine sipped his whiskey and stared thoughtfully at him. "Look," he continued at last. "You don't even have to give me all the details. Just tell me *enough* so I can believe you, and we'll fight this thing together."

"I appreciate the offer," said Redwine carefully. "I truly do. But everything's under control. Victor can't do a damned thing."

"He can pull you off the *Comet*."

"It won't matter. Everything's taken care of."

"How about Suma?"

"Suma was taken care of three days ago. All she is now is an unemployed, oversexed teenager."

"You make it all sound very simple."

"It is," said Redwine.

"If it's that simple to fuck around with the Vainmill Syndicate, how come nobody's ever gotten away with it before?" asked Rasputin.

"Maybe nobody else has known where all the bodies are buried," answered Redwine.

"And you do?"

"Some of them," nodded Redwine.

"And you think that makes you safe?" demanded Rasputin with a harsh laugh. "Jesus, Harry—I knew you were a liar and a saboteur, but I never thought you were *dumb*!"

"What do you mean?"

"I mean if you know half of what you think you know, your life expectancy once they find out you've double-crossed them is, not to be too pessimistic about it, maybe ten minutes."

"I'm taking steps to extend it just a little beyond that," replied Redwine.

"Then let me help you," insisted Rasputin. "Show me you're working to save the *Comet* and give me what you've got on these people, and I'll hide it on so many worlds that nobody'll ever find it all." Suddenly he stared intently at Redwine. "Or do you think I'm one of them?"

"No. I know you're not."

"Well, then?"

"Let me talk about it with the Madonna," replied Redwine slowly. "Maybe, it's time we let someone know exactly what's going on here."

"It's *past* time, if you ask me."

"There'll be conditions," continued Redwine.

"Such as?"

"That you play it our way. You're going to want to jump the gun, and you can't give them time to regroup."

"You convince me that you're telling the truth, and I'll play it any way you want."

"All right," said Redwine. "I'll discuss it with her tonight, and get back to you in the morning."

"Do you want me to keep an eye on your pal in the meantime?" asked Rasputin.

Redwine chuckled mirthlessly. "If you can keep an eye on Victor, this is going to be easier than I thought."

Rasputin cursed. "How the hell come everyone on this ship has a skeleton card except the Security chief?"

Redwine uttered a genuine laugh at Rasputin's frustration.

"You're in the wrong department. They're much easier to come by in espionage."

"Very funny."

"Being funny doesn't stop it from being true," noted Redwine.

"I suppose it doesn't," admitted Rasputin, walking to the door. "Well, I guess I'll hear from you tomorrow."

"One way or the other," promised Redwine.

He secured the door after Rasputin had left the office.

Then he poured himself another drink, sat back down on the couch, withdrew the small plastic cube from his pocket, and forced all thoughts not pertaining to the Madonna and the farm on Pollux IV from his mind.

16

"This was a hell of a good idea," said Redwine, chewing thoughtfully on a piece of cheese and peering down into the lagoon.

"I had a feeling you might like it," said the Madonna, reaching into her wicker picnic basket for a golden, grape-like fruit from Gamma Sigma IV.

"Like it?" repeated Redwine, looking around the fantasy room. "I could spend the rest of my life here!"

"Not unless you plan to die before eleven o'clock tonight," she replied with a smile.

"The *Comet*'s got lots of fantasy rooms," he said. "Let 'em use one of the others."

"They're using *all* the others. I really think four hours is about the limit that I can get away with claiming that the Tropical Paradise is getting a maintenance inspection."

"Well, I suppose it's better than nothing," agreed Redwine. "And I've been wanting to come back here since the first day I saw it." He shrugged. "I guess it's pretty damned silly to bitch about having to leave in three and a half hours. I mean, hell, we just got here." He scanned the artificial horizon, then turned to her. "I don't suppose Pollux IV looks anything like this?"

"I've already told you: *no* place looks like this."

"Well, then I know what I'm going to dedicate the rest of my life to," said Redwine.

"Oh?" said the Madonna. "What?"

"Proving you're wrong."

"We could see a lot of worlds in the process," she said. "It might be fun at that."

"Why the hell not?" he agreed. "I've always wanted to travel."

"I thought you traveled quite a bit."

"Yeah, but I'd like to do it without looking back over my shoulder to see who might be gaining on me. There are some pretty interesting worlds out there."

"I know."

"Ever hear of Vasor?"

"No."

"Small world, out near Aldebaran," he said. "I've never been there, but I've heard about it. The inhabitants have huge skinny legs, fifteen or twenty feet long, and they spend every minute of the day following the sun over the horizon."

"When do they eat or sleep?" asked the Madonna.

"How the hell should I know?"

"Well, it sounds wrong."

"My friend, the romantic," he said with a mock grimace. "We'll go and see for ourselves."

"It's a deal."

"Well," he said, "that takes care of *my* future. Now, isn't there some world *you'd* particularly like to see? Maybe take a trip back to old Earth, or go hunting on one of the jungle worlds on the Inner Frontier?"

She shook her head. "Not really. Once I wanted to go back to Seascape, but that was a long time ago."

"Your home world?"

"Yes. After I'd been madam for a couple of years I tried to arrange a trip there, so I could show everyone how rich and successful I was." She frowned. "But I cancelled it. Their attitudes about what I do are, well, pedestrian. And over the years impressing people just seemed less and less important." She shrugged. "Besides, everyone I knew there has probably either died or emigrated by now."

"You never mention your parents," remarked Redwine. "Are they still alive?"

"No. They died before I left Seascape."

"Maybe we'll go back for a week or two, anyway. I've always wanted to see a world named Seascape."

"It's called Beta Hydri II," she replied. "Seascape was just the colonists' name for it."

"Anything with 'Sea' in its name holds a certain appeal for me," said Redwine.

"That's right," she said. "You grew up on Delta Pavonis IX, didn't you?"

He nodded. "Dryest place this side of hell. We had to import all our water." He smiled ruefully. "The colonists were so damned busy trying to save enough money to get the hell off of Delta Pavonis that they never bothered giving it a nickname." He paused. "You know, I never took anything but a chemical bath or shower until I was nineteen years old, and it cost me twenty thousand credits to learn how to swim when I got to Binder."

"Do you care to put those lessons to some use?" she suggested, rising to her feet.

"I was afraid you'd never ask," he grinned, starting to unfasten his tunic.

A moment later they had left their clothes behind, hers folded neatly next to the picnic basket, his dropped casually on the ground, and had jumped into the water. It was invigorating without being cold, clear without seeming sterile, and they swam and splashed like children for the better part of five minutes.

Then the Madonna climbed out, and Redwine followed her a moment later.

"Where are the towels?" he asked, overtaking her just before she reached the basket.

"Just lie out on the grass," she replied. "The sun will dry you off."

"But that's not really a sun."

"I know. It'll dry you that much faster."

She walked over to the grassy knoll by the thatched

hut and lay down on her back, and he followed her example.

"What time is it now?" he asked suddenly.

"Harry, we've got hours left," she said. "The room will tell us when it's time to go."

"How?"

"It'll be twilight in another hour, and then night. When the sun rises again, we've got fifteen minutes to gather our gear and leave."

"It's on a four-hour cycle?" he asked.

"No. You tell the computer how long you plan to be here, and the cycle adjusts to it. I'm surprised you didn't notice it when you used your card to secure the room."

"Shit!" he muttered, walking over to his clothes and withdrawing his security card. "I was so excited about being here that I forgot." He made a couple of adjustments on the card, replaced it, and then lay back down beside the Madonna.

"Try not to look so upset, Harry."

"I don't like being spied on."

"They're there for a reason," she continued.

"I know," he said. "Look, in your line of business, you're probably much safer when someone is watching everything you do, but *my* line of work requires that no one be able to see what I'm doing. It's difficult to adjust."

"I know," she agreed. "It was difficult for me at first, too."

"It was?" he asked, curious.

"Contrary to what you may think about prostitutes, Harry, none of us were brought up to screw in front of an audience. But after a couple of lives get saved because Security sees a problem developing, and after you realize that they're not simply a batch of drooling voyeurs at the other end of the monitors, you come to accept and appreciate them, and after a while you don't even think of them at all." She paused. "One of the first things a prostitute learns how to do is not think of things, especially while they're happening to her."

"You don't seem especially bitter about it," he remarked.

"Why should I be? It's work of my own choosing, it pays very well—and if I hadn't been aboard the *Comet*, I'd never have met you."

"I still can't see why you don't aim your sights a little higher."

"Because I'm comfortable with you," she replied.

"There are lots of comfortable people in the galaxy," he said.

"Then aren't you lucky that I haven't found any of them yet?" Suddenly her face became serious. "Harry, if you haven't figured out by now that money and looks aren't important to me, what can I tell you? I've been lonely, and you make me feel less lonely. I've been an object, and you make me feel like a person. I've been asked to do a lot of kinky things, but you're the very first man who ever asked me to talk to him when there was an empty bed in the next room. I have a farm I haven't visited in six years, and suddenly you make me want to settle down there. What the hell else do you want me to say?"

"Nothing, I suppose," he replied. "I guess I still can't believe my good luck."

"Wait until we visit a world where prostitution is still a dirty word, and somebody recognizes me, and then tell me how lucky you feel."

"Then we won't visit any worlds like that," he said.

"There are more of them than you might think. That's why the *Comet* was built in space."

"If you can live with a man who throws innocent people out of work, I suppose I can live with a woman who makes them happy," said Redwine. "Now how about changing the subject?"

"Did you have a particular subject in mind?" she asked him.

"Well, I had a little talk with Rasputin this afternoon,"

he began. "I think it's time we took him into our confidence."

"You've been adamantly opposed to doing that for weeks," said the Madonna. "What changed your mind?"

"Because I'm probably going to have to leave with Victor," replied Redwine with a sigh. "Like you said, we can't have him getting suspicious. And once I'm gone, I want to know you've got an ally on the ship."

"What do I need an ally for?"

"I don't know. But I know you're going to have three enemies aboard the *Comet*—Suma, Gamble, and Lena—and I want to make sure that there's also someone on your side."

"It's his job to protect me whether he knows what's going on or not," she pointed out.

"True. But this way he'll know who the hell he's protecting you *from*. It might make a difference."

"And how do you know he won't turn you in?" she persisted.

"To who—Victor?" asked Redwine with a smile. "I think he'll believe me—after all, I can prove what I'm saying to him the same way I proved it to you—but even if he thinks I'm lying, there's nothing he can do about it until long after I'm beyond his jurisdiction."

"Do you want me there when you tell him?" asked the Madonna.

"I don't think it'll be necessary. Knowing him, he'll probably come to you to corroborate what I've said, anyway."

"Okay, if that's the way you want to do it—but I can't help feeling that you're over-reacting."

"Maybe. But five'll get you ten that Victor manages to talk to Suma before tomorrow morning—and since we've no way of knowing what they'll be saying to each other, I think I'd rather be safe than sorry." Suddenly the artificial sun sank behind the artificial horizon, and Redwine smiled. "Twilight comes fast in the tropics."

"It'll get chilly in a few minutes," replied the Madonna.

"Not *cold*, but the temperature will drop. Would you like to go into the hut?"

He shook his head. "I'm sure we'll find some way to keep warm."

"I take it you've never made love beneath a full tropical moon?" said the Madonna with a smile.

"I've never made love beneath *any* moon," he replied. "One of the drawbacks of a career in accountancy."

"Harry," she said as he leaned over her.

"Yes?"

"It just occurred to me: this might be the last time we do this for a few months."

"Nonsense," he said. "I'll be here at least four more days."

"Victor could change his mind and make you leave tomorrow."

"I'd like to see him try."

"Just the same, let's make love as if it was the last time—just in case."

"You're being silly."

"Then humor me."

He smiled. "I'll do more than *humor* you," he said, lowering his lips to hers.

And, unlike his session with Suma, this one was *truly* memorable.

17

Victor Bonhomme, comfortably ensconced in a form-fitting lounge chair, took a sip of his drink and looked once again at the pornographic entertainment on his holoscreen. A beautiful gold-skinned girl, whom he was sure he had seen earlier in one of the restaurants, seemed intent on setting some sort of record for accommodating the most partners at one time. Five young men were safe and snug in various orifices and hands, but the final member of her sextet of lovers seemed unable to find a lodging for himself.

Jaded as he was, Bonhomme found himself fascinated by the pulsating tableau before him, and actually had to restrain himself from offering suggestions to the life-sized images. He was absolutely sure that the sixth man would eventually make some kind of connection, and he could almost imagine a tote board down in the casino giving odds on where that connection might take place. Probably the Duke would have to appoint a steward to process claims of foul from disgruntled losers.

Suddenly there was a knocking at the door to his suite.

"In a minute!" he shouted.

He stared intently at the seven writhing figures for another thirty seconds, then sighed and deactivated the screen, making a mental note to check the results later.

"Open," he commanded the door, after adjusting his skeleton card.

The door slid back into the wall, and Suma, dressed in one of her more exotic outfits, entered the parlor.

"And whose little girl are *you?*" asked Bonhomme.

"Your boss's," she replied.

"Then you must be Suma. Forgive me for being forward, but do you mind if I asked you a very personal question?"

"Not at all."

"How many men can you take on?"

Suma grinned. "How many have you got?"

"I mean at the same time," said Bonhomme. "It's something in the nature of a bet."

"With who?"

"Myself."

"Seven," she answered promptly.

"*Seven?*" he repeated, certain that six had to be any woman's absolute physical limit. "Are you sure?"

"I've done it. In fact, it's probably available on one of the video channels."

"Wasn't it . . . *crowded?*" persisted Bonhomme.

"That was half the fun of it."

"This is some place, this ship!" said Bonhomme, shaking his head in amazement. "Can I offer you a drink?"

"Later, perhaps."

"A cigarette, then?"

"I don't smoke."

"How about a chair?" he asked, making a sweeping gesture with his arm.

"Thank you," said Suma, walking over to a plush, tufted sofa and seating herself.

"Now, then," said Bonhomme, sitting down on the lounge chair, "to what do I owe the pleasure of this visit?"

"We have a number of friends in common," replied Suma, "so I thought we might have a little chat."

"Does this mean you're not going to rip my clothes off and rape me?" asked Bonhomme with mock disappointment.

"It depends on how our conversation goes," said

Suma with a feline smile. "And we've got a lot to talk about."

"Do we?"

"Oh, yes, Victor, we certainly do. By the way, is this suite secure?"

"Secure from what?"

"You know, Victor, the longer you play stupid, the longer it's going to take us to get to bed," said Suma. "I know Harry has some kind of device he uses to jam the security system. I assume you have one too."

He stared at her for a moment, then shrugged. "It's secure."

"I thought so, when the door wouldn't open on my command."

"I'm just a guy who likes his privacy," said Bonhomme.

"Of course you are." She paused. "I assume one of our mutual friends told you about my message?"

"I heard something about it," responded Bonhomme. "He mentioned that you were feeling distressed, and asked me to look in on you." He stared at her. "You look just fine to me."

"I am."

"Then why did you tell him otherwise?"

"It got you out here, didn't it?" said Suma. "I was rather hoping he'd come himself, but I suppose an underling is better than no one at all."

"You think I'm an underling?" he asked, amused.

"I *know* you are."

"Well, then, speaking as one underling to another, what seems to be your problem?"

"*I* don't have a problem," said Suma. "*You* do."

"Oh? And just what *is* my problem?"

"The Madonna fired me earlier this week."

"I'm heartbroken to hear it," said Bonhomme. "However, people get fired all the time. I hardly see that it's any of my concern—although I must say it seems profligately wasteful of so beautiful a young woman."

"Oh, it's your problem, all right. I don't intend to stay fired."

"Good," he said. "I like a woman with spunk." He walked over to the bar. "Are you sure I can't fix you something?"

"No," she replied. "But don't let me stop you from making yourself a drink. I think you're going to need it."

He stared at her for a moment, then pulled out a bottle, uncapped it, and poured a few ounces of its contents into a tall glass. "Shall I assume your being fired precipitated your message?" he asked.

"Of course."

"Then why didn't you mention it at the time? The extra charge for one more sentence would have been minimal." He took a sip of his drink, added a couple of ice cubes, and returned to his chair.

"If I had mentioned that I was fired, you wouldn't be here now, and our mutual friend would be turning cartwheels in his executive office."

"You make him sound like a spiteful man," noted Bonhomme.

"No," said Suma. "Just greedy."

"Everybody's greedy," replied Bonhomme. "He just happens to be a little more efficient at it than most of us."

"He's not as efficient as he thinks," said Suma. "For that matter, neither are you."

"Okay," said Bonhomme pleasantly. "I'm sitting down, I'm relaxed, I've fortified myself with liquor—so tell me how this is all my problem, and then let's get on to the fun part of the evening."

"All right," she said. "I met our mutual friend about a year and a half ago."

"I know," interjected Bonhomme. "He came home raving about you."

"He came back almost every weekend," continued Suma. "He was a very nice man. He always had a gift or two for me." She held out her hand so that Bonhomme could see her diamond-and-platinum bracelet. "This was one of his presents."

"It probably wouldn't ransom more than two or three emperors," commented Bonhomme dryly.

"It's very pretty, isn't it?" she said. "Anyway, when my vacation came up eight months ago, he insisted on flying me all the way to Deluros."

"He can be very generous to people he likes."

"I know. While I was there he begged me to quit the *Comet* and become his mistress." She smiled at the memory. "He offered me a penthouse, and a country home on Earth itself, and all kinds of money."

"You should have taken him up on it," said Bonhomme. "He's a very successful man."

She shook her head. "I've got more money than I need, and I sure as hell didn't plan to spend the next ten years sitting around waiting for him to sneak away from his family." She paused. "But because he was nice to me, I decided not to hurt his feelings, so I simply told him that my contract with the *Comet* had three more years to run."

"Well, this is a fascinating melodrama in the life of a lovely young girl," said Bonhomme, "but I fail to see what it has to do with me."

"We're just coming to the good part," said Suma with a smile.

"Oh?"

She nodded. "Do you know what he said to me when I told him about my contract?"

"I haven't the foggiest notion."

"He laughed and told me not to worry, that in less than a year I'd have more time on my hands than I knew what to do with."

"Now, how could he have known the Madonna was going to fire you?" asked Bonhomme.

"Oh, I don't think he did. I got the distinct feeling that he thought the *Comet* would be out of business in a year's time."

"Did he say so?"

"Not in so many words, but that was the impression he gave." She paused. "He also mentioned your name."

"He's a good man," said Bonhomme with a sigh, "but he talks too much in bed. Always has, always will."

"Anyway," she continued, "I put two and two together, and I decided that he planned to wreck the *Comet*. I even figured out that you would have something to do with it."

"You've got an overactive imagination," said Bonhomme.

"Perhaps," she said. "At least, a lot of my patrons seem to agree with you."

"You should listen to them. You're building some kind of paranoid fantasy here. Why the hell would anyone want to destroy the *Comet*?"

"You know, I asked myself that very question," replied Suma. "And when I couldn't answer it, I asked a number of rather intimate friends. Do you know the answer I came up with?"

"Would you like me to guess, or will you just tell me?"

"I found out that his main competitor for the chairmanship of the Vainmill Syndicate is the head of the Entertainment and Leisure Division. Now, I never really thought he meant to blow the ship out of the sky—but it certainly makes sense for him to tamper with the books so he can show that we've been hiding enormous losses, doesn't it?"

"You think it makes sense for a member of the Vainmill board to let a twenty-billion-credit investment sink without a trace?" said Bonhomme with a mocking laugh. "Suma, I think you'd better stick to staring at the ceiling for a living. You'll never make it as a detective."

"The investment won't sink," replied Suma. "Just the business. He'll find some other use for the ship."

"Do you know how quickly they'll laugh you out of court with that accusation?" said Bonhomme.

"Yes, I do. That's why I decided to back my word up with some evidence."

"Evidence?" said Bonhomme, frowning. "What evidence?"

"I made friends with a woman in Security—you'll forgive me if I don't tell you her name—and had her make a copy of all the existing financial records six months ago." She grinned at him. "Can you guess what I had her do last week?"

"You tell me," said Bonhomme grimly.

"I had her make another copy, after Harry Redwine had been working on the books for a month."

"Where are these copies?"

"In a safe place," replied Suma with a smug smile.

"Why in the world are you suspicious of Harry?" asked Bonhomme. "He's just an old friend. He's never worked for me in his life."

"Perhaps not," said Suma dubiously. "But he's an accountant, and he's from Deluros, and he's sleeping with the Madonna."

"What does sleeping with the Madonna have to do with anything?"

"It's a business move, nothing more," said Suma. "You don't really believe he could prefer her to the rest of us, do you? It's just a way to protect his ass, and to get her to fire anyone who knows what's going on."

"Like you?" suggested Bonhomme dryly.

"Exactly. And of course our friend would be delighted if he knew, because he'd think it meant I was available."

"There are worse situations to be in," said Bonhomme. "Why don't you take him up on his offer?"

"Victor, you don't seem to understand what I'm telling you," said Suma patiently. "I'm not letting *anyone* kill the *Comet*—not you, not your boss, not Harry. If you persist in trying, I'll turn the records over to the head of Entertainment and Leisure and a couple of other division heads whom I happen to know on a very personal basis."

"Have you spoken to anyone else about this?"

"No—except to say that if anything happens to me, I want the records turned over to the press." She smiled pleasantly. "I also told my bodyguard that if any harm comes to me tonight, you're the one who should be held responsible."

"You've got a bodyguard?"

"Gamble DeWitt," she said proudly.

"*He's* on the *Comet*?"

"Yes. And he's very loyal."

"I can just imagine," said Bonhomme. He finished his drink and stared at her for a long moment. "Why are you telling me all this?" he asked at last. "You're holding all the aces, so why don't you just go public and be done with it?"

"Because I don't like hurting people," she answered.

Bonhomme laughed aloud. "You have a delightful sense of humor."

"Really," she said. "And of course, there's an alternative."

"I have a feeling that we just came to the gist of this conversation."

"Yes we did, so pay careful attention," said Suma. "Because if we *don't* reach an accommodation, I'm afraid I won't have any choice but to expose all of you."

"Which would no doubt cause you great emotional pain," said Bonhomme sardonically. "Go ahead. I'm listening."

"The *Velvet Comet* must stay in business."

"I'm sure once our friend finds out what you've got on him, he'll be the very soul of reason," replied Bonhomme. "Is there anything else?"

"Of course."

"Somehow I had a feeling there would be," he said. "What is it?"

"I want the ship to have motive power. We can do much better traveling from one solar system to another, rather than making all the patrons come to Charlemagne."

"Motive power for the *Comet* can run into a lot of money."

"We'll make it back," she said confidently. "Every time we take up orbit around a planet, we'll be world-wide news. Planetary governments will bid for the privilege of having the *Velvet Comet* visit them for a month or two."

Bonhomme sighed. "I suppose it can be arranged."

"And there's one thing more," continued Suma.

"Isn't there always?" said Bonhomme wryly.

"It's for your own protection."

"How thoughtful of you. Go ahead."

"The Madonna has to have some notion of what's been going on," began Suma. "After all, she's been living with Harry for more than a month." She stared directly at Bonhomme. "The Madonna loves this ship almost as much as I do, and she's a very stern, moral woman."

"Not reasonable, like yourself?" suggested Bonhomme.

"Totally unreasonable," agreed Suma. "If she gets her hands on the data, she'll almost certainly blow the whistle on you."

"Whereas if *you* became the madam, you could keep the lid on everything?"

"I'm glad to see that we understand each other," she said with a smile. "Either way, the *Comet* is going to survive. But if you leave the Madonna in charge, you're not going to survive along with it. She's not as conciliatory as I am."

"Obviously not."

"It's time for a change, anyway," said Suma with a smile that was a mixture of arrogance and triumph. "People like you and Harry and the Madonna can stockpile all the yesterdays you want, but tomorrow belongs to me. You're the past, I'm the future; it's inevitable that I wind up in control of the ship. Besides," she added, "the Madonna has been very stupid."

"Oh? In what way?"

"She forgot the prime axiom of a whorehouse: that there's a difference between love and sex. Her job is dispensing sex, and instead she fell in love with the man who's rigging the *Comet*'s books. It was a very unprofessional thing to do."

"I have a feeling it's a pitfall you'll never have to worry about," commented Bonhomme.

"Never," echoed Suma. "Anyway, as far as I'm concerned, that makes her expendable, even if she didn't have all her other faults."

"I gather her major fault is that she's got a job that you want."

"She's had it long enough. It's my turn now—and I'll do it a damned sight better than she ever did."

"Perhaps," said Bonhomme. "But allow me to point out that you're not the only person with a contract. The Madonna has one too."

"Contracts can be broken."

"Not if she's toying with blowing the whistle, they can't."

"Contract signers can be broken, too," added Suma softly.

"I hope you're not suggesting murder," said Bonhomme. "Because I won't have anything to do with it."

"I'm not suggesting anything," she replied. "I merely made an observation."

"Well, let *me* suggest that murder is out of the question," he said firmly.

"What if the Madonna were to have an accident?" asked Suma. "Not a fatal one, but one that put her in the hospital for a few months?"

"We'd certainly need an acting madam during that period," said Bonhomme carefully. "And of course, if it should be decided that she really wasn't fit to return to duty, the position would probably become permanent." He lit another cigarette. "Mind you, I'm not recommending anything of the kind."

"Of course not," said Suma.

"I would never recommend anything illegal," he continued. "And if something illegal were to occur, I wouldn't want to know anything about it."

"What could occur?" asked Suma innocently.

"Who knows?" replied Bonhommme with an eloquent shrug. "It's a big ship. Doubtless there are numerous health hazards around."

"Doubtless," agreed Suma.

18

The Madonna was still asleep when Redwine left the apartment. He had a quick breakfast in one of the restaurants, then took the tram over to the Home, and shortly thereafter was ushered into Rasputin's office.

"Good morning, Harry," said the Security chief, looking up from his desktop computer. "I've been waiting for you."

"I'll just bet you have," said Redwine, sitting down opposite him. "Got any coffee?"

"I'm afraid not," replied Rasputin. "But I can send for some."

Redwine shook his head. "No. Once we secure the room, I don't want to be bothered."

"You're the boss," said Rasputin with a shrug. "Cigar?" he added, opening his desk drawer and withdrawing a pair.

"I've got my own," replied Redwine, pulling one out of a pocket and lighting it.

Rasputin touched a quartet of small squares on his computer, then turned back to Redwine. "Okay, Harry, the room's sealed off."

Redwine withdrew his skeleton card and manipulated it. "Just to make sure," he explained.

"All right," said Rasputin, leaning back on his chair. "Shall we get down to business?"

"That's what I'm here for," said Redwine. "But we need some ground rules first."

"You name 'em, and I'll tell you if I can live with 'em."

"First off, everything I tell you is confidential."

"Forever?" asked Rasputin.

"Until either the Madonna or myself releases you from your promise."

"That's acceptable," said Rasputin after some consideration.

"Also, I want you to keep a 24-hour-a-day watch on the Madonna—and I'd prefer that she didn't know about it."

"How much danger is she in?"

"I don't know," admitted Redwine. "I wish I did."

"I'll take care of it," said the Security chief promptly. "Anything else."

"Yeah. One more thing."

"What?"

"I'm leaving with Bonhomme in a few days, and I don't want your team at the airlock inspecting my luggage."

"That'll depend on your story," said Rasputin.

"Fair enough," agreed Redwine.

"All right," said Rasputin. "Are there any other conditions?"

"No. If those are acceptable to you, we can begin."

"They're acceptable."

"I imagine you've got a pretty good general idea of what's going on," began Redwine.

"Probably," said Rasputin. "But you tell me the details, and I'll let you know if I was right."

"All right. I was sent here to doctor the *Comet*'s financial records."

"Not exactly a surprise, given your prior record of accomplishments," commented Rasputin dryly.

"True," said Redwine. "The surprise came a little later. I committed the one sin that's unforgivable in my line of work."

"The Madonna?"

Redwine nodded. "I became emotionally involved with the person I was being paid to victimize."

"You know," said Rasputin, puffing on his cigar, "we can save a lot of time if you'll just give me a blow-by-blow account of this whole operation from start to finish."

"All right," said Redwine, launching into a brief history of his previous jobs for his unknown employer, his instructions regarding the *Velvet Comet*, and the manner in which he had sabotaged the books.

When he was through, he noticed that his cigar had gone out, and he re-lit it.

"Now, let me see if I've got it straight," said Rasputin at last. "As things stand now, the *Comet* is hiding a sixty-three-billion-credit deficit, accumulated over the past nine years."

"That's right."

"And the computer is rigged to revert to the original figures in ten months?"

Redwine nodded. "Unless the Madonna decides to move the date up or back. I'll be keeping her informed of conditions on Deluros while I'm trying to hunt us up a protector."

"Can anyone un-rig the computer?"

"Not without a skeleton card. All we've got to do is keep Victor from getting suspicious for the next three or four days." He paused and stared at Rasputin. "And if your men inspect my luggage while Victor and I are waiting to leave, he's going to be more than suspicious. The second he sees the copies I made of the financial records he's going to know what they are."

"Would he want copies for himself?" asked Rasputin slowly.

Redwine uttered a harsh laugh. "He'd have a stroke if he thought anyone had made them. I mean, hell, they could put him behind bars for a dozen years."

"Then we've got a little problem," continued the Security chief.

"Oh?"

Rasputin nodded. "A few days ago you pulled up

some records from the main computer bank. I don't know what you did with them, but I know which ones you pulled." He paused. "That was the night you figured out that Suma was the plant."

"I remember," said Redwine.

"But along with Suma and Gamble DeWitt, you also pulled the file on Lena Boatswain. I didn't know why you were interested in her, but since she works for Security, it made *me* interested too."

"And?"

"You're not the only person on board who's made before-and-after copies of the financial records." Rasputin leaned forward. "Now, if she didn't do it for Bonhomme, who *did* she make them for?"

"It had to be for Suma," answered Redwine with a frown.

"What does Suma plan to do with them?" asked Rasputin. "Blackmail you?"

"I think she's after bigger game than me."

"Bonhomme?"

Redwine shook his head. "She's the plant, remember? She knows who my employer is." He exhaled deeply. "My guess is that she's after *him*—or her, as the case may be."

"Will it work?"

"It doesn't make any difference."

"I don't think I follow you."

Redwine allowed himself the luxury of a large grin. "If he pays her off, he's going to be buying her silence for a crime that won't exist a year from now."

"Then who becomes the next chairman?"

"I don't give a damn. The *Comet* will stay in business, which is all the Madonna cares about. And to tell you the truth, that's all *I* care about at this moment."

"If I were you, I'd find a little more to care about," commented Rasputin. "Even if no one figures out what you've done, it's going to cost you your job."

"I'm tired of my job."

"You might get tired of being the Madonna's permanent houseboy," remarked Rasputin.

"She's quitting too," answered Redwine.

"How soon?" asked Rasputin sharply.

"Once this whole thing is resolved, and she can choose her successor."

"I take it that Suma isn't exactly a prime candidate?"

"Suma's got twenty-six days to get her pretty little ass off the ship," replied Redwine. "She was fired, remember?"

"I have a feeling that this isn't quite as neat and tidy as you're making it sound," said Rasputin. "Did you know that she paid a visit to Bonhomme last night?"

"I'm not surprised," answered Redwine. "Were you able to monitor them?"

The Security chief shook his head. "He sealed off his room the minute he arrived."

"You really ought to get a skeleton card," chuckled Redwine.

"I didn't know that one skeleton card could overpower another," remarked Rasputin.

"It can't—but it can *negate* another card. If your security system is working, it comes to the same thing."

"He's going to be on the ship for a couple of more days, isn't he?"

"To the best of my knowledge."

"Then there's always a chance that he'll meet with her again," continued Rasputin. "Why don't you show me how that damned card works, and maybe I can listen in on them next time."

Redwine shrugged. "Why not?"

"Can we do it from right here?" asked Rasputin.

"Yes, but we'll have to unseal the room first. Right now no signal can get in or out."

Redwine withdrew his card while Rasputin adjusted his computer.

"Ready when you are," said the Security chief after a moment.

"Let's get on with it," said Redwine.

Raputin touched a number of squares on his console, then frowned as an orgy appeared on the screen.

"I must have the wrong room," he muttered, and reached for the console again.

"No," said Redwine suddenly. "That's Victor there on the bed."

"And that looks like Suma over there on the lounge chair," added Rasputin, squinting at the picture.

"They must have the whole damned Demolition Team in there with them," commented Redwine. He turned to Rasputin. "I thought you told me the room was sealed off."

"It was," answered Redwine. "I guess there's a little exhibitionist in all of us."

"Maybe," said Redwine, frowning.

Rasputin chuckled. "Why *else* would he stop jamming the monitors?"

"I don't know," said Redwine. "Unless . . ."

"Unless what?"

Suddenly Redwine sat bolt upright.

"Unless they needed an alibi!"

"What are you talking about?"

"Get the Madonna's room—quick!" demanded Redwine.

The Security Chief touched six squares in quick order, and the Madonna's office flashed on the screen.

It appeared empty at first, but an instant later they heard a crashing noise and Rasputin transferred to a different camera.

The Leather Madonna, blood streaming down her face, was backing away from Gamble DeWitt, who was throwing furniture out of his path as he slowly, almost casually, pursued her around the room.

"Get a Security team there on the double!" yelled Redwine.

Rasputin reached for the computer console, then cursed and jumped to his feet.

"Come on!" he snapped, rushing to the door.

"What's the matter?" demanded Redwine.

"Lena Boatswain's on duty on that level! This thing was set up!"

They reached the tramway in less than a minute, then spent the longest eighty seconds of Redwine's life traversing the two miles beneath the mall. They ran to an elevator bank, shoving prostitutes and patrons aside as they went, and burst into the Madonna's apartment another minute later.

DeWitt, a look of fury on his handsome face, had the Madonna in a corner of the room and was slapping her, first forehand and then backhand, with a quick, savage rhythm. Her eyes were glazed, and from the swelling and miscoloration of her face it was obvious that her nose and left cheekbone were broken. Most of the furniture in the room had been shattered, and the floor was littered with chess pieces, broken glass, and splintered wood.

Redwine instantly hurled himself at DeWitt's back, knocking the athlete into a wall. Though surprised, DeWitt responded quickly, catching Redwine on the throat with the flat of his hand and knocking him to the floor.

During the momentary confusion the Madonna began stumbling groggily toward the doorway. DeWitt saw the motion out of the corner of his eye, caught her in a single stride, and landed a tremendous blow on the back of her head.

Two cracking sounds followed simultaneously, one from the Madonna's neck and the second from Rasputin's hand weapon. DeWitt spun completely around and, cursing at the top of his lungs, charged across the room toward the Security chief, a huge bloody spot just under his left shoulderblade. Rasputin fired again, and DeWitt collapsed in a heap and lay totally motionless.

The Security chief knelt down next to the Madonna's body and examined it briefly. Her bruised and bloodied head was twisted at an impossible angle, and he tried to straighten it out.

"Stay where you are, Harry," he said softly, as Redwine got painfully to his feet and began approaching him. "You don't want to see her like this."

Redwine uttered a moan that was more animal than human, then ran to the Madonna's side and pushed Rasputin away. He placed an arm under her terribly battered body and began speaking incoherently as tears streamed down his face. After a moment he took one of her lifeless hands and began rubbing it vigorously.

"It's no use, Harry," said Rasputin. "She's dead."

"No she's not!" snapped Redwine. He rubbed her hand for another few seconds, then lowered his mouth to hers and vainly tried to breathe life back into her body.

"Where's your card, Harry?" asked Rasputin after another minute had passed.

Redwine looked uncomprehendingly at him.

"Your skeleton card, Harry," repeated Rasputin, articulating each word slowly and carefully. "We've got to seal off the room."

"My pocket," mumbled Redwine, turning his attentions back to the Madonna.

Rasputin approached him, gently removed the card, and secured the apartment, as Redwine, again oblivious to him, cradled the Madonna in his arms.

Redwine remained absolutely motionless for another moment, then stood up and dried his face with the sleeve of his tunic.

"I loved her," he said softly.

"I know," replied Rasputin.

Redwine pulled a handkerchief out of his pocket, then seemed to forget what he had wanted it for.

"We were going to live on her farm in the Pollux system," he said in a faraway voice. He paused, momentarily disoriented. "Why would anyone want to kill her?"

"I don't know if he did," replied the Security chief thoughtfully. "I think we startled him. If he had come here to kill her, she'd have been dead long before we arrived."

Redwine stared at the Madonna's lifeless body.

"I didn't even know her name," he said at last.

"You knew everything you needed to know about her," replied Rasputin gently.

Redwine was silent for another moment.

"It's back," he said at last, in a dull, dead voice.

"What is?"

"The emptiness." He paused. "It was gone while I knew her, and now it's back."

"I don't understand," said Rasputin.

"You don't have to. *I* do." Redwine's expression hardened. "Someone besides me is going to be sorry this day ever happened," he announced at last.

"Can you be ready to leave the ship in half an hour?" asked Rasputin.

"Who's leaving?" asked Redwine distractedly.

"*You* are."

"Not until I see Suma and Victor."

"Harry, if you kill them, I won't be able to protect you. You'll go to jail."

"It doesn't matter."

"There's a better way," persisted Rasputin.

Redwine looked at him blankly.

"Deluros, Harry," said Rasputin, articulating each word carefully as if speaking to a child. "Take your copies of the records and go to Deluros. You'll not only take care of Suma and Bonhomme, but you'll save the *Comet*."

"What do I care about the *Comet*?" said Redwine.

"*She* cared."

Redwine looked down at the Madonna's body.

"All right," he said at last.

"Good," said Rasputin briskly. "Now we've got to get you out of here."

Redwine remained motionless.

"Harry, are you paying attention to me?"

"I want her buried on her farm on Pollux IV," said Redwine, never taking his eyes from the Madonna.

"I'll see to it."

"And I don't want Suma to have any of her things. I'll see them burned first."

"Is there anything of hers you'd like to take with you?"

Redwine looked slowly around the room.

"The chess set," he said at last.

"Where's the container?"

"In the bedroom closet," said Redwine. "And bring the briefcase that's next to it; it's got the data copies."

Rasputin left the office and returned a moment later with the briefcase and the ornate wooden box. He laid both on the floor, then dropped to his knees and began gathering up the chess pieces.

"I'm going to give you the first shot at this, Harry," he said as he began collecting the scattered chessmen and placing them carefully in the box. "But if you fail, I'm going to see that Suma gets what's coming to her."

Redwine made no answer, but merely stood there, trying to adjust to the terrible reality of the situation, to the fact that the Madonna would never read another book, or laugh at another joke, or greet him at the end of a day, or ever again walk the decks of the *Velvet Comet*.

Rasputin put the last piece in the box, locked it, and got to his feet.

"Harry, I've got to ask you a question."

"What?"

"It's about your skeleton card."

"You can't have it," said Redwine. "I'll need it on Deluros."

"You said before that it could negate Bonhomme's card."

"So what?" said Redwine dully.

"Damn it, Harry—try to concentrate!"

Redwine looked at him. "What about the card?"

"I don't know all the intricacies of working it," said

the Security chief. "Is there a way you can stop Bonhomme from jamming his suite's monitors before you leave?"

Redwine stared at him for a moment, then nodded. "What room is he in?"

Rasputin gave him the number, and Redwine walked over to the fruitwood secretary, activated the small computer inside it, and made a quick adjustment.

"It's done," he said.

"I wish to hell *I* had one of those," muttered Rasputin. He picked up the briefcase and the box. "All right, Harry. The sooner we get you off the ship, the better."

"You go ahead," said Redwine. "I want a minute alone with her."

Rasputin nodded and left the room, and Redwine knelt down beside the Madonna once more.

"I waited forty-three years for someone like you," he said softly, "and then we only had five weeks together." He lowered his head and kissed her for the last time. "It shouldn't have ended like this"—he sighed—"but it was worth the wait."

He stood up, blew his nose once, and then walked out the door and followed Rasputin to the airlock.

19

Night had fallen on Deluros VIII, the enormous planet that would shortly become Man's capital world. Seven billion bureaucrats had returned to their dwellings, secure in the knowledge that they had advanced the cause of the sprawling Republic for another day. Traffic in and out of the ten thousand orbital hangars had slowed to a manageable flow, half a million restaurants had closed their doors for another day, all but a handful of the five hundred holographic video stations had switched from prime time entertainments to reruns and low-budget epics.

And yet not everyone on Deluros VIII had ceased working for the day. Five million police patrolled the streets and byways of the major cities, a third of a million bars remained open, a sanitation force the size of a small army was preparing the planet for another day's assault by its busy minions. The Planetary Governor was hosting a party for a trio of alien ambassadors from Lodin XI, the Department of Commerce and Trade was holding an all-night session to explore means of combating the current recession, the Federation of Miners was polling its deadlocked membership regarding the Republic's latest contract offer.

And, on the eighty-sixth floor of the Vainmill Building, a very old woman sat in a sumptuous office, studying flow charts on a tabletop computer. A cup of tea, cold and forgotten, rested on a corner of her desk. Every now and then she would utter a brief command to the computer, but for the most part she merely watched the endless display of charts and statistics.

Suddenly she heard a door slide into the wall, and looked up to find herself facing a middle-aged man. The man touched a small card he held in his hand, and the door slid shut again.

The two stared at each other in silence for a long minute.

"Come in, Mr. Redwine," said the old woman at last. "I've been expecting you."

"You know who I am?" asked Redwine, surprised.

"Of course," she said. "I make it my business to know *all* my major employees, even those I haven't met before."

"You also make it very difficult for them to talk to you."

"I'm a busy woman. If what they have to say is important enough, they usually find a way to see me, as you seem to have done." She paused. "How did you get past my security people?"

Redwine held up his skeleton card.

"I can't quite see what you have there," said the old woman. "Please step a little closer."

"It's dark in here," commented Redwine, approaching her desk.

"The light hurts my eyes. Ah—a skeleton card! You show remarkable initiative, Mr. Redwine. Do sit down."

Redwine seated himself on an overstuffed chair about ten feet away from her.

"May I offer you some tea?"

"No, thank you."

"To what do I owe the honor of this visit, Mr. Redwine?"

"Like I said, we have to talk."

"That sounds remarkably like an order, Mr. Redwine," said the old woman. "And I don't take orders. I *give* them."

"I'm afraid you'll have to take this one," said Redwine. "I've sealed off your office."

The old woman smiled and touched a button beneath her desk. An instant later the door slid open.

"We'll have our talk, Mr. Redwine," she said as Redwine manipulated his card to no effect. "But you must understand that I am consenting to this meeting because *I* want to, not because you have told me that I must."

She moved her hand and the door slid shut.

"Now," she continued, "what is so important that you are willing to risk your career and even your life, just for a few minutes of my time?"

"I've come to tell you that you have a saboteur in your organization," said Redwine bluntly.

"I have *many* saboteurs in my organization," replied the old woman calmly. "Including you."

"What do you know about me?" he asked sharply.

"More than you suppose," said the old woman, taking a sip of her cold tea, making a face, and adding some sugar to it.

"Then you know why I was sent to the *Velvet Comet?*" he persisted.

"Certainly."

He frowned, puzzled. "Are *you* my employer?"

"Not in the sense that you mean."

"But you know I was sent there to falsify the financial records?"

"Of course, Mr. Redwine. It is my business to know such things."

"Do you also know a murder was committed just before I left?"

"It was most unfortunate.

"*Unfortunate?*" snapped Redwine.

"A poor choice of words," said the old woman. "It was tragic."

"Someone's going to pay for it," said Redwine grimly.

"Oh?"

He nodded, withdrew a small package from inside his tunic, and tossed it onto her desk.

"The original records and the ones you forged?" asked the old woman.

"That's right," said Redwine. "It's everything you need to nail whoever's been sabotaging your companies."

"And you're giving them to me?" she asked.

"Yes. But there's a price."

"There usually is," she said with a wry smile. "All right, Mr. Redwine. What is your price?"

"Two other people have to take the fall along with my employer."

"Victor Bonhomme and whom?"

He stared at her for a moment, startled. "A girl named Suma."

"Ah, yes, Suma. A lovely young woman."

"She killed the Madonna."

"I was under the impression that a former athlete named Gamble DeWitt killed her, and was killed in turn."

"He was her weapon."

"You, of course, have certain knowledge of this?" asked the old woman.

Redwine stared at her. "Do we have a deal?" he said at last.

"I'm afraid not, Mr. Redwine."

"Why not?" he demanded.

"First of all, the only person implicated by those records is yourself."

"You put me on a witness stand and I'll have Victor Bonhomme in jail in five minutes' time."

"Even if it meant you had to go to jail yourself?"

"Even so," he said resolutely.

"You loved her that much?" asked the old woman, curious.

"I don't know what you're talking about."

"I think you do."

"My motives aren't important," said Redwine. "Do you want the records or not?"

She took another sip of her tea.

"No, I do not," she said.

"But I'm giving you this guy's head on a silver platter!"

"I have enough heads and enough platters, Mr. Redwine. I don't need any more."

"I don't think you understand what I've been saying," persisted Redwine. "My employer has been systematically sabotaging Vainmill operations all over the galaxy."

"Do you really think I wasn't aware of that?" asked the old woman. "What a low opinion you must have of me, Mr. Redwine."

He stared at her, trying to comprehend her answer. Finally he shook his head. "It doesn't make any sense!" he said. "Are you just going to let him keep bankrupting your companies?"

The old woman took another spoonful of sugar and spread it on her desk.

"Do you see this sugar, Mr. Redwine?"

"Yes."

"Even in a single spoonful, there are tens of thousands of grains. Let us pretend that it represents the Vainmill Syndicate." She wet her finger. "Now let us remove the nine companies you have successfully sabotaged, as well as the *Velvet Comet*." She placed her finger down at the edge of the sugar, then took it away away. "Do you see a difference?"

"What's the point of this?" said Redwine.

"The point, Mr. Redwine, is that Vainmill is too big and too powerful and too far-flung to be diminished by the removal of ten companies, just as this pile of sugar remains just as full and potent despite the removal of ten grains. Do I make myself clear?"

"Do you mean you're going to let this bastard get away with what he's done, just because you can afford it?" demanded Redwine.

"In essence, that is precisely what I am going to do," she replied.

"You're crazy!" he snapped.

"No, Mr. Redwine. I'm old, and I'm tired, but I am

definitely not crazy. I plan to retire next year, and must leave behind me the most able successor possible."

"The most able criminal, you mean."

"Corporations are not human beings, Mr. Redwine," said the old woman, "and they cannot be ruled by human laws. If your employer is bold enough and ruthless enough to pull this off, then he is my logical successor."

"But he's *not* pulling it off!" insisted Redwine. "I've got the evidence to put him away."

She shook her head. "You're a wild card, Mr. Redwine. You don't count."

"What are you talking about?"

"If you hadn't committed the unpardonable error of falling in love in a whorehouse, you wouldn't be offering me your evidence. Your employer gets a free pass for that."

"Then I'll go to the press."

"No you won't, Mr. Redwine," she answered. "This entire conversation has been monitored by two of my most trusted security personnel. If you kill me, you won't leave this room alive—and if you allow me to live and try to take those records with you, I have five hundred security men prepared to take them back before you reach the nearest exit."

Redwine slumped back in his chair. "What will you do with them?"

"Destroy them, of course."

"And let my employer keep bankrupting your companies?"

"If he can," she agreed. "This is survival of the fittest, Mr. Redwine."

"Or of the least moral," he said bitterly.

"It comes to the same thing in the end," she acknowledged pleasantly. "And don't speak so harshly of survivors, Mr. Redwine. You used to be one, before you got sex and love all mixed up."

"And what will become of the *Comet*?" he asked.

"Oh, Eros always survives, of course," she replied.

"The *Velvet Comet* is much too impressive a showcase to be allowed to die."

"Who will run it?"

"Suma, I suppose. She's a very ambitious young woman. In fact, she reminds me a lot of myself when I was younger—not that I was ever a prostitute, you understand." She paused. "I am told that Mr. Bonhomme has already agreed to make her the madam and to give the ship motive power."

"She'll have your job in ten years' time," Redwine predicted.

The old woman shook her head. "She's not subtle enough. Still, I suppose I'll have to keep an eye on her."

"How can you do that if the *Comet* has motive power?"

"Then I guess I can't allow it to have motive power, can I?" she said with a smile. "I think we'll put it in orbit around Deluros VIII, just for safe-keeping."

"And what happens to *me*?"

"You?" she said. "Why, you're free to leave whenever you wish, Mr. Redwine—just so long as you leave your package on my desk."

"There's something I want to know first," said Redwine.

"And what is that?"

"Who is my employer?"

"I'm sorry, Mr. Redwine," replied the old woman, "but I can't see that any purpose would be served by telling you. You're still distraught over the Madonna's death, and I'm not sure you can be expected to behave in a rational and intelligent manner."

"So that's it?" said Redwine. "The Madonna is dead, and everyone responsible for it keeps right on working for you?"

"Life goes on, Mr. Redwine."

He glared across the desk at her.

"You're worse than the rest of them."

"Not worse, Mr. Redwine," she said. "Just harder. I have to be; it's the nature of my job. And now," she added, "if there's nothing further, I really must get back to work. It's been a very enlightening conversation." She smiled at him. "You will undoubtedly wish to hand in your resignation. I'll arrange for a very generous severance fee to be desposited in your account."

"It's not necessary."

"I realize that, but we'll do it anyway."

"I don't want your money!"

"Oh, it's not *mine*, Mr. Redwine. It belongs to all the people you put out of work over the years."

He glared at her and made no answer.

"Oh, I see," she said with mock sympathy. "You had forgotten them during our little discussion. I suppose it's just as well. It would never do for a man playing the tragic lover to have so many people on his conscience." She paused. "Or was this supposed to be the noble act of expiation that would mitigate all your prior actions?" She chuckled. "I suppose I shall have to remind Suma never to underestimate the redemptive power of love."

"You were right," said Redwine bitterly as he got up from his chair.

"About what, Mr. Redwine?"

"Suma will never replace you."

"I'll assume that's a compliment."

"Assume any damned thing you want," he said, walking to the door.

"Mr. Redwine?" said the old woman as the door slid into the wall.

He turned and faced her. "What?"

"You probably won't believe it, but I am truly sorry about the Madonna."

"You're right about that, too," he replied, and stalked out of the office.

20

Rasputin was sitting at his desk, carefully studying the Lady Toshimatu's every move at the poker table on his holographic screen, when the door to his office slid back and Victor Bonhomme entered the room.

"Good morning," said Bonhomme. "I hope I'm not intruding?"

"Not at all," replied the Security chief as he deactivated his monitor. "Have a seat."

Bonhomme pulled up a chair, sat down, and lit one of his blue-tinted cigarettes.

"Do you find my company irresistible," asked Rasputin, "or does this visit have some purpose?"

"I think it's time you and I had a little talk," replied Bonhomme, exhaling two thin streams of smoke from his nostrils.

"I like talking as well as the next man," said Rasputin. "Did you have any particular subject in mind?"

"Business."

"I especially like talking about business." Rasputin paused. "In fact, if you hadn't stopped by, I was going to hunt you up later today."

"Oh? What about?"

"It can wait a few minutes. I'd like to hear what you have to say first."

"Fine," said Bonhomme. "I'll get right down to cases. How happy are you here?"

"I like my work."

"Do you like your salary?"

Rasputin shrugged. "It's adequate."

"But you'd like more?"

"Who wouldn't?" replied Rasputin with a smile.

"In that case, we may be able to work something out," said Bonhomme. "Harry thought very well of you." He paused. "You heard about what happened, didn't you?"

"I know he's dead," said Rasputin. "I don't know how it occurred."

"The poor dumb sonofabitch killed himself," said Bonhomme. "He must have gone a little crazy when the Madonna died. I don't know all the details, but I guess he went back to Deluros, broke into the Vainmill Building, and then went home and hung himself in his apartment. It must have been . . . oh, three or four weeks ago." He paused. "By the way, how did you find out? Even Suma doesn't know yet."

"Harry told me."

"I don't think I follow you," said Bonhomme.

"He sent me his skeleton card and the Madonna's chess set," explained Rasputin. "He'd never have done that unless he knew he was going to die."

"You've got his skeleton card?" asked Bonhomme sharply.

"That's right."

Bonhomme frowned for a moment, then shrugged. "Maybe it's for the best, at that. Have you learned how to use it?"

"It's not that difficult," said Rasputin. "Why?"

"I don't know if you're aware of it, but Harry did a little undercover work for Vainmill from time to time. Now that he's gone, I'm going to be needing someone to replace him."

"I'm not an accountant."

"To be perfectly honest about it, Harry had almost outlived his usefulness to us. I only had one more job lined up for him." Rasputin made no comment, and

Bonhomme continued. "He seemed quite taken with you, so I checked out your credentials. They're very impressive: fifteen years in Intelligence, decorated three times, two degrees in computer technology, twelve years as Chief of Security." He paused. "It's a hell of a record. I especially like those computer degrees; the word I get from the computer experts back on Deluros is that they're going to be installing a number of new fail-safe devices to make them tamper-proof."

"How very interesting," commented Rasputin.

"Well, what do you say?" asked Bonhomme. "Do you think you might be interested in working for me?"

"Which particular companies did you want me to destroy?" asked Rasputin pleasantly.

Bonhomme frowned. "Harry always did talk too god-damned much."

"He was a good man who got in over his head and couldn't get out."

"Harry was a fool and a loser," answered Bonhomme. "Why romanticize him just because he's dead?"

"He tried to redeem himself," said Rasputin. "Who knows? He may even have succeeded."

"We seem to be getting away from the subject," said Bonhomme. "I came here to offer you a job, not to argue with you about a dead man."

"To tell you the truth, Mr. Bonhomme, I don't think I'm interested in your job."

"You're sure?"

Rasputin nodded. "I find my current work very satisfying."

"Well," said Bonhomme, getting to his feet, "I guess that's that. I'll expect you to return Harry's skeleton card, of course."

"I'm afraid your expectations aren't going to be fulfilled, Mr. Bonhomme," said Rasputin.

"What are you talking about?" demanded Bonhomme.

"Please sit down. We're not quite through yet."

Bonhomme stared at him questioningly.

"I had some business to discuss with you, remember?" said Rasputin.

"I thought you didn't want the job."

"Espionage is *your* business," said Rasputin. "Mine is the security of the *Comet*." He activated his computer. "I've got a little something that I want you to see."

Bonhomme glanced at his watch. "Is this absolutely necessary? I'm a very busy man."

"Oh, I think you'll find it rather interesting," replied the Security chief, touching a number of squares on his computer console. "One might even say fascinating."

Suddenly the holographic screen flickered to life, displaying two figures in animated conversation.

"That's Suma and me!" exclaimed Bonhomme, surprised. "How the hell did you—?"

"Shhh," interrupted Rasputin with a smile. "I wouldn't want you to miss a word of this."

"But how did it happen?" Bonhomme was demanding of Suma.

"I don't know," she replied with a shrug. "He must have lost control of himself."

"I told you to disable her, not kill her!" Bonhomme snapped.

"Rasputin killed Gamble before he could talk, so what difference does it make?" responded Suma.

Rasputin touched another square and froze the holograph.

"It goes on for another ten minutes, but I think you get the picture," said the Security chief. "Now let me ask you a question, Mr. Bonhomme," he added pleasantly. "Do you know the penalty for being an accessory to murder?"

Bonhomme glared at him. "All right, you bastard. How much do you want?"

"I don't want your money, Mr. Bonhomme."

"What *do* you want?" demanded Bonhomme.

"A favor."

"What kind of favor?"

"I want you to fire Suma."

"I don't have the authority," said Bonhomme.

Rasputin smiled. "You're a resourceful man, Mr. Bonhomme. You'll find a way."

"And if I do, you'll destroy the recording?" asked Bonhomme.

"Not a chance," said Rasputin with an amused laugh. "Work in this place long enough and you run out of trust in your fellow man. But if you fire her, I won't turn it over to the authorities."

"That's not much of a bargain," complained Bonhomme.

"I've got the recording," replied Rasputin easily. "I don't *have* to make much of a bargain."

"Since, as you point out, you've got the recording, why don't you simply use it to put us both in jail?" asked Bonhomme.

"Nothing would please me more," admitted Rasputin, "but since you both have friends in high places, you could probably fight this thing for years before you were finally convicted. I'm willing to let you go free to get her off the ship now."

"Why her instead of me?"

"Because Gamble was following her orders, not yours. If I can only make one of you pay, it has to be her."

"That's not much of a reason."

"You should be thanking me instead of arguing with me, Mr. Bonhomme," said Rasputin, smiling at Bonhomme's sudden discomfort. He paused. "And, for what it's worth, there's another reason: I promised Harry."

"You're as crazy as *he* was!" snapped Bonhomme. "*He* tried blackmail too, and look where it got him."

"He never understood that corruption starts at the top," responded Rasputin calmly. "If I went after your boss, whoever he might be, I'd probably get slapped down. But you and me, we're small potatoes, Mr. Bonhomme. Nobody will ever know or care what we agree to today except the two of us."

"Well, what the hell," said Bonhomme with a shrug. "She was a dangerous little bitch to have around anyway.

We'll probably all be much happier once she's gone."
He frowned. "How the hell am I going to stop her from
blowing the whistle?"

"That's not my problem," said Rasputin. "I'm sure
you'll think of something."

"What do *you* get out of all this?" asked Bonhomme.

"The same thing Harry and the Madonna got," replied Rasputin. "The satisfaction of doing my job well."
He paused. "Do we have a deal?"

"Of course we have a deal, you son of a bitch. What
choice have I got?"

"Not much," agreed Rasputin. "You might try looking at the bright side, however. You'll still be free to
sabotage other businesses."

"You know," said Bonhomme thoughtfully, "it's not
such a bad goddamned deal at that. The *Comet* is going
to be out of business in a year, anyhow."

"Oh, I don't know," replied Rasputin. "It just might
outlive us all."

Suddenly Bonhomme's eyes narrowed. "You know
something else that you're not telling me, don't you?"

"Like what?"

"I don't know. But I've suddenly got a feeling that
you know more about the *Comet's* books than anyone
suspects." He paused. "You're a man of many qualities,"
he said admiringly. Suddenly he grinned. "That job I
offered you is still open."

"Even though I've just blackmailed you?"

"Especially because you've just blackmailed me. You
have a capacity for doing what's necessary. I can use a
man like you."

"I don't think I have any use for a man like you," said
Rasputin.

"That's what Harry always used to say," replied
Bonhomme with a confident grin. "But he always came
back to work."

"Until he found what he was looking for."

"All he found was a cheap whore and an early grave,"

said Bonhomme contemptuously. "What are *you* looking for?"

Rasputin's gaze moved to the holograms of his family, then returned to Bonhomme. "I found it a long time ago," he said at last.

"What the hell are you talking about?" asked Bonhomme, scanning the walls and trying to figure out what Rasputin had been looking at.

The Security chief smiled. "Something tells me that you wouldn't understand."

Bonhomme shrugged, got to his feet, and walked to the door.

"I'll hold the job open for another week," he said. "You might change your mind."

"I doubt it."

"You never know," replied Bonhomme confidently. "I might even arrange for you to choose a traveling companion from the other end of the ship."

Rasputin stared at him without answering, and after a moment he walked out into the corridor.

The Security chief lit a cigar, then leaned back in his chair, put his feet up on the desk, and sighed heavily. The insular little world of the *Comet*, he reflected, was starting to resemble a mortuary. Harry was dead, the Madonna was dead, Gamble DeWitt was dead, Suma was on the way out. Bonhomme was still intact, but he promised himself that he wasn't through with Bonhomme yet, not by a long shot.

Only the *Comet* had emerged unscathed, and he had a feeling that it would be a living, thriving, functioning entity long after all the surviving players in this little drama had passed from the scene.

Suddenly he felt very old and very tired, and wondered if perhaps it wasn't time to pack it in and go find a nice quiet job on a nice quiet planet. Possibly he might take a look at Pollux IV; there would be a farm up for sale there very soon.

Then he remembered the Lady Toshimatu, and a moment later he was staring intently at his screen, scrutinizing her every movement as she delicately picked up her cards, appraised them, and pushed a pile of chips to the center of the table.

Pollux IV could wait. The *Velvet Comet* was still in business, and he had work to do.

A moment later he emitted a cry of triumph.

"I've spotted it, you wily old bitch, you!" he yelled happily. "After all these goddamned years, I've finally got you!"

All thoughts of regret and retirement had vanished from his mind by the time he reached the casino.

About the Author

MIKE RESNICK was born in Chicago in 1942, attended the University of Chicago (where, in the process of researching his first adventure novel, he earned three letters on the fencing team and was nationally ranked for a brief period), and married his wife, Carol, in 1961. They have one daughter, Laura.

From the time he was 22, Mike has made his living as a professional writer. He and Carol have also been very active at science fiction conventions, where Mike is a frequent speaker and Carol's stunning costumes have swept numerous awards at masquerade competitions.

Mike and Carol were among the leading breeders and exhibitors of show collies during the 1970s, a hobby which led them to move to Cincinnati and purchase a boarding and grooming kennel.

Mike has received several awards for his short stories and an award for a nonfiction book for teenagers. His first love, though, remains science fiction, and his excellent science fiction novels—THE SOUL EATER, BIRTHRIGHT: THE BOOK OF MAN, WALPURGIS III, SIDESHOW, THE THREE-LEGGED HOOTCH DANCER, THE WILD ALIEN TAMER, THE BEST ROOTIN' TOOTIN' SHOOTIN' GUNSLINGER IN THE WHOLE DAMNED GALAXY and THE BRANCH—are also available in Signet editions.

JOIN THE *TALES OF THE VELVET COMET* READERS' PANEL

Help us bring you more of the books you like by filling out this survey and mailing it in today.

1. Book Title: _____

   Book #: _____

2. Using the scale below, how would you rate this book on the following features? Please write in one rating from 0-10 for each feature in the spaces provided.

	NOT SO GOOD		O.K.			GOOD		EXCELLENT
POOR								
0 1	2 3	4	5	6	7	8	9	10

RATING

Overall opinion of book . . . . _____

Plot/Story . . . . _____

Setting/Location . . . . _____

Writing Style . . . . _____

Character Development . . . . _____

Conclusion/Ending . . . . _____

Scene on Front Cover . . . . _____

3. About how many Science Fiction books do you buy for yourself each month? _____

4. How would you classify yourself as a reader of Science Fiction?
   I am a ( ) light ( ) medium ( ) heavy reader.

5. What is your education?
   ( ) High School (or less) ( ) 4 yrs. college
   ( ) 2 yrs. college ( ) Post Graduate

6. Age _____ 7. Sex: ( ) Male ( ) Female

Please Print Name_____

Address_____

City _____ State _____ Zip _____

Phone # ( ) _____

Thank you. Please send to New American Library, Research Dept., 1633 Broadway, New York, NY 10019.